After the Prodigal Returned

CASSANDRE
BRISSOT

Acknowledgments

"This is a trustworthy saying, and everyone should accept it: "Christ Jesus came into the world to save sinners"—and I am the worst of them all. But God had mercy on me so that Christ Jesus could use me as a prime example of His great patience with even the worst sinners. Then others will realize that they, too, can believe in Him and receive eternal life (1 Timothy 1 vs. 15-17)."

Maman Tout, words fail me. I cannot thank you enough for your devotion to Christ and your inspiring walk with Him that has inspired my own. Just by being who you are, a mighty woman in The Lord, you have stirred many hearts to Christ. You are a jewel in The Father's crown, a blessing to all who encounter you, and an inspiration to all who watch you. Thank You, Mommy, and may your eyes behold all the good fruit of your hard labor.

Devoue Pour Christ, thank you for being a refuge, a rampart, and a high tower for the oppressed to run into and encounter God. Thank you, everyone, for the prayers, the encouragements, the birthday wishes and cards, and for cheering me on. Your prayers matter. They move mountains. Keep praying. Keep believing. Keep the faith.

Mom, Thank you for always blessing me. Everything I did, from washing the dishes to getting you a glass of water, earned me a blessing. I know God heard your heart's cry. I'm living those blessings now. Thank you for teaching me God is real and to put my hope in Him, even in the darkest of nights. That is the greatest inheritance you could have ever given me. Thank you for all the time I was fast asleep and woke up to you praying over me and pronouncing God's blessings over my life. Thank You for doing your very best and giving us all you had, withholding nothing.

Dad, thank you for coming into our lives and bringing joy, laughter, and lightheartedness into our home and hearts.

Jude, thank you for being part brother, part father, part friend. I'm proud to call you my brother.

Anthony, your humility, kindness, and generosity cannot be appreciated enough. Thank you for being a sounding board when I needed one.

Herbert, you're an honorable man, a great father, and a good husband. Thank you for being the best brother-in-law.

Emanuella, my biggest cheerleader, thank you for being a loving, supportive sister and always cheering me on.

Emmily and Perrine, my Sunshine and Periwinkle, you two have made our family infinitely better. Auntie loves you.

Thank You All.

Contents

Chapter 1

Catching Up

Coffee sloshes in the mug in front of me, splashing on to the tabletop at the same time the half-eaten plate of French toast begins to rattle. I grip both edges of the small table to stop the violent shaking. I almost let go when my fingers come into contact with something wet and tacky, but I suck it up and hold on for dear life.

"Sorry." Cashmere Sage flushes, then as quickly as it started, the shaking stops.

"My bad."

I scan the unbothered faces of the diners around me and realize Cashmere must have been bouncing her knees beneath the table. I wipe my sticky hands on a napkin and throw it into my plate while keeping an eye on her. She's drumming her long orange fingernails against her water glass. The tiniest of cracks splinters from beneath her nails.

"What's—"

"Do you—"

"Sorry, Leah," she says, chuckling. "Go ahead."

"It's cool. I think you should go. You obviously need to get something off your chest."

Cashmere pushes the raven locks of hair falling into her eyes behind her ears and sits up taller in her seat. "Do you remember all that time I spent with Brice before I was eliminated from the competition?"

All thoughts fall out of my head except one. More than any of my other *Star Quality* cast mates, I miss Brice. Most days, I'm positive the five weeks I spent as a contestant on *Star Quality* nine months ago was a colossal mistake from start to finish. I let Trent convince me an acting competition show was my best and last shot at stardom. As a broke twenty-seven-year-old Haitian-American aspiring actress and former pageant queen turned ad sales representative for thelist.com, I believed him. Like the desperately lost fool I was, I believed everything Trent said.

I moved into the cast house with six strangers, let the cameras follow, and film me twenty-four hours a day. I did the scene performance challenges at the end of each week and always rose to the occasion. I did everything Trent told me to, yet ended up right back in the one-window peach bedroom in my mother's basement.

It's my fault. I was living outside of God's will and wouldn't heed the warnings He sent me. To anyone else, recurring nightmares would be an unmistakable sign that something isn't right, but not to me. I kept trucking right along, further and further away from Jesus. Small wonder Trent turned out to be a snake.

Some good things did come out of that painful experience, though. I learned God cares about me and has a plan for my life, although that's hard to remember at times. And I made friends. My castmates and I grew close. My friendship with Cashmere was unexpected but has endured outside the competition.

And I met Brice.

I haven't heard or spoken his name—Brice Young—aloud in months, but he's nearly always on my mind. We clicked immediately, becoming confidants—best friends—until what would be both of our last nights in the cast house. The dynamic between us had begun to shift before then because of Trenton Shaw, the executive producer of *Star Quality,* and my fiancé. But on that night, we imploded.

I went downstairs in the middle of the night for a glass of water. I came across Brice in the living room, rehearsing for the next day's elimination performance. During better times, Brice and I met there every night to talk—coincidentally then later purposely. But we hadn't spoken in days. I was distancing myself from him, and Brice let me do it. I planned on getting my water and going back up to my room, but Brice followed me into the kitchen. He was clearly looking for conversation. I for sure wasn't. I was upset with him for brushing me off a few days earlier and not about to let him off the hook.

I slammed my cup onto the countertop, only minutely concerned with waking the remaining castmates or being caught on camera. "You were my best friend," I half yelled at Brice. "You were my rock. Now you won't talk to me; you barely even look at me." Just then, the lights filtering in from the floor-to-ceiling windows shifted, completely illuminating Brice. He looked different—more handsome, less haunted. That's when he changed us forever; Brice embraced me. Locking eyes with me, he said, "Everything. That's what I'm asking of you. Let me love you, Leah; let me love you with the love of Christ."

I wanted to respond. I just didn't know how. I didn't see it coming. I thought Brice was still in love with his dead fiancé, Seriyah, and he and Cashmere were bonding in a way I couldn't define. I now know I misinterpreted their friendship, but even if I hadn't, I wouldn't have guessed the truth. I didn't see how it could be true, that Brice could want to be with me. Maybe I didn't want to see. I was still engaged. There was nothing I could do about his feelings...then.

Sometimes I wonder if Brice still feels the same way about me. Then I tell myself there's no point in wondering about something I already know the answer to. If he did, he would have called. Other times, I reason maybe he's waiting on me to call. I've thought about it. I've even dialed his number a few times, but I never press Send.

There's much between us left unresolved. He poured out his heart to me, and I said nothing, I didn't have an answer for him that night; I don't have one for him now, so he doesn't call, and neither do I. Sitting across from Cashmere hearing his name, what I want more than anything is to hear his voice.

"Leah."

"Huh?" I come to with a start and notice the group seated in the booth behind Cashmere and me look over at us with curious expressions.

"Sorry." One of the women at the table nods in what I assume is a gesture of acceptance of my apology, then they return to their meal and conversation. I do the same.

"Sorry, Cash. I completely spaced," I say, shaking my head a bit, "but I'm back now, and yes, I remember all the time you spent with Brice." I answer with a tight smile.

Cashmere rubs her hands down her arms like she's trying to get warm. It's cold in New York City in the middle of March, but it's warm in the restaurant. Not for the first time today, I think, *What is Cashmere so nervous about?*

"Believe it or not," she says, cutting short my reverie. "Most of that time we spent talking about Jesus. *Ummm,*" Cashmere starts then stops. She averts her eyes and begins tapping on her glass again.

I don't want to be insensitive to whatever's going on with her, but the suspense is killing me. What's weighing on her, and what does it have to do with Brice? I master myself and wait—thankfully, not very long. Finally, after closing her eyes and taking a deep breath, she's talking again.

"You know how it was for me growing up—no one ever loved or cared about me until Ms. Figero," she says, sounding too neutral. Moments like this I remember that behind her provocative demeanor is a girl who spent her formative years only ever being noticed to be abused. Cashmere's not the emotional type. Growing up with a violent alcoholic mother then being abandoned as a teen made her tough. If she was going to survive the group home, she couldn't go around crying regardless of the situation warranting it. She'd have been easy pickings. Even now, as an adult, it's hard for Cashmere to be vulnerable.

"You, Ms. Figero, and Brice are the only people who've ever been kind to me without expecting something in return. I now realize it's because of your faith. It compels you to treat others better than they deserve."

I don't want to be held in the same regard as Brice or Ms. Figero, but I don't interrupt her.

"There I was in my fabulous apartment, with all my pretty things, the ink still wet on a six-figure deal with a major beauty brand, and I was depressed," she says, shaking her head. "I should've been happy. I wasn't, though. I was empty. Hollow."

I nod along because I understand how it is to finally have everything you've worked for yet feel unsatisfied.

"When I did feel anything, it was this all-encompassing sadness. I couldn't bring myself to post, film, or talk to anyone."

"Not even to your followers?"

"Nope." She shakes her head. "Especially not them. All I could do—wanted to do—is relive the worst of what I've been through. I couldn't escape the memories. Then, as if dropped into my mind, I had my first clear thought. The dead rest in peace."

I open and shut my mouth like a guppy flopping around on dry land. Somewhere in my brain, I know she didn't do it. If she had taken her own life, Cashmere wouldn't be around to tell the story, but knowing that doesn't make it easier to hear. I don't know what to say or do.

"It's okay." Cashmere swipes at a lone tear gliding slowly down the right side of her face. "I didn't go through with it, although I meant to. I was good and drunk when I decided to down a bottle of painkillers left over from my wilder days. I got them from my medicine cabinet but passed out before I could take any."

"Weren't you afraid?" I ask.

"Of what? Dying?" She gives a noncommittal shrug. "I thought it was the only way. One moment I'm fumbling at the bottle, ready to find out what happens after life. The next moment, I'm waking up hours later on the bathroom floor, disoriented, with an incessant pounding in my ears. It took me a minute to realize the pounding was knocking."

"Did you answer it?" I interject, unable to stop myself.

"Yeah, but not because I cared who was at my door. I just wanted the noise to stop. It was giving me a headache. Then again," she says more to herself than me, "it might have been the bottle of Jack I downed before passing out, catching up with me."

I smile because for a second, I get a glimpse of the fearless and funny friend I made in the most unlikely of places.

"I picked myself up off the floor and answered it. It was UPS. Not my usual deliveryman, though. This guy wouldn't stop talking, even though I didn't say not one word to him."

Cashmere turns away, her gaze out the window. When she turns back around, the tip of her nose is red with the effort of keeping from crying.

"I slammed the door in his face. From the other side of the hallway, I heard him say, 'God bless you.' That's when I remembered. A few days before I was eliminated from *Star Quality*, Brice and I were hanging out on the couch in the living room. I was teasing him about how much of a Boy Scout he is and his devotion to his faith when he tensed up. I tried apologizing, but he cut me off.

"'If someone died in your place,' he said, 'left you as an heir to their inheritance and guaranteed you that no matter what you would ever go through, they would never leave you, wouldn't you be devoted to them too? And what if they knew you—I mean, really knew you, your every mistake, and the things you try to hide from the world yet loved you perfectly enough to cause you to overcome those things? And what if that person's love transformed you? Wouldn't you be faithful?'

"Without thinking, I answered 'yes' because my whole life, what I've wanted is to be loved that way. Brice smiled and said, 'Someone did do all of that for you.'"

I match Cashmere tear for tear, neither of us able to hold them back.

"I fell on my knees right at my front door," she says, clinching her hands. "I cried out to Jesus asking for His love. I needed it then, more than ever before. I had everything but nothing. I felt empty, unworthy, alone. I was honest with Jesus. I told Him I'd never bothered trying to get to know Him—ever. I'd done things, a lot of which I'm not proud of. Now I was desperate and hurting."

Her voice is powerful and urgent.

"I'd been told He alone could make me whole. I asked God to please do it, put my broken pieces back together. You know what?" she asks, looking lighter than she did seconds ago.

"I think God heard me. Taking my life didn't feel like something I needed to do anymore. Peace came over me—a peace I've never known before."

I try and fail multiple times to say something that expresses the depth of the empathy I feel for the pain that led her to that dark moment and my joy that Jesus led her through it. No words feel big enough. Cashmere comes to that conclusion at around the same time I do and puts my attempts to rest.

"I didn't share that with you so you'd comfort me. Jesus did that already. I told you because I'm thinking I want to give Christianity a try. I don't know much, but I think I might need the support of other believers. You and Brice are the only ones I know. Since you're both here in New York City, it makes sense that I be here too. I can film and post from anywhere, so here I am."

"Cash, Brice lives in Charlotte."

"No. He used to live in Charlotte. Now, he lives in New York City. He moved here Labor Day weekend." With wide eyes and dawning understanding, she says, "Wait. Did he not tell you?"

I'm numb. Brice has been in New York for four months and hasn't contacted me once. Things between us are complicated, no doubt, but how could he be in my city and not call?

"No," I admit. "The last time I spoke to him was seven months ago, right after he was eliminated."

She shakes her head. "Wow. I thought he would have kept in touch with you for sure."

I hate the pity in Cashmere's eyes. I hate my anger and jealousy even more. Brice kept in contact with her, not me. How real could his feelings have been if he was able to easily discard me but hold on to his friendship with her? I stop short at the thought that this is exactly how Cashmere feels about Trent and me, and that maybe, the pity I see in her eyes is carefully disguised glee.

"Yeah, well," I say, "he hasn't. What would make you think Brice would have kept in contact with me? We were just cast mates."

"Listen, I'm not trying to cause drama between you and Trenton. I know you're together and in love or whatnot but—"

"I know you're not trying to stir things up," I interrupt. "Please, speak your mind."

"Okay then. I will," she says, drawing a deep breath. "I'm pretty sure Brice is into you." She puts her hands up, palms facing me. "Mind you, he never said this to me." She shrugs. "But I'm positive it's true. Again, I'm not trying to cause any drama in your relationship. I just thought you should know."

I almost forgot I hadn't told Cashmere I broke it off with Trent; she'd already been eliminated by then. I want to tell her about it to put her at ease. I want to tell her about Brice, too, but that's what happens when friends have romantic history with the same men. Open, honest conversations are difficult to have, especially if it's a particularly complicated past.

Despite everything that's happened between her and Trent and Trent and me, Cashmere's my friend. I don't want any more of the awkward tight rope–walking chats.

I lean forward and prop my elbows on the table. My fingers meet and interlace. "You don't need to worry about causing drama in my relationship because I'm no longer in that relationship. And as far as Brice goes..." My shoulders rise and fall. "I don't know."

"What? You and Trent aren't together anymore? When? Why? How?"

I weigh my words, deciding how much more to say. My natural inclination is to not elaborate because I can't answer that question without talking about things I'm not sure I'm ready to discuss. No one knows the specifics of what happened between Trenton and me. My sister Antonia, and my oldest friend Amanda Moore know we're no longer together, but not the cause for the breakup. I haven't told anyone that. But Cashmere trusted me with a painful truth. To hold back from her would be wrong.

"Because he was the executive producer," I begin, "Trent saw a lot of the footage of my interactions with Brice. He didn't like them. He thought there was something more there, so I had to put some distance between us for the sake of my relationship. You were there. You remember when Brice and I stopped hanging out."

She nods.

"Yeah, that's when he and I became chill. Come to think of it, it's why too. Brice looked like he needed a friend—both of you did. I thought it might have been because of something like that, but you never said anything."

"I mean," I say, shifting in my seat. "What could I have said that wouldn't have been uncomfortable?"

She's completely silent. When the embarrassed space grows ridiculous, I rush to fill it because really, what could she say?

"It ended up being for nothing since Trent and I called off our engagement anyway."

Cashmere's eyebrows lift so high on her forehead they're nearly touching her hairline. "You called off your what?"

I could kick myself. I forgot no one—well, no one besides Brice, who only accidentally found out—knew about the engagement. I could have gladly taken that to the grave with me; now, there's yet another thing I have to explain.

I lean back, sink lower in my seat, and cross my arms over my chest. "Trent and I were engaged for about a second. It didn't work out."

"I don't get it," she says, shaking her head. "That man was so in love with you, he ..."

She lets the rest of the sentence go unsaid, but it isn't difficult for me to guess. He was so in love with me that he let her go. Cashmere dated Trent before he and I officially met. Although he was not on my radar, I stayed on his for six years until we crossed paths at a club nine months ago. We were both interns at Premier network seven years ago. I worked at the downtown location; he worked at the midtown location. At the end of the summer, interns were invited to a party in our honor. That's when Trent saw me for the first time. He showed up late, and I left shortly after he arrived. We never got to meet.

Seven months ago, while still, contestants on *Star Quality,* Cashmere told me the reason she'd been horrible to me up to that point. She'd dated Trent, loved him, and wanted to be with him, but he admitted he was in love with a girl who didn't know he existed. At the time, that flattered me. I thought it meant I was special. Today, I regret every second I spent with him. Cashmere doesn't know it, but of the two of us, she's the fortunate one.

"He did you a favor." Cashmere looks up at me, brow furrowed. I can tell she's puzzling out what I mean.

"He's not a good man," I blurt out. "I was just too much of a mess to see him for the snake he is. Mad as I am at Trent—and I'm really mad at him—I'm more upset with myself. I knew better. Something was always off about us. We never seemed to be reading from the same book. He was my contrast in almost every way, definitely in everything major. I went along with it though, despite the part of me that knew he was toxic because he's beautiful and persuasive, especially when I know he's wrong."

I yank my wallet out of my purse, grab a few bills, and toss them down onto the table without counting. It should be enough to cover both our meals. I throw my wallet and phone back in my purse, stuff my hands into my sleeves, and pull the jacket up the rest of the way. I can't believe I just spilled my guts to Cashmere.

Without looking at her, I mumble, "Good luck with everything."

I'm nearly gone from the table when she says, "When I decided to live, I felt God had given me a second chance at life, a chance to do things better." Her voice is far away and reverent.

"At first, I was excited, then I became afraid. All I could think about was messing up; I was so sure I would mess up. Then I remembered what Brice told me. 'Jesus loves us perfectly enough to help us overcome ourselves, our mistakes, our wrongs.' So it doesn't matter that Trent was a mistake. Jesus can right the worst of what we've done."

I haven't thought about it that way before. I sit back down under the weight of her words and the thought I've been struggling with ever since I quit *Star Quality* and went back home. It's the first thing I thought about when I woke up this morning in my peach bedroom with the one window in my mom's basement. It's what I think about when I'm helping customers at the boutique and on the train ride home. Am I forgiven, and what happens now?

For months, I dreamed about forks in the road and choosing "the good way." I finally understood God was speaking to me about surrendering to His will. He wanted me to quit the show, leave my relationship, and return home. I did return, and I did everything else, but I'm right back where I was nine months ago. If I'm forgiven, shouldn't my life be different? Why are my struggles the same?

"I get your fear of messing up," I confess while leaving out the part about constantly feeling like I can't do right myself. "You're looking to me like I'm some kind of expert on living a Christian lifestyle, but the truth is..." My breath hitches in my throat. I'm on the verge of another purge. The truth is fighting to be acknowledged. My brain is saying be quiet, but my mouth won't quit.

"Maybe...Maybe you should find a good church home to give you spiritual guidance."

"Yeah. I've been looking into that. Any suggestions?"

"Not really. I haven't committed anywhere yet. I've been to my mom's church a few times. It was nice, but I'm on the fence."

"Really? I would've thought you had a place you attend regularly." If she notices that I flinch, she doesn't mention it. Cashmere goes on, unaware she's hit a nerve. "Oh well. I'll just ask my followers for recommendations and kill two birds with one stone—post new content and get helpful suggestions." Cashmere's voice fades into the background as I try out the words shouting in my head.

"None of us are worthy of forgiveness, but we are given it freely by His grace. Take it and never look back." I repeat the words exactly as they come to me.

"What?"

"None of us are worthy of forgiveness," I slowly repeat, "but we are given it freely by His grace. Take it and never look back."

I went to Bible study with my mom a few weeks ago. The topic was forgiveness—God's forgiveness. I asked Brother Germain, the leader of the Bible study, how God could forgive us. What I meant, though, was how could God forgive me. His response was, "None of us are worthy of forgiveness, but we are given it freely by His grace. Take it and never look back."

"Did you read that somewhere?" Cashmere asks hesitantly.

"No. Brother Germain said it to me."

"Who's Brother Germain?"

"He leads Bible study at my mom's church."

Cashmere nods to herself. For a second, I think she's going to drop it, then she asks, "That thing you said, what does it mean?"

"It means...it means..." The answer comes to me suddenly. "Forgiveness isn't a question of worthiness. If it were, none would receive it. Forgiveness is a gift from God through the Blood of Jesus. Receive it and press forward."

"In that case..." Cashmere takes a deep, satisfied breath. "That's exactly what I'll do."

I give my first genuine smile in months. "Yeah. Me too."

"So, what are you going to do about Brice?" Cashmere asks.

I lean forward and put my elbows on the table. "There's nothing to do." I blew it. Whatever Brice may have felt for me nine months ago has clearly passed or else he would have reached out to me by now.

"What do you mean there's nothing to do?" Cashmere tilts her head and pauses. "Stop playing. You and I both know you and Brice are into each other."

"No, you and I don't," I say, sitting up and crossing my arms.

"Whatever, Leah. You're just upset he hasn't called you—"

"I'm not upset," I argue. Cashmere presses her lips into a thin line. "Fine," I say, huffing. "Why hasn't he called me, Cash?"

"Why haven't you called him? You have his number, right?" I nod. "Then what's the holdup?"

"I don't know what to say."

"Maybe he doesn't either. So, why don't you stop being pigheaded and call him?" She picks my cell up from the table and holds it out to me. "Call him."

Chapter 2

It's Too Late to Apologize

"I'm coming. I'm coming," I shout, running up the stairs. The doorbell rings again the precise moment my feet hit the landing. I nearly slip, but I catch myself before I fall. I run through the short hallway through the kitchen all the way to the front door. I pull it open and peer at the young deliveryman.

"Package for Leah Albanese," he says.

"That's me," I say, panting between words. "Sorry. I'm out of breath. I ran to get the door." I unlock the security door and take the medium-sized manila envelope from the deliveryman.

"That's fine. Sign here for me, please, ma'am." He hands me an electronic device with an attached pen. I shift the envelope under my arm, scribble something, and hand the device back to the deliveryman.

"Hey, *ummm,* this doesn't have a return address on it," I say, looking the lightweight manila envelope over for the umpteenth time.

Without looking up from the device he handed me for my signature, the deliveryman says, "A return address isn't required."

"Right." I nod. "But the sender had to give some information, or else how did they pay for the services?"

"Ma'am, I get that you want to know who the package is from, but you're asking me a question you already have the answer to." He points to the envelope. "Open it."

I watch the deliveryman walk back to his van and pull away from the curb before I shut the front door. Of course he's right, but for some reason, I'm afraid to open the envelope. I put it on the nightstand in my bedroom and go back to preparing dinner.

Dinner is a disaster. I leave the chicken breast in the oven too long, and it comes out rubbery and dry. The rice is overcooked, mushy, clumpy, and sodden. And the greens taste unwashed which they might be. I don't actually remembering washing them. It's that stupid envelope; I've been distracted ever since I got it. Halfway through trying to choke down the meal I give in and return to the letter.

I turn the envelope in hand over and over, searching for a clue as to who sent it. Eventually, I accept the deliveryman was probably right. The answer of who is in the envelope. I rip it open and pull out a single sheet of folded legal pad paper filled in with a familiar slanted script in heavy black ink. The writer is no mystery after all.

My hand feels heavy, the muscles in my arm are taut with the strain of holding the featherweight letter. I let it go and watch it float all the way down to the carpeted floor, all the while in disbelief.

Trent isn't the admit-your-wrongs, swallow-your-pride-and-beg-forgiveness type of guy. I caught him in a passionate moment with Beverly in the house we were supposed to move into after we were married. Instead of apologizing, he tried to flip the script on me and somehow make it my fault.

Trent claims I was slipping away from him, that the competition and Brice were driving us apart. He didn't want to lose me, so he eliminated the things that stood between us and our happily ever after.

According to Trent, Beverly was just an employee on his payroll, that there was no love between them. She did whatever he asked her—hijack my monologue, tell the judges about my panic attacks, whatever it took to make me less attractive to them. Her fee? Winning the competition. Trent got Beverly's services at a bargain. He's the executive producer. It was no sweat off his back to make sure Beverly won.

Funny thing, Trent never guaranteed me I'd win. The entire time he was pitching me on joining the cast of *Star Quality,* he only ever offered the possibility of winning. I didn't want to win because my fiancé fixed the competition in my favor. I wanted to deserve the W. But it hurts that he took away my chance of winning and gave it to someone else as payment for her role in his subterfuge.

I didn't believe Trent's explanation. His actions weren't the desperate acts of a man in love. Trent's too calculated to ever be desperate. No. It was his plan all along to bait me into his sphere with promises of everything I ever wanted then prevent me from getting them. Trent wanted me utterly dependent on him for my joy, success, self-worth—all of it. I saw him for the first time that day.

He wasn't my dream guy who wanted to give me the world. Trent was a monster who gave everything he promised me to another woman. He gave it all to her—the movie role he wrote for me, first place in *Star Quality,* and his affection. Regardless of what Trent said about his arrangement with Beverly, it wasn't strictly business. There was nothing he could say to fix things. I broke up with Trent and returned to the cast house to get my stuff. I didn't want to be there anymore.

My emotions were all over the place. I was still reeling from my confrontation with Trent and having to say goodbye to Brice only a few hours before it all went down. I was distraught when the judges announced Brice was going home. Hours after confessing his true feelings for me, he was eliminated from the competition. I'd never see him again. I cried more than he did. Brice just hugged me and told me he'd left something for me in my dresser drawer before we left the house. The last time he left me something, it was his Bible. Mine had been stolen by Beverly- well, I thought it was Beverly. Actually, I thought it was Cashmere first, but it turns out it was neither of them. Trent did it. Trent stole my Bible to drum up drama between the other women in the cast house and me. I got into a nasty confrontation with Cashmere and Beverly over it. My Bible was never returned to me, but when Brice saw how worked up I was over it, he gave me his. I didn't open my Bible once the entire time I was on *Star Quality* but having it with me made me feel like I wasn't as far from God as I actually was.

I look over to my nightstand. My eyes linger on the worn, loved cover of Brice's Bible. I kept it even though I had another Bible at home. Brice has notes in the margins and obvious signs of a person hungering for God's Word in their life. His faith is still inspiring me even now. My eyes flick back to the letter on the floor from Trent. Brice wrote me a letter, too, once. That's what was in my drawer. Actually, it was after I read Brice's letter that I went looking for Trent.

In the letter, Brice described a dream he had about me. I was stunned at how much his dream mirrored the nightmares I'd been having since I moved into the cast house. It was disturbing enough that we were sharing dreams, but the why sent me to the brownstone looking for Trent. I loved him—at least I thought I did—but I wept over Brice leaving, and we were obviously connected. I needed to be sure Trent was the man for me. I got my answer.

Catching Trent with Beverly brought things into focus for me, though. I finally understood my recurring nightmares. For weeks, I dreamt of a fork in the road, a beautiful colonial to the left, a house in need of repairs to the right. Chased by a Beverly-led mob, I'd come to the fork. A voice would call me to "choose the good way." Every time I chose the house on the left, and every time it came alive with horrors as soon as I crossed the front gate.

18

Hands reached for my ankles from below the dry, cracked earth where vibrant green grass stood seconds before. They held me down while the house moved closer. The front door would fling open, revealing a terrifying darkness inside. Fear, visceral fear, would overcome me. I scream, but my mouth doesn't work, or the scarier version; the sound is trapped in my throat.

In his dream, Brice saw me cowering on the front porch of a menacing house, screaming as things crept out of the darkness toward me. Brice said he woke up terrified something had happened to me. He went to my room, but I wasn't there or in the living room, where we usually met when I woke up from a nightmare. I was with Trent at the time. Brice doesn't know that, or maybe he does.

My nightmares usually ended with me belatedly noticing the house I didn't choose with sorrow and regret. Although the house needed repairs, it was beautiful, and someone was working on it the entire time. That was the point of the dream. God showed me He was working on my life. It may look like a major construction site, but it would be worthwhile. If I went with Trent, the beautiful colonial, the ramifications would be painful and irrevocably detrimental.

Amy, the thorn in my side of a producer, caught me shoving clothes into my suitcases and demanded to know what I was doing. I told her I quit. Amy lost it. She couldn't believe it. All I had to do was get past Zack and Beverly. Amy didn't know I knew Beverly would win; maybe I knew more than she did about the winner. Either way, I was through. It was time to return home.

I left Trent standing alone in his brownstone and came back home sure I'd never hear from him again, and I was more than okay with that. Why was he trying to get in contact with me now, and writing me letters no less? I was supposed to live my life while Trent lives his, with our paths never to cross again. Why couldn't he honor that? If he couldn't hold up his end of our unspoken no-contact agreement, I'll just have to hold up mine and not read the letter.

I sit on the edge of my bed and turn on the television. Two hundred channels yet nothing to watch. I flop back and stare up at the ceiling. I wonder… What could it hurt to read the letter? It's not like a phone conversation; this is different—harmless really. I peek over at the floor. It's still there. The last letter Trent wrote me was beautiful. It put to rest all my doubts about him, for a time. Then again he did steal that letter from me and give it to Beverly, so there's that.

I should have trusted my gut and not Trent's words when I saw Beverly all over him at the network's cast party. He brushed Beverly off as just another girl pressed for his attention. Trent admitted they dated for about a second when I pushed back but convinced me that what they had was over. He said casting Beverly on *Star Quality* was him helping out a friend, nothing more. My feelings for Trent were beyond rationale at the time. I believed him over myself even after I moved into the cast house and Beverly straight up told me she was going to make the competition miserable for me. I believed Trent when he said Beverly wasn't a threat to me after Cashmere admitted all the ways she and Beverly had tried to sabotage me. In the end, Beverly got the guy and everything else, so why is he writing me?

"Hmmm." I get up and go to stand over the letter. It doesn't look like a bomb or threatening at all. It looks like an ordinary sheet of yellow paper. "I'm making way too much of this," I say, shaking my head. There's nothing Trent can say to change anything between us, so why not read the letter? I pick it up, unfold it, and begin to read.

L,

I don't know how to begin to put into words all the things I've felt since you walked out the door, straight out of my life. Sorry is not nearly enough to express the magnitude of my sadness for hurting you and destroying us in the process, but I am. Believe it or not, that wasn't my intention. I wanted to give you the world. Somehow, it came crashing down on us instead. I won't try to explain away my actions, I'm not sure I can. Something good did come from all of this though.

I'm not the same man you knew. I've changed—for the better. Maybe one day you'll give me the opportunity to show you. I shouldn't say this although I will anyway: I miss you. Every day without you is the day I think I'll die. I'd wait another six years, L. I'll wait a hundred more if I have to. I won't go quietly.

I Love You,

Trent

I crumple up the letter, toss it on the floor. "Ugh. The nerve of him," I shout, pacing the short length of my bedroom. He's as arrogant and without a clue as ever. Once upon a time, I would have read that handwritten letter riddled with vain sentiments and been simply over the moon. Now, I see it as further confirmation that leaving Trent was the right thing to do.

All he did was go on about how he feels, how he's changed, how he'd wait another six years, and that he'll never stop fighting for me. Where was the accountability for betraying me? I pick the letter back up, smooth it out, and scan it. *Sorry is not nearly enough to express the magnitude of my sadness for hurting you and destroying us in the process, but I am.*

"Ha. What a sorry excuse for an apology."

Believe it or not, that wasn't my intention. I wanted to give you the world. Somehow it came crashing down on us instead.

"Somehow? Somehow?"

Has he forgotten he sabotaged my chances of winning *Star Quality?* The irony is I wanted no part of it. I didn't want to be a reality TV personality; I wanted to be taken seriously as an actress. Then Trent explained *Star Quality* was an acting competition, not a reality television drama. I was already twenty-seven, well past the age of being "discovered," and the show seemed legit. The judges were all industry heavyweights. There was a cash prize, agent representation, and a feature film role for the winner. All of that if I won, and

I had Trent, the most gorgeous man I'd ever seen. It was everything I wanted for my life in one fell swoop; all I had to do was what I already wanted to do: act.

Every week, all cast members—seven of us to begin with, Cashmere, Beverly, Aiden, Zack, Corey, Brice, and myself—were given a performance challenge, monologues, scene work, and the likes, then we were ranked from best to worst. The lowest ranking cast members were put in the bottom two. One would be saved, the other went home.

The first week we had to perform a monologue that revealed something about who we were. I did a Leonardo DiCaprio monologue from *The Wolf of Wall Street*. It was all I could think of on such short notice. After Beverly performed my original piece exactly how I rehearsed it earlier in the week, I had to think fast. I only had the time it took her and Brice to finish their performances before I was up. Months of working at thelist.com selling ad space to small businesses and being forced to watch the wolf of Wallstreet himself, Jordan Belfort, shout at his employees to be telephone terrorists every single day, had the scene permanently burned in my brain. With the pressure on, it came to mind.

I was a great Jordan Belfort. It was probably my best performance to date, but I was burning mad. At the time, I thought Amy, the producer who hated me, had given Beverly my rehearsal footage, then set her loose. It wasn't Amy, though. It was Trent. He taunted, mocked, and seduced me into the worst version of myself then played me.

I was a mess before I got involved with him, but he definitely added layers of turmoil and complication to my life. I listened to him when he told me to embody a new bolder, sexier persona for social media, even though I was uncomfortable with it. I let him persuade me there were multiple ways to the same end despite the loud protestations of my spirit. I gave in to him, in other ways too. I wanted to abstain, but Trent's love required mine to prove its feeling. It's ironic that he believes every day without me may be the day he dies because every day I spent with him could have been the day I died.

I was dying a slow death, my spirit suffocating at the hands of my flagrant disregard of it. I can't blame Trent for that though. He didn't force me to do the things I'm guilty of. It was my choice to go down a dark path. I wanted the fame and success he promised even at the expense of my soul, though I didn't know it at the time. Now, what I want from him is to forget I exist.

I rip the bedside lamp right out of its socket. It crackles and pops before plunging the room into darkness. I hear rather than see the lamp crash against the peach wall then fall onto the floor. I'll regret it later. Right now, it's satisfying to break something.

Chapter 3

Wise Woman

Since I've been back home, I've been putting one foot in front of the other. Like a baby learning to walk on wobbly legs, I've been taking it one step at a time. It's been more difficult than I imagined, but I've gotten into a rhythm of sorts, yet it's taken less than two days and the reemergence of three people I thought I'd never speak to again to throw me off beat.

"Leah?"

The sofa scrapes against the hardwood floor above me. My mom must be sitting in the living room; at least she was. She's on her way downstairs now. The floorboard creaks under the weight of her heavy tread.

"I'm fine, Mom," I call, hoping she goes back upstairs. She's deciding on what to do. I can tell because her footsteps have stopped. They're not going up or down. Seconds pass.

"Okay. Be careful," she says.

I breathe a sigh of relief. "Will do," I call. Her steps resume, this time heading back upstairs. I love my mom. I don't want to talk about this with her, though. I don't feel like hearing I told you so. She warned me not to get involved with Trent or do the show. I didn't listen then ended up back on her doorstep two months later, proverbial hat in hand.

I walk over to the light switch and turn on the harsh ceiling lights. It takes my eyes a few seconds to adjust. The bright lights spotting my vision eventually give way to strewn pieces of the broken porcelain lamp.

"Yup," I say to myself. "I regret it."

My head snaps in the direction of my nightstand at the sound of heavy vibrations against wood. I practically leap to it and grab my phone. My heart sinks. It's just an email, not a text. It's not him. It's not Brice. Twenty-four hours have passed, and he still hasn't answered my text. Is he really going to leave me on read?

Dear Miss Albanese,

This is the third communication we've sent you in regards to the Star Quality reunion show. As the date rapidly approaches, your confirmation of attendance is urgently required. We do remind you as per our existing agreement, your participation is contractually obligated at all promotional events, unless otherwise specified. Please find attached additional details including a calendar of important dates. We await your speedy response.

I run to the bathroom. The door flies inward, bounces off the wall, and swings shut. I'm bent over the toilet heaving before I hear the telltale click of the door closing behind me. My body racks and contorts with the effort, but nothing comes up. After the third time, there's nothing left in my system to expel. I lay down right there on the mat until I'm strong enough to get up. When I do, I clean up then make my way slowly back to my bedroom. I collapse on my bed, pull out my phone, and read the email again. It hasn't changed.

My phone ends up stashed beneath my pillow—out of sight, out of mind. I pull the covers up over my head and lower myself into the mattress. I can't believe the nerve of production lauding the contract over me. Where was their professional acumen when they let Trent decide Beverly would win? The contract I signed said the show was unscripted. A winner is selected by a fair, unbiased process of elimination. They didn't honor their end of the deal, so why should I honor mine? I curl up in fetal position and turn to my right facing the wall, but after a minute a dull ache starts in my hip. I flip onto my back. How dare they threaten me with legalese? I didn't let the contract stop me from quitting. It won't force me back into their grasp either. It's no use trying to get comfortable. I've never been a back sleeper.

They could send ten more emails for all the good it'll do. I turn over onto my stomach. I've spent the last few months barely picking up the pieces of my life, trying to put the past behind me. I can't go back there.

My mouth starts secreting spit at an alarming rate, which means another trip to the bathroom. I sit up, prepared to make a quick dash and wait for the sickness to come. I signed a contract. I was allowed to quit without reprisals— probably Trent's doing, a twisted apology for cheating on me with Beverly among other things, but my absence from the *Star Quality* reunion episode won't fly. If I skip it, there will be retaliation, production as good as promised. The queasiness subsides, but I still feel sick. I'm without options. I have to do the reunion. My nausea returns.

At this point I'm not sure if my body racks with the effort of being ill or shame, at how easily I gave into the worst decision of my life. Amanda, my oldest friend, warned me the night I met Trent that something was off about him. I agreed with her and pretended to be hot and bothered by his arrogance, presumption, and nerve. Truthfully, I had already decided in my heart way before I did in my mind that I would break all the rules for him.

I splash cold water on my face and stop when I catch my reflection in the medicine cabinet mirror. I look like the same girl, the one who walked into a nightclub disillusioned with her faith and noticed the most handsome man she'd ever seen sitting in VIP.

I was wildly attracted to Trent—every woman is. He's painstakingly handsome. He's six feet two inches with smooth ebony skin, perfectly squared jaw, broad shoulders, and luminous chocolate eyes full of mystery. If you can move past his attractiveness, there's his energy to contend with. It's untamed and exciting. You never know what he's going to do next, and when he looks at you—into you—there's nothing you won't agree to, just to make sure he never stops looking. A more irresistible man I've never met.

I like to think it took a lot of convincing and manipulating on Trent's part to get me to join a reality show, become a social media vixen, and turn my back on my friends, family, and beliefs. Truth is, he didn't have to try that hard. I wanted what he was offering; that I didn't agree with how he wanted to give it to me didn't matter nearly as much. Only, deep down it did.

To be fair, I started spiraling before Trent, evident in that I ignored the big neon *trouble* sign flashing over his head. If I hadn't been ripe for the picking, I would have known him for what he is. A lie. The kind of lie you convince yourself into believing because no matter how wrong the boy is for you, you're going to be with him anyway. Imagining he's not so bad—that you can change him—makes you feel better about the mistake you're about to willingly make. That kind of frailly constructed mirage usually falls apart quickly. Trent and I were no exception.

Filming was the stone that shattered our glass house. Everything I had with Trent came crashing down around me, releasing me from the cage that kept me captive. Yes, I was upset and hurt, but mostly, I felt set free. Trent was poisonous to my soul; I didn't even enjoy being with him anymore. However, until that moment, I couldn't break away. I left Trent and the competition behind me that day.

The irony is, while I was in a place that if I was right with God I would have never been, I heard God's voice most clearly. God spoke to me through my dreams. He showed me how my life would be with Trent versus the life I could have if I trusted Him. In a way, I was more aware of God and His will than I had ever been.

Star Quality is also where I met Brice. Witnessing his faith was instrumental in helping me come back to my own. I regret a lot of things—most things—from that time. Not him, not Brice.

Would we have met if I hadn't veered off the path? I don't know. What I am certain of is if I had it to do over again, I'm almost sure I would choose differently. I mean, I might look exactly the same—the same caramel complexion although slightly flushed from all the activity, the same russet eyes, and even the same naturally curly hair, but I'm not.

I mean yes, I still want some of the same things. Who doesn't want financial freedom and success? And I don't completely hate the limelight, but I'm different now. I study the mirror with hawklike attention to detail. That's when I find what I'm looking for, evidence of my change. I pull on two short gray strands tightly coiled within a thick lock of chestnut hair. They weren't here before.

"I've changed," I scream at the reflection in the mirror.

I walk over to the tub and sit on the edge of it. A crystal-clear image of Trent the night we met pops into my head. Like that night, a shiver goes through me, and I'm back up at the mirror looking for the two strands of gray hair. I can't find them. What if they were never there in the first place? What if I imagined them? I run out the bathroom in search of help.

She's seated in her favorite chair in the living room wearing her reading glasses. She looks at me from the top of them. I glance to her lap, and as suspected, her Bible lays open there. It's the only book she reads.

"Hey, Mom."

"What's on your mind?"

I forgot the other thing my mom reads: me. It's been that way from as far back as I can remember. She can always tell when something's bothering me. I abandon the doorway separating the living and dining rooms and plop down onto the ottoman at the foot of her chair. I try to be conscious of my posture, but I end up slumping in my seat.

"I've been getting emails from the producers of *Star Quality* inviting—insisting—I participate in the reunion episode." I tip my head back, casting my gaze upward for a second. "I don't want to do it, Mom, but if I don't, they'll take legal action against me."

"I'm not surprised," she says while shifting her Bible from her lap to the coffee table.

"You—you're not surprised," I stutter.

"I'm not surprised," she says, pausing, "that after all you've been through, all you've learned, a test has presented itself."

Several thoughts chase one after another: What kind of test? Who's administering the test? What happens if I fail? I can't bring myself to ask any of them. There's no point anyway. I know my mom as well as she knows me. She won't give me the answers. There is one thing she will do though.

"Mom, I'm scared," I say, whimpering. "Please pray for me. Pray I won't fall. I'm trying my best, I really am, but I feel weak. Please ask the Lord to strengthen me."

First my posture crumbles, then my chest is heaving with loud, uncontrollable sobs I try to hide behind my hands. When I decided to return to my mother's house in Brooklyn—return to my faith—I thought things would fall into place. I thought things would be easier, but they're not. I'm struggling to hold on. Whenever I think I'm finding my footing, I get the wind knocked out of me. As many steps as I take forward, I'm always two steps behind.

My mom pulls my hands away from my face, but I let my head fall to my chest. I can't face her. Then I feel her hand beneath my chin tipping my head back up, forcing me to look at her. I can barely see through my tears. Everything's a blur, except her fierceness.

"I know you're trying," she says, "but you can't succeed in your own power. Apart from Jesus, you can do no good thing. You need His strength in every situation." She scoots down from her seat into mine. I collapse against her, weeping. She hugs me tight. I want to be strong enough not to need consoling, but I'm not. I hold on to her, allowing myself to be a daughter in need of her mother.

"Some things the Lord will deliver you from; others, He will deliver you through. We all must go through times of testing. None of us can escape that. It's how both our faith and character are refined. Those times aren't meant to destroy you. They're meant to bring you to your knees—in prayer—that you may stand in strength. After you've been tried in the crucible of fire, you emerge as a servant of the Lord."

Gently, she shifts me off her shoulders. Personally, I'd stay there, where it's safe, all night, but she won't allow it. My mom's a warrior. She's tried her best to instill that in my sister, Antonia and me. She could never be anything less.

"I understand your tears, Leah. You've had a difficult year, but I—and I'm sure the Lord, would agree with me—would much rather see your faith."

I try to compose myself, allowing my mother's words to comfort and fortify me. When I've stopped sniffling, I tell her about the other thing that's bothering me.

"*Star Quality* premieres tomorrow night."

With no social media, I've been out the loop. If I hadn't looked at the calendar the producers attached to the email, I wouldn't have known. I wish I didn't know. Then I could pretend it wasn't happening.

With her penetrating eyes trained on me, my mom looks more like the version of herself in my recurring dreams than the one who held me a few minutes ago. My nightmares changed sometimes; they were essentially the same but with meaningful variation. My mom showed up at the fork in the road one night, except she didn't exactly look like her. She looked powerful. She was still five feet four inches, but she felt taller. She spoke with such authority when she told me to "choose the good way." It was as if she were divinely commissioned. That's what she reminds me of now as she holds me in place with her knowing eyes.

"We knew this day was coming. Now it's here. You can't change what you've done, your mistakes, or errors in judgment. Nevertheless, God can give them intention. Romans eight twenty-eight tells us all things work together for good for those who love Him and are called according to His purpose. We know that and believe it. Now, dry your eyes."

I sit up and wipe my tears with a corner of my shirt.

"There you go," she says, squeezing my free hand. "Obedience isn't easy, Leah. You took the first step in returning home. That was the easy part. Persevering. That's where most stumble. But God gives grace to those who return to persevere."

My steps slow as I approach the non-assuming door hidden in the recesses of the plain cement building. Left and right my head swivels, searching every face milling around the trucks: food trucks, equipment trucks, and trucks that serve purposes of which I'm unaware. Every vaguely familiar face sends me into a tailspin. My heart races, and my skin tingles with anticipation until...realizing it's a false alarm, it's not him.

Down the block, a small group of crewmembers walk toward me. None of them are tall enough to be Trent, but what if Amy's in that group? I'm not exactly looking forward to seeing her either. Between her, Beverly, and Trent, I'm not sure who made my time on the show more difficult. The group's closer now, much closer. They'll be upon me in a matter of seconds. What to do?

A familiar jingle blares from my purse. My phone is ringing. I'm so elated I could actually cry.

"Thank God," I nearly shout, stepping into the recesses of the building. Whoever it is has my undying gratitude. I put the phone up to my right ear to hide my face from view and answer.

"Hello."

"This is dealer services calling to inform you that your manufacturer's warranty is almost up."

This is the point where I usually hang up the scammy calls, but from the corner of my eye, I make out the group walking past me.

"Great. Thank you so much for letting me kn—"

"Leah? Leah Albanese?" I turn in the direction the voice is coming from.

"There you are."

I point to myself to make sure he isn't looking for a different Leah Albanese.

"Yes. You." He looks incredulous. "I've been waiting for you. Your call time was five minutes ago."

The credentials hanging from the lanyard around his neck, the clipboard in his hand, and manic expression he wears so like the other producers I've worked with identify him as part of the production crew. This makes me only slightly less apprehensive. I hang up the phone and slip it back in my bag.

"Come, come, come," he says, waving me over to the door he's holding open. "Pick up the pace."

He whisks me through the door past security. I'm nearly jogging to keep up with him and still falling behind.

"Where have you been?" he bemoans, though not genuinely desiring an answer. "Whatever. It doesn't even matter. Your first stop's makeup, then hair. Wardrobe will meet you in your dressing room. If you would've gotten here on time," he says, shooting me a backward glance, "I could've taken you to catering to get breakfast. As it happens, you didn't."

We rush past plain gray door after plain gray door, distinguishable only by their numbers then come to an abrupt stop. He turns to face me.

"We're walking down to set at thirteen hundred hours. You'll be reunited with your cast mates then. For now, you're being kept separately." He opens the door and nudges me in. "I'll be back for you."

Three hours later, my stomach is in knots, and my mouth feels stuffed with cotton, but I've never looked better. Not a hair out of place. I tug at my figure-skimming gown as the door swings open.

"Whoa." The rude production assistant that dropped me off at hair and makeup stares wide eyed at me.

"What? Is it too much?" I ask, spreading my hands over my gown.

"Not at all. You look great."

"Thanks," I say, blushing. That's the first nice thing he's said to me all day. Maybe now he'll stop being so short.

"I just came to let you know we'll be walking in five minutes. If you have anything else to do, do it now. I'll be back in exactly five minutes."

He's gone before I can promise I'll be ready. So much for warmer communication. Truth be told, I'm grateful for the extra time. I'm a little nervous about my outfit. It's splashier than anything I've ever worn, including three years' worth of pageant dresses.

I walk to the mirror to give myself the once-over. The voluminous honey-blond tips of my ponytail balancing between my bare shoulders and back momentarily distract me. I'm still getting used to the color. As soon as I sat in the stylist's chair, she suggested we add some highlighted extensions. She convinced me it would complement my caramel complexion. I wasn't so sure at first, though seeing it against my pale gold sequin gown, I know she was right. I have no idea what it's going to be like for me out there, but I'll face whatever happens with style.

I breathe deeply with every step I take, readying myself to face the thing I've been trying hard to forget. Focusing on my breathing usually helps to soothe me. Not this time. I feel like I'm on my way to a reckoning; maybe I am.

Tim, the production assistant, great at his job horrible at interpersonal skills, looks right at me and cautions me to watch where I'm going. He doesn't seem to notice my angst. That's a good thing. If he didn't pick up on how dangerously close to a panic attack I am, hopefully no one else will. Everyone still probably thinks I'm crazy thanks to Beverly. It'd be best that I not legitimize that theory.

We step over cords and maneuver around crew working hard backstage to make the taping a success.

Breathe, I remind myself. *It'll be okay.* Truth be told, I don't know exactly what it is I'm afraid of. I don't want to see Trent, I can do without a reunion with Beverly, and things between Brice and me are uncertain at best, but I don't think any of those things in themselves are the reason my teeth are chattering.

Three wooden walls hammered together replicating a makeshift house sit in the middle of the soundstage. Overhead, bright lights fix on their objects of illumination inside the roofless construct. Dread I haven't felt since my nightmares stopped sits like a log in the pit of my stomach. Despite the intense air conditioning, a lone bead of sweat travels from the pit of my arm down my side. Somehow, through a jaw that feels wired shut by fear, I tell Tim I can walk the rest of the way to set alone. He regards me skeptically but doesn't challenge my request. I make sure he's out of sight before I duck behind one of the walls of the set.

This is where it all started for me, my downward spiral. Not here exactly, not this particular set in this studio. I mean here, as in my desire for the bright lights. I was willing to do anything, I nearly did, and where did it get me? Nowhere. The last time I was on a set, I was tragically lost. I don't ever want to be that again. I'm afraid today will teach me I'm still the same person I was nine months ago.

Chapter 4

Setting Around

*I*t's okay. *You've got this. You're not the same desperate girl who joined* Star Quality *nine months ago; you're different.* I close my eyes, take a deep breath, then release it slowly. *Walk in with your head high, shoulders back, and remember to breathe.* I shake out my arms and blow out five short breaths, a technique my acting coach, Andy, taught me to control my nerves.

Andy jokes in every class that I enjoy the breathing exercises more than acting. There's some truth to that. A year ago, when I had panic attacks what seemed like every ten minutes, breathing deeply helped me get through them. And Brice. The panic attacks came before *Star Quality,* but they followed me there. Brice found out accidentally; I had a bad episode in front of him one night, and he helped me through it.

I got back to the cast house late. It was dark, and I was sleep-deprived. I hadn't gotten a full night's rest in days because of the nightmares. Usually, when they got too bad, I'd find Brice. He was typically awake himself, sitting on a windowsill in the living room. Bad dreams kept me up. Grief over the death of his fiancé Seriyah five years prior haunted him. That's how we became friends; we bonded over the things that kept us up at night.

We'd stay up and talk. Sometimes Brice would pray for me, but I always wound up asleep. The nightmares never came when I was with him. Trent saw the footage from some of those nights and got really upset. It didn't help that the producers were working a romantic angle between Brice and me in the editing process. No matter how many times I told Trent nothing was going on between Brice and me, he didn't believe it. I had to cut Brice off to save my relationship, which meant I couldn't go to him when the nightmares came.

The night Brice found out I had panic attacks, I was so fatigued I was delirious. I didn't notice him sitting on his favorite windowsill. When Brice got up and started walking toward me, I didn't know who he was. I thought I was in a nightmare. I freaked out, tripped, and hurt myself, but Brice took good care of me. He ran to my side, talked me down, and iced my bruise.

Once I calmed down, I was mortified. If my knee wasn't injured, I would have run and hidden in my room. Brice picked up on how embarrassed I felt. To put me at ease, he told me about the time he had a panic attack. His roommates at the time thought it was a heart attack. A doctor checked him out at a hospital, told him nothing was physically wrong with him, and suggested seeing a therapist. Brice went to see a counselor, which helped some. What worked most, though, was leaning into his relationship with Jesus.

I haven't had a panic attack since I realized the significance of my dreams. I've found comfort in knowing God is working on something for me. Although, lately, I've begun feeling the gnawing of those same old fears and desires about my life in the pit of my stomach. What if this is it for me? What if I work as a sales associate at a boutique and live in my mom's basement the rest of my life?

I put my hand against the wall and breathe deeply and slowly. *Stop it. This is not your end. There's more for you on the other side if you hold on.* I suck in a deep breath and hold it. *You survived five weeks of filming twenty-four hours a day. What's three hours?* I let the breath go slowly. *You can do it, Leah. I can do it.*

I step out from behind the wall, take another deep breath, and walk the few steps to the set entrance. I hear Aiden's laughter before I see him and automatically feel at ease. The stage is busy and noisy, with about a dozen crewmembers speaking to one another and walking back and forth to and from the set.

The crewmembers are easy to spot. They all look like Tim, not physically but in their movements. They do everything briskly. Although their demeanor is far from relaxed, their dress is very much so; everyone's wearing jeans, sweatshirts, sneakers, and walkie-talkies except for a small group of guys. They're standing around the chairs and couches that I assume are there for the cast to sit once we begin filming.

My heartrate picks up. Brice is here. His back is facing me, but I know him as soon as I see him.

"Leah." Aiden turns, sees me, and comes rushing my way. I fight the urge to look at Brice and keep my eyes on Aiden's smiling face.

"Aiden," I shout back.

"I'd hug you, but I'm afraid to touch you," he says, lifting my hand over my head and twirling me.

"I'm happy you're here," I say, beaming. "This reunion would be way too stuffy without you." Aiden's positive vibes all the time—he doesn't take himself too seriously; he doesn't allow you to take yourself too seriously either. You can always count on him for a good time.

"Oh," he says, raising his brow, "So you've been looking forward to seeing me, huh?"

"Oh, Aiden," I say, rolling my eyes. "You're still a shameless flirt, I see."

"Yeah, well, I like to play the odds."

"Clearly," I say, laughing.

"Come say hi to the guys."

"Which guys?" I ask, feeling flushed.

"Leahz, don't tell me you forgot about the other guys already," he says with an impish grin. "I know they're not as handsome or as funny as me, but you should try to remember the people you live and work with."

39

"Aiden…" I shove him, not hard enough to hurt but to get him to be serious. "Who's here?"

"*Hmmm…* Let me see."

"Aiden," I shout.

"Okay. Okay." He laughs. "I left Zack, Corey, and Brice in the corner back there."

I turn left and right, but the set's dense with crew, I can't make him out. "Where is he?" I ask, still looking around.

"He?"

"They. Where are they?" I quickly correct.

"Follow me."

Corey sweeps me up in a bear hug. Unlike Aiden, he isn't concerned about wrinkling my dress or accidentally moving a hair. I remain perfectly still, hoping to avoid a wardrobe malfunction of the slipping or popping-out variety.

"Leah," Zack says, then places a chaste kiss on my hand.

"Dude, you're not in one of your Shakespeare plays," Corey jokes. Standing impossibly straight in an imitation of Zack, he turns to Aiden. "I say, my good sir, doth thou knoweth of what I speaketh?"

Never one to decline a laugh, Aiden joins in. "Sir, 'tis all hum drugeon." Zack playfully throws a fist at Aiden, who easily sidesteps it. Corey steps in, and the three of them are horsing around, just like old times.

"Where's Brice?" I ask over the noise of the set and their roughhousing.

"I'm not sure," Zack says. "I thought he said he was going to the restroom, but that was some time ago."

"I do believe so, sir," Corey says right before Zack cuffs him on the ear. Zack does have the tendency to sound a bit stiff sometimes; it suits him, though.

I back away from them right into Brice. After seven months, it's like seeing him for the first time—better in fact because I allow myself to really look. He's so much more handsome than I remember, which is hard to be. He's suave in a mauve suit, ivory shirt, no tie, and cognac wingtips. I've never seen him this dressed up before. Maybe that's why he feels distant.

We stare, neither one of us speaking or moving. The awe in his eyes pins me in place. Suddenly, after months of not knowing what I would say to Brice if we ever met again, I become overwhelmed with too many words clamoring to be spoken.

"Brice, I'm—"

"I have to go."

Without thinking, I grab hold of his arm. I'm not strong enough to stop him from leaving if that's what he wants to do, but I hope he doesn't.

"Wait."

His eyes hold mine. In them is a familiarity time hasn't erased. I see when he decides to hear me out. His expression is pained, but his arm relaxes, so I let go of my grip. He's hesitant of me; he's never been that before. Why now?

"Thank you." I bite my lip, unsure of what to say next. None of what I wanted to say a second ago feels right anymore. How can I apologize to him for all the time I spent not seeing exactly what I had in front of me when he's this guarded?

"H–How are you?" I stutter.

"In this very second." He shrugs.

"What does that mean? Are you not okay?" I ask, looking him over from head to toe.

"I'm fine, Leah—or should I call you Mrs. Shaw?"

"Mrs. What?"

"What, you didn't take your husband's last name?"

He thinks I'm married. Brice thinks I married Trent. That's why he's standoffish and why he didn't answer my text, not because he doesn't care about me anymore. He thinks I'm married. Before I can stop myself, I'm laughing because he's so wrong. Brice's face crumples, and he turns away from

41

me for the second time. I grab his arm again. This time, he isn't slowing down. To his back, I shout, "I'm not married."

Brice whips around, confusion and hope in his eyes. "You...You're not married?"

"No. I'm not," I say, still holding on to his arm.

He takes a step closer to me, staring deep into my eyes. He asks, "Are you getting married?"

"Someday, God willing. Not now. Not to him."

With reckless abandon, Brice pulls me into a hug too intimate with cameras around to enjoy. I don't push him away, though. I've done enough of that as it is. Besides, I miss being in Brice's arms, close to his heart.

"*Awww,* you two."

Aiden, Corey, and Zack choose that exact moment to amble over and turn our intimate moment into a group thing. I love them ninety-nine percent of the time. The way I feel about them right now falls into that other one percent.

"I missed you guys," Corey jokes.

"Actually..." I let go of Brice, causing everyone else to let go of one another too. I turn to Corey who's behind me. "I did miss you," I say, staring up into Corey's pale, lightly freckled face. "I was devastated when you were eliminated." I couldn't be sorry for being saved from the bottom two, but I was sad that my staying meant he had to go.

He puts his heart over his hand. "Leahz, you're gonna make me cry. Tear." He traces the trail of his imaginary tears down his face, but even in his joking, I know he's touched.

"It's true," Zack confirms. "I found her in our room basically in tears after you left."

"I wasn't crying. My eyeballs were sweating. It was hot out that day,"

"Aww. Leahz, you're so sweet," Aiden says, trying to pinch my cheeks.

I swat his hands away from me. The guys erupt in laughter.

"Seriously, Leah, you really are the sweetest," Aiden says. "It's crazy how the producers got that completely wrong."

"Yeah," Zack says, nodding.

"Yeah," Corey agrees.

"Yeah." If I didn't know any better, I'd say Brice sounds upset. "It's okay, Leah. There are still six episodes left in the season. That leaves six more episodes for the viewers to see the real you."

"Thanks, Brice. Thank you—all of you—for trying to make me feel better."

I smile at them because I appreciate what they're trying to do, but even I wouldn't like me if I were a viewer. I have editing to thank for that—and Amy probably. They've edited me into a raging, promiscuous, crazy zealot.

"It's not all bad," Zack says. "You actually have a huge fan base on Twitter."

"I noticed that—"

"I thought you deleted all your social media accounts," Aiden says.

"I did," I begin, my face growing warm. "I disconnected after the competition, but I enabled Instagram and Twitter again the night the show premiered. I was thinking about tweeting you and Corey during the show."

I'm not sure it was the right thing to do. The comments were harsh. People actually accused me of being jealous of Cashmere and Beverly. In their defense, it wasn't a hard conclusion to jump to when every other scene is me getting into it with one of them. Somehow the camera never caught the inciting action, though.

Everything I said or did painted me as the villain. Every story needs one. I learned that from Trent. Since I abruptly quit the show, I drew the short straw. I didn't make it to the end of the episode. I couldn't. I shudder at the fun they undoubtedly had with the footage of me confronting Cashmere over my missing Bible.

That wasn't a good moment all on its own, even before it got to the editing room. I was incensed, ready to strike, and the cameras were there to catch every second of that exchange. I was positive it was Cashmere who'd stolen from me, either of her own design or as part of a plan she and Beverly were working. Turns out she was innocent. The same couldn't be said of Beverly.

That was her first move against me, sanctioned by Trent, of course. Which is another thing the viewers don't know. They probably think I'm an unhinged psychopath. Given the biased depiction of me, I don't blame them.

By the end of the hour, I had to disable my comments and make all my social media accounts private. The viewers found me, and they wanted me to know exactly what they thought about my television debut. The reactions were surprisingly mixed. Don't get me wrong: A lot of people hated my guts, but I had fans too. #TeamLeah was trending.

This was what Trent promised. This was reality TV fame: viral, instant, and hollow. I hated what I saw of the show and my representation. I didn't like being harassed on social media or praised for being a debased version of myself either. But like my mom said, I can't change what's happened, but I can allow God to give it purpose.

Corey slings a long, lanky arm around my shoulder and squeezes. "Don't worry, Leahz. All publicity is good publicity. Just sit back and enjoy the #TeamLeah ride." I squirm my way out from under his arm, troubled by how much like Trent he sounds.

"Ahem."

I look over my shoulder to find Cashmere in an all-black strapless, backless ensemble. It's severe, but she pulls it off.

"Am I a ten or what?" she asks, striking a *Vogue* cover-worthy pose.

"Definitely a ten," Corey replies without hesitation. Aiden, Zack, and Corey move closer to Cashmere for a better look, leaving Brice and me standing alone.

"Hey," he says, stuffing his hands deep in his pockets.

"Hey, back at you," I reply, tilting my head in his direction.

Brice gives one of his rare million-watt carefree smiles, making me blush. He takes the few steps between us, igniting a flurry of emotion. Gently, Brice takes my hand in his.

"I've missed you," he says.

"I've missed you too." I don't say how much or how glad I am just to be able to look at him outside of my mind's eye. The Brice of my imagination pales in comparison to the real thing. The real Brice's cheeks flush, and his skin smells like citrus underneath his musky cologne. He radiates light, and his eyes soften when they look at me. Everything looks different standing next to him—impossibly better.

Brice clears his throat. "Zack was talking about getting the gang together for dinner after taping, afterward...can you and I go someplace and talk?" Brice's cheeks flush, deepening the faint red hues in his rich terracotta complexion.

My chest fills with a light airiness, a stark contrast from the dread I've felt since I woke up this morning. I search Brice's face. He's so handsome. Why did it take me this long to appreciate that? After Cashmere told me he'd moved to New York City, but I hadn't heard from him, I was sure I'd imagined the night Brice said he loved me. Then I thought maybe he stopped, but he's here, and he obviously still cares. I'm not going to blow it with him this time around.

"I'd like that," I answer.

"Yeah," he asks. I nod.

"So would I," Brice replies. He squeezes my hand lightly. I squeeze his back. "Let's go," Brice says. He nods toward the small circle of our friends and former castmates. "Cashmere will chew us both out if we don't go compliment her dress."

"Facts." I chuckle softly. "I'm not trying to feel Cashmere's wrath today." Brice leads the way to the rest of our castmates, my hand in his.

What was I so afraid of? Trent's not here, but Zack, Corey, Cashmere, and Aiden are. Best of all, Brice and I are finally going to have our moment. I completely overreacted; so did my mom. I don't see any test. This is shaping out to be a great day.

"This is ridiculous. Where is she?" the associate producer, Stephanie Piscano, asks the room at large for the umpteenth time. "Beverly should've been here an hour ago." She paces the length of the set. "We can't shoot a *Star Quality* reunion without the winner of *Star Quality*."

Complete quiet covers the set; everyone's afraid of being noticed by Stephanie who's on the verge of a total meltdown. Serves her right. Beverly shouldn't have been a contestant on the show, let alone the winner. Her acting skills are nonexistent. She was consistently the weakest performer every week, but she got the contract, the money, the agent, the role, and the guy in the end. I'm trying to keep in mind the decision was above Stephanie's pay grade; she's just another producer. Trent was the one calling the shots. But her attitude is making it a difficult task. She suddenly storms away without a word to anyone, signaling it's okay to exhale to everyone on set.

"I was hoping someone else would ask," Zack says, looking about as serious as I've ever seen him. "However, since none of you have, I guess I will. How on earth did Beverly win?"

My eyes meet Cashmere's briefly, a pact not to tell what we know. I told her about Trenton and Beverly's arrangement. She helped him sabotage me, and he made sure she won *Star Quality.* I can't share that with Zack or anyone else, though, except maybe Brice later.

"That's a good question. I thought Leah or maybe you would win," Aiden says to Zack. "Never Beverly, though. I mean, she's worse than you, bro." He ducks, narrowly avoiding Corey's playfully aimed punch.

"Hey, watch it," Cashmere shouts at them.

I'm usually okay with their horsing around, but I'm with Cash on this one. If I have to sit on this couch underneath the warm lights this close to Cashmere, Aiden, and Corey, play fighting will not be tolerated.

"How'd you get eliminated, Leah?" Corey asks, straightening up his jacket.

"She wasn't," Zack says, from his seat behind me. "She quit the same night Brice was eliminated. I was in the top two with Beverly."

"You quit?" Aiden, Corey, and Brice ask in unison.

I squirm beneath the hot lights, the curious expressions of my castmates, and all their questions. The conversation was bound to come up today at some point; I just wish I had an answer ready. I really should have been more prepared.

"Yes, I quit."

"Why?" Corey asks, although, by the expressions they wear, I know the whole cast is wondering the same thing. "You could've won."

I shift in my seat, hoping to get more comfortable, and end up with my back pressed against the arm. I don't know what to say. Other than Brice and Cashmere of late, my castmates aren't religious. How can I tell them I had to leave because it's what I knew God wanted me to do? They'll think I'm crazy. I can't tell them about Trent's involvement with Beverly either because that would mean having to reveal my involvement with Trent. They'll think I'm just as bad as Beverly.

"I quit...I quit because I just didn't want to be there anymore." I catch Brice's eye. He's the only person I'd risk looking at now. The wheels are turning in his mind. I owe him a real conversation later, but that'll have to be good enough for everyone for now.

We've been waiting almost two hours for her, yet when Beverly comes sashaying on set wearing a fire engine–red blazer dress and a haughty sneer, no one's happy to see her. Except Stephanie whose more relieved than anything else. Without any salutations or acknowledgment that she was wrong to hold up shooting, Beverly swaggers around the couch and sits on the empty stool between Zack and Brice.

Cashmere and I share a covert glance in disbelief of how brazen Beverly is.

"That's your friend," I mouth, shaking my head.

Cashmere rolls her eyes then mouths back, "For about a minute."

I guess their mutual dislike of me wasn't enough to build a lasting friendship, especially after Cashmere and I became friends.

I have my reasons for disliking Beverly; if things were different and those reasons didn't exist, we'd be in the exact same place. She's an equal opportunity anti-hero—no one's favorite person. It's hard to stomach her, which I'm starting to believe is intentionally done.

"Everyone's finally here," Stephanie says, aiming an irritated look Beverly's way. "Let's get this shoot back on track. Places, people. Last looks."

Hair and makeup hurry on set, powdering noses and chasing stray hairs.

"Okay, my dear," Nancy, the lone makeup artist on set, blots my nose then stands back, assessing me. She nods. "You are ready for the world."

"Thanks for helping me look my best, Nancy," I reply.

"Please. You were born with it, honey." Finished with me, Nancy moves on to Cashmere.

"Corey," Stephanie says, "switch places with Beverly. Take the stool at the end, and Beverly," Stephanie waits for Beverly to look at her before continuing, "sit at the end of the couch here." Stephanie points at the now empty seat next to Aiden.

I stay perfectly still, refusing to acknowledge Beverly. Thanks to Stephanie, Beverly is now sitting a lot closer to me than I like, but it's okay. We may only be separated by two bodies, but as far as I'm concerned, it might as well be an ocean.

"Hey."

I half-turn. Brice is leaning forward in his chair to whisper to me. I almost forgot how strategically placed my seat is, close enough to speak to and always be in Brice's line of vision, but far enough to give him space to admire me.

"Hey back at you."

Brice tilts his head slightly to the left, cutting off the view to our castmates, making it just him, his unreadable expression, and me. "Why'd you come today?"

I see his lips move and hear the words, but I have no idea what just happened. One minute he's gazing what I thought was adoringly at me, the next he's asking why I'm here. I turn back around in my seat, inwardly seething. I don't want to be here, but I have as much a right to be as anyone else.

I turn back around to face him. "I–I," I stammer at the tender expression on his face. For a split second, I almost forget his offense and let him off the hook, then I remember.

"I came for a few reasons," I say, fueled by the hot fire coursing through my veins. "First, because it's my right. I was a cast member just like the rest of you. Second, because I could. I was invited just like everyone else here. Third, because I had to—if I didn't, I would've faced legal repercussions—and last… Actually, I'm not going to tell you my fourth reason."

I turn back around, arms folded across my chest. Fourth, I came to see Brice, but there's no way I'm telling him that now.

Brice leans back into my space over my shoulder. I see him out of the corner of my eye though I choose to ignore him. I can't reverse time and make it so I'm not here, but I can give him the next best thing, the cold shoulder.

"Don't give me your mad face," Brice says, laughter coming through his voice.

"My what?" I ask, immediately breaking my resolve not to speak to him for the remainder of the shoot.

"Your mad face," he replies, the corners of his mouth twitching.

If he thinks he's going to be rude one second, playful the next, and I'm going to be cool with that, he is sadly mistaken. I've dealt with enough skittish male behavior from Trent to last a lifetime. I'll pass, thank you very much. I turn slightly to my left, entirely away from him.

"Leah." Silence. "Leah," he sings. More silence. "Leah."

"What?" I crack.

"Can you please not give me your mad face?" The gentleness in his voice irks me, but two can play that game.

"I don't have a mad face," I say as sweet as pie, turning to face him again.

"Yeah, you do," he says, laughing. "You usually don't use it with me, though, except twice."

"I have no idea what you're talking about. First, I don't have a mad face, and second, when have I ever been upset with you?"

His smile slips, but his mouth retains traces of laughter. "You don't remember the conversation we had the last night in the house?" I suck in a breath. I hope he doesn't hear. I can't believe he brought that night up. I've thought about it a lot myself. *I want to talk to you about it and tell you I have feelings for you too, just not right now.* "I'd say you were plenty mad at me. Look, you're not upset anymore; your eyes are back to normal," he says, jumping from one thought to the next.

"You know, you're the only person I've ever met whose eyes actually darken when they're angry. I've always thought of brown eyes as kind of ordinary. Not yours, though. They're mesmerizing."

My eyes drop, unable to hold his any longer. My ears feel hot, and I know I'm blushing too. I'm not used to Brice openly admiring me. I can't be too mad at him when he's painting me at my worst in beautiful detail, but I still resent his question.

"When you put it that way..." I shrug. My stomach flutters when our eyes meet again. He's not getting off that easily, though. "Hypothetically speaking, if I did, in fact, have a 'mad face,' it would be reserved exclusively for you at the moment."

"Wrap it up, people," Stephanie shouts, cutting through our conversation. "Last looks." She punctuates every word with clapping. "Where's Ileyana?" Stephanie turns in a circle. Realizing Ileyana, the host, isn't on set, she says, "How is it this whole time no one thought to bring her to set? Come on, people, work with me. Someone get her here now." It's funny how worked up Stephanie is over something she didn't think to do before now, either.

My neck's starting to hurt, and Brice can't possibly be comfortable hunched down leaning over as he is to talk to me. Still, I much prefer this conversation to any other one I could possibly be having with anyone else. Brice's eyes flit from my face to somewhere off set and back; it's a casual gesture though I read in his expression he sees something he doesn't like.

"What I asked you before, about why you came," he says, "it wasn't meant to insult you. I asked because I needed to know how to handle things." I shake my head. "Trenton. He's here."

"W–What?"

Trent has never shown too much interest in *Star Quality* except where I was concerned. He created the concept, then sold it to REAL TV, and stayed on as executive producer, but he gave Stephanie a lot of creative control. He only intervened to ensure Beverly won and I didn't. Still, Trent showing up was always a possibility. It's one of the main reasons I didn't want to do the reunion, but after being a no-show all morning, I thought he'd decided to stay away. I hoped he'd stay away. I thought my silence was clear enough communication; I didn't want anything more to do with him. I should have known better. He said he wasn't giving up; this is him being true to his word. He picked a great time to start doing that.

I grip my elbows to steady my body. Every ounce of calm I've felt since reuniting with my castmates is gone. Maybe I can say I'm sick—the way I feel right now, it wouldn't be pretending. I'm terrified of turning around and seeing him. The day I left the competition, I cut Trent out of my life, just lifted him right out. I didn't consider what I would do if I saw him again—at least not seriously. I imagined I'd yell a lot, maybe bruise my knuckles against his jaw, but I don't want to scream or fight. I don't want to be bothered with him at all.

"The Lord is your light and your salvation whom shall you fear?" Brice's large hand comes down on my shoulder; warmth spreads from that spot to the rest of me. He's solemn and urgently wanting me to know something. For the time being, we're not on set—our castmates aren't here, Stephanie isn't yelling into her walkie-talkie, even Trent's gone.

"The Lord is the stronghold of your life—of whom shall you be afraid? When the wicked advance against you to devour you, it is your enemies and your foes who will stumble and fall." He looks past me again, most likely to Trent, then back. "I'm sure he's here out of a desire to see you, not out of any obligation to the show."

I nod, knowing he's right.

"I'm sure he will do anything he can to manipulate this situation to get what he wants, which is you. If you want him back, too, this conversation doesn't matter. That's why I asked why you came today. If it's for him, then mission accomplished. However, if you're here out of obligation like you said and you want nothing more to do with Trenton, know the Father, the Son, and the Holy Spirit's got you first; I've got you second."

In the midst of it all, I smile at the slight blush creeping up Brice's face. He clears his throat and continues without the color in his face, though clearly in his voice.

"It can be difficult getting an ex, especially one you felt very connected to, out of your system. With God's help, you can sever that tie, but it's up to you what happens next. I'm here if you need me."

I reach up and take hold of Brice's hand, squeezing gently; he returns the pressure. I'm still not thrilled about seeing Trent, but I'm prepared. I didn't come here for him. It doesn't matter what his intentions or designs are; they don't affect me, I tell myself. I take a deep breath and turn around. My gaze darts to every face, every corner. No sign of him. I relax my shoulders for the time being. He's always had a talent for lurking. He'll make his presence known sooner or later.

"Leah."

"Yeah," I say, turning toward the source. I lock eyes with Beverly. She grins and waves, sending a chill up my spine. Guess she plans on making this a reunion to remember.

Chapter 5

A Reunion, the Reunion, and Our Reunion

"**B**everly, congratulations on your well-deserved win," says Ileyana, the host of the reunion episode. She hosted *Star Quality* too. She was at every performance challenge serving as a moderator between the contestants and the judges. Her role's different today though. She's definitely giving Oprah.

In the forty-five minutes we've been filming, Ileyana's gone through the pleasantries as well as Aiden and Corey's segments. She hasn't addressed me yet except to compliment my reunion look. It was easy to gush about the excellent job hair, makeup, and wardrobe did. The hard part's answering questions about myself, one question, in particular; what am I doing now?

When Ileyana asked what projects he's currently working on, Corey revealed he filmed a pilot that's recently been picked up by one of the major four networks. She asked Aiden the same question. He's been cast as a series regular on a successful sitcom. All my castmates are doing exciting things except me. I'm scared Ileyana's going to ask me what I'm working on. What will I say, that I went from almost winning *Star Quality* to working at a clothing store? It's Beverly's turn in the hot seat now. Like Zack and Corey, she's been cast in a huge project. I know this because Trent gave her the role in his upcoming feature film that he wrote for me. That was part of their deal. Beverly sabotages me, and Trent gives her the win and the movie role.

Dread burrows its way into my chest again. One second, my body's taut with tension. The next, it's fluttering with tiny trembles all over. I can barely hear Ileyana and Beverly over the chattering of my teeth. I clench my jaw and clasp my hands together tightly in my lap, praying to stay as still as possible. I hope no one notices. I just want to get through my turn and be done with this.

"Beverly, how did you feel when you won? Describe that feeling to us," Ileyana says.

"I was excited but not surprised. I knew I was going to win," Beverly says. I forget to be afraid and look at Beverly.

She can't possibly be about to tell everyone the competition was rigged, can she?

Beverly turns her head slightly in my direction. She doesn't meet my eyes, but she wants me to see and hear her every word. Beverly's not admitting anything; she's gloating. Beverly tosses her long blond hair off her shoulders.

"I was born to be a star," she says.

"Okay," Ileyana says, "you weren't surprised that you won. Is there anything that did surprise you about the competition?"

"I don't surprise easily." Beverly chuckles. "But finding out from production right after Brice was eliminated that Leah had to withdraw from the competition to check into a mental wellness center came as a shock."

"What?" Aiden exclaims.

"Is that true?" Zack asks.

"Why didn't you say anything, Leah?" Corey questions.

Total chaos erupts on set; I don't know who's saying what. The questions are coming from everywhere. Everyone's speaking over one another, wanting to know if what Beverly said is true. Like my castmates, this is the first time I hear this version of events, although it doesn't surprise me. Amy, the producer who disliked me probably as much as Beverly, promised something like this would happen if I walked out on the competition. Actually, I'm impressed they were able to put together such a credible story. It was a stroke of brilliance on their part.

Beverly revealed I suffered from panic attacks during week three. The judges were concerned I wouldn't be able to deal with the pressures of the industry. According to the producers, my apparent hostility, violent outbursts, and sudden departure proved I couldn't. The groundwork was laid long before I left the competition. All they had to do was pour the cement.

I look past Aiden and Cashmere at Beverly; she's the picture of unbothered. To her credit, she doesn't give anything away. She was able to maliciously answer Ileyana's question without appearing to be so. It's the best acting she's ever done.

I could just let it go, take the high road, but I'm not in a let-it-go kind of mood. I sit up taller in my seat, blood simmering.

"Leah," Brice whispers behind me, his voice a plea to exercise restraint. I appreciate his concern, but my mind's made up. He's not talking me out of this.

"Actually, I left because I discovered the show was rigged. Beverly was going to win no matter what."

"Cut." Stephanie storms on set, blue eyes ablaze.

"What was that?" she screams.

I don't bother responding. It's more of a rhetorical question, plus there's no explanation needed. Stephanie's as aware of the truth as I am. My bombshell won't make the final cut. I know that. I just didn't want Beverly, Trent, and *Star Quality* to continue to get away with humiliating me. It was impetuous and gutsy. Beverly can easily tell everyone about Trent and me, though I doubt she will. I'm sure Trent's made it worth her while not to.

"You," Stephanie says, staring murderously at me, "come here."

"No. I'm fine right where I am," I reply with a smile. Her anger, which should intimidate me, only stokes the embers of my own anger. I'm tired of playing their games. They can force me to be here, but I won't be their punching bag. "If you wish to speak with me privately, you can," I say, returning her stare, "provided you ask again, nicely."

Next to me, Aiden whistles through his teeth. I get it. That might have been reckless, but I'm not backing down. I won't let this show take any more of my life or self-respect.

"Be quiet," Stephanie yells above the murmurs of the cast and crew.

I can almost see the steam coming out of her ears. No way will she let me get the better of her, and I won't give her the satisfaction of responding to a summons. She folds her arms over her chest, waiting for me to get up. I fold my arms across my chest, waiting for her to ask with respect. We're at an impasse.

"Leah."

If I weren't already sitting, I would need to. All the strength leaves my body, and my knees go weak. Trent walks on set looking like the devil he is in a tailored red suit, not all that different in color or cut from Beverly's dress.

I feel a wealth of things at the sight of him: anger, hurt, fear. But then there's part of me—the part I hate—that swoons a little too. A few months apart hasn't changed him or lessened the thing in me that's thrilled at the sight of him. We lock eyes. I hold my breath. Otherwise, I might scream.

"Would you please do me the favor of speaking to Stephanie and me privately for a moment?"

It isn't that he asked. It's the nakedness with which he's looking at me that makes me get up and follow him and Stephanie off set. I turn to look at Brice before he's entirely out of my line of vision. I smile. He doesn't smile back.

"You're the crazy one if you think for one second I'll go along with that ridiculous storyline," I yell. "What I am willing to say is I received news from home that made it imperative I return. The show had to go on. It did, without me."

"No. We will continue as planned with the previously stated reason for your abrupt departure. Need I remind you, you signed a contract? *Star Quality* and the network have the power to use your likeness, performances, conversations, et cetera, in perpetuity whichever way we choose. This matter is no longer up for dis—"

"We'll say Leah left to deal with a family crisis." Trent's voice is measured, without hardness or intimidation but also without room to be disagreed with.

Stephanie looks at Trent like he's an idiot, but she doesn't put up a fight either. She stomps away, yelling, "Places" as she goes.

I make to follow her. I don't want to be alone with Trent, but he stops me. I jerk my arm away, repulsed by the conceit that led him to think he could touch me.

"L," he pleads, letting his hand fall away. He takes a step forward; I take one back. Whatever it was I briefly felt when I saw him is gone. The only thing I want from Trent is to be left alone.

"I'm sorry, L, I shouldn't have touched you. I just want you to hear me out."

"No." I leave him standing alone without a backward glance.

"My next question is for you, Leah."

I tense up in anticipation of what Ileyana's about to ask. She's left me alone for the most part, but I guess it's my turn to be in the hot seat.

"We've heard from your castmates about their projects post *Star Quality*. What about you? What have you been doing since your abrupt departure from the show?"

Straightforward question, complicated answer—actually not so complicated answer, which is the problem. I'm a sales associate at a small boutique. The closest I've come to my dream is the expensive acting classes I take every week. I'm just as talented, if not more, than my castmates. I obeyed

God. I left the guy, the fame, the money all behind. What do I have to show for it?

Biting back tears, I smile and say, "I'm happy for the success of my castmates. I don't have anything as major to report, but I am weighing a few offers."

"Anything you can tell us about?"

"No, Ileyana, not yet."

"That's because she doesn't have any offers," Beverly says.

"Cut. Let's go again from 'Anything you can tell us about?' And this time, keep your comments to yourself." Even Stephanie feels sorry for me. I cross my legs to hide their shaking and take a deep breath to keep from crying; my throat aches with the effort.

From behind me, Brice whispers, "Remember: God's got you."

We're rolling again. There's no time to thank him, but that was exactly what I needed—to be reminded God cares.

"Anything you can tell us about?" Ileyana asks.

"No. Not yet." This time around, Beverly keeps her mouth shut, but it doesn't matter; she accomplished what she set out to. Everyone knows I've accomplished nothing, I have nothing, I am nothing.

"Leah, there's something I've been dying to know. You came into the competition in a serious relationship. Yes?"

"*Ummm...well,*" I sputter, blindsided by the question. "Serious isn't exactly the word I would use. However, yes, I was in a relationship."

"Was? Does that mean you're no longer in a relationship?"

I nod, hoping she'll move on from this line of questioning.

"Inquiring minds want to know: Was Brice the reason for your breakup?"

Before she's through asking, I'm already shaking my head.

"I see you saying no, but we also saw you two growing pretty close. Am I right?" she asks my castmates.

To their credit, no one responds.

"Come on, spill it. What's going on between you and your gorgeous costar?"

My difficult-to-articulate relationship with Brice is a central storyline of the show. I know that. I knew it coming here. Trent told me as much, yet, I didn't imagine I'd be badgered about it. Why is Ileyana pressing me for an answer? Did Trent put her up to this?

"I—" The sound of blood pounding in my ears is deafening. I can't think or speak.

"I got to the cast house thinking the most I could get out of the experience was a win," Brice interrupts.

I let out the breath I didn't know I was holding and decide to let him do all the talking.

"Fortunately, I was wrong. No cash prize equals the value of the relationships I've made. I have a bond with every one of my castmates, including Leah. Though every relationship I gained is special and unique, my friendship with her is..."

My body tenses waiting to hear the word he would use to describe what we have.

"Refreshing. We're able to talk to each other about anything. Partially, I think, because we have similar beliefs and tastes; mostly because Leah's great. She's one of the best friends I have. However, I do emphasize that she is a friend."

I don't know what I wanted him to say—definitely not a passionate declaration of love, not an emphasis on friendship either. I wish I knew where we stand.

"Leah, do you have anything to add?" Ileyana asks.

"I wholeheartedly agree with Brice. Like he said, we're great friends." I smile as brightly as I can manage; I hope it doesn't look as fake as it feels.

"Dinner first, party later," Aiden suggests. He pauses, probably waiting for one of us to object. No one does, so he continues. "Since Zack, Corey, Bev, and myself are tourists, you three," he says, pointing to Brice, seated behind him, then to Cashmere and me beside him, "are responsible for showing us the best places to do that." With a self-satisfied grin, he leans back against the ugly blue couch in Zack's greenroom, where we've been holed up since we wrapped.

"Thanks for volunteering us for the location committee, but Cashmere and I are new here ourselves. Leah's the native," Brice corrects.

I try to catch his eye, to let him know I don't appreciate him making me the group's tour guide, but he never looks my way. Not now, not once, from the time I returned to set. He hasn't so much as glanced in my direction since I walked off with Stephanie and Trent. Yeah, he tried to comfort me when Beverly attacked me, but that's just who he is. That had nothing to do with any special regard for me.

"I'm not exactly an authority on hot spots," I say, holding up my phone, "but we can search thelist.com app and social media for what's trending."

Without delay, everyone gets on their phones. Brice has his phone out too. I'm not sure what he's doing; I remember from our time on the show together that he wasn't big on social media. I think he said he has an Instagram account he rarely checks. He could be on there now though I doubt that. I want to ask to try to break the tension. I don't think he wants to talk to me, though.

I get why he's upset. I got all worked up about seeing Trent then, as soon as he asked, I gave him my time. Nothing happened—I wouldn't even let Trent speak to me, but Brice doesn't know that. All he knows is I've been careless with his feelings in the past; however, I'm not about to do that again. Trent showing up and me agreeing to speak to him has zero to do with what

Brice and I have going on. Nothing's changed for me. I'm still looking forward to going somewhere with Brice to talk later. He needs to know that.

"By the way," I say, fixing my attention on Brice, whose attention is still on his phone, "I'm cutting out after dinner." I get what I want. Brice finally looks at me, although it's not what I expect. His expression is guarded and unreadable. He's...I don't know what he is actually, not mad though, something else.

"What do you mean you're cutting out early?" Corey asks. "We've spent the last fifteen minutes making these plans. You can't just bail on us."

"I'm not bailing out. I'm going to dinner, just not partying afterward."

"Why not?" Cashmere asks. "I hope it's not because of Beverly and that stunt she pulled. She probably won't even show; you saw how fast she ran off the set. I don't think she wants to see you off-camera."

"Don't take it personally. Beverly's horrible to everyone," Zack says, laughing. "Imagine a whole week alone in the cast house with her."

Aiden clasps him around the shoulder. "I'm so sorry for you, bro."

"I was sorry for myself. If the competition hadn't ended when it did, I would've quit too," Zack says.

"I'm not afraid of Beverly," I scoff. She's the last thing on my mind. "I don't want to go to the club because it's not my scene."

That may not be my sole reason for not wanting to go, but it is one of the reasons. Just because I can go anywhere doesn't mean I should. The last time I went to a club, I met Trent.

"Let's just focus on finding a restaurant so we can get out of here. I'm starved."

"Me too," Brice says placidly.

"*Shush.* Do you hear that?" Corey asks. We quiet, listening. "There it goes again."

"What is it?" Aiden asks.

"My stomach saying it's time to eat. I vote we go to the Cuban place near the train station. All in favor say *aye*."

"Aye," we sing in unison.

"Alright," Aiden says, "Let's go."

"So, what gives? What's the real reason you don't want to hang out with us?" Cashmere asks.

"I didn't lie. The club was never my scene; it's even less so now," I say over the howling wind and the New York City sounds. "What's the point anyways? You get dressed up, spend crazy money on alcohol, get drunk, dance, and make bad decisions. I'm still recovering from my last bad decision; I can't afford another one. I'm trying to do better, so thank you, but I'm going to sit this one out."

I push my hands deeper into my coat pockets, hunching my shoulders against the cold. We're not far now, the restaurant's at the end of the block. I look back, checking to see how much farther behind us the guys are before I tell Cashmere my other reason.

"And…"

"And what?"

"Brice and I might go someplace to talk." I leave out the part about not being sure if that's still the plan. I want to; I'm just not sure he does.

Cashmere stops short, forcing the stream of pedestrians to split to the left and right of us. "I knew it," she shouts. "I knew I was right about you two."

"Hush." I slap my hand over her mouth, turning my head in the direction of the guys. They're deep in conversation, completely unaware of us. "Quieter, okay?" I say before letting her go.

She nods.

"I knew it." I give her a pointed look. "I knew it," she repeats, much quieter this time. "When you walked off stage with Trenton..." She hesitates. "I thought it was over for Brice. Then when he came to your defense, I thought, *Good for him. He's not going down without a fight.*"

"You think he was defending me?"

"Yeah. Don't you?" Cashmere asks.

We stop in front of the restaurant but don't go in; we decide to wait for the guys to catch up. They aren't far behind; they should be here any moment. I see Brice first. He's easy to spot because he's head and shoulders above most people. He's with Aiden, Corey, and Zack but somehow apart from them too. I've always admired his ability to stand on his own. He doesn't need the validation of a group. Maybe he feels my gaze on him because Brice turns his head mid-conversation with Aiden and locks eyes with me. *I wish I knew what he was thinking.*

"You didn't answer my question," Cashmere says, calling my attention back to our conversation."

"What question was that?" I reply without breaking eye contact with Brice.

"Do you think Brice was defending you?" Cashmere asks.

Brice looks away first. Aiden said something to him, and he looked away.

"I don't know what to think," I say, looking back Brice's way. He isn't looking at me. "I'll tell you one thing though: It didn't feel like it."

"Leah, it's clear as day to anyone paying attention how much Brice cares for you. He's not like Trenton." Her voice shakes, but she keeps going. "Whatever you're thinking about him is wrong. Stop being offended and give him the benefit of the doubt."

The restaurant's small and ordinary, but it smells delicious. It's reasonably empty, too, which is a good thing. We have the tendency to get rowdy when we're all together. Fewer customers equal fewer complaints, hopefully.

With Corey's help, the petite hostess pushes two tables together to accommodate our large party. He's not ordinarily chivalrous; he just crushes a lot. He goes as far as helping her rearrange the chairs to fit seven though we're only six. Aiden sent Beverly the obligatory text about our plans. According to him, she said go ahead without her. She might catch up later. I hope she doesn't. I've had about as much of her as I can take.

"Bro," Corey says to Aiden. "I promise she likes me. She's just playing hard to get."

"Seriously doubtful, man. You did all that heavy lifting, and she wouldn't even give you her Instagram handle. I don't blame her though. I was standing next to you the entire time. She probably took one look at me and thought, why settle on you."

Zack weaves to his left, avoiding a paper ball to the face courtesy of Corey. He picks it up from where it landed on the floor and tosses it across the table to Brice, who easily catches it.

"Personally," he says, tossing the ball back and forth between his left and right hands. "I don't think there's anything wrong with working for a woman's attention or affection."

Corey holds out his fist to Brice for a pound, ignoring Zack and Aiden's loud disagreement. "Finally," Corey says, "someone who understands the game."

Aiden turns slightly to his left, facing Brice. "You don't genuinely believe that," he accuses. "Odds are you're only saying that because right now you're into someone who's about as into you as Corey's future wife over there is into him." Aiden nods to the hostess standing at the door waiting to greet the next dinner.

I watch Brice like a hawk for any sign Aiden's correct about him being into someone, preferably me, but he only shrugs, noncommittally at that. Which can mean anything or nothing.

"All I'm saying is if I have genuine feelings for someone—the kind of feelings that don't fade or diminish with time, distance, or circumstance—

then she's who I want to be with. Her. Not someone else. If I have to move a few tables to get her to notice me..." He shrugs again. "I'm okay with that. Look at Jacob; he worked fourteen years for Rachel."

"Fourteen years?" the table exclaims.

Everyone except me. I know the story.

"I was with you until you said fourteen years," Corey says. "No girl's worth that."

"Yeah," Zack adds, "and who are Jacob and Rachel? Are they another celebrity couple I accidentally purposely don't follow?"

"They're a Biblical couple," I say. I catch Zack's frown before he looks away. *What's that about?* "Long story short," I continue, ignoring the sour look on Zack's face. "Jacob met Rachel and was immediately taken with her. Out of the gate, he knew he wanted her to be his wife."

"Wife," Corey and Aiden exclaim in unison.

"Yes, wife. Jacob was a man of action; he always took his shot." I casually flick my eyes to Brice, then quickly back to Corey and Aiden; Zack seems to have checked out. "Anyways, Jacob began working for Rachel's father, Laban. Instead of wages, he asked that Laban agree to give Rachel to him in marriage after he'd worked for him seven years."

"Why is he working to earn her? That sounds crazy to me." Zack's tone matches the derision on his face. The idea of a bride price may be foreign in our culture, but Zack's refined and well-read. He's familiar with the notion.

"Because," I say, trying not to give Zack the attitude he's putting out, "it was the cultural practice of the time. Jacob made Laban an appealing offer, seven years of free labor, for his daughter. Laban agreed to the arrangement, thus began Jacob's labor for her."

"I thought you said fourteen years," Cashmere says.

I turn slightly in my seat to look at her.

"He did end up working fourteen years for Rachel. See, Rachel had an older sister, Leah."

"Her name's Leah, like yours," Corey says, pointing out the obvious.

I nod. "Yes, exactly. Leah wasn't beautiful like Rachel was—"

"So, not like you then," Brice interjects.

Our eyes meet across the table; the steadiness of his gaze causes my stomach to flutter. "Thank you," I say softly. This time I look away first. "*Ummm...What was I saying?*"

"That Leah wasn't cute," Cashmere says.

"I don't think I put it that way, but that's the general point. In ancient near eastern culture, the oldest sister had to be married before the younger one. Laban tricked Jacob into marrying Leah. Because the wedding garments for a bride included a veil that covered her face, Jacob didn't know it was Leah he marrying. The next morning when Jacob realized he'd married Leah, he was upset. Laban told him he should have known the cultural rules. Rachel couldn't be married until Leah was. Laban's solution was that Jacob marry Rachel too. However, he'd have to work another seven years for her, and that's exactly what he did."

"That could not have been me," Corey says. "I would have cut my losses. Miss one bus; the next one comes in fifteen minutes."

Seriously, bro." Aiden laughs and shakes his head. "Fourteen days is crazy, let alone fourteen years."

"Not if it's the right girl," Brice says to Aiden. "In your twenty-eight years of life, you haven't met one woman worth the investment of your time and energy?"

Aiden pauses as if thinking then collapses into laughter. "Nah," he says through laughs. "I've never met anyone worth that many years of my life."

"To Jacob, it was nothing," Brice says. "The Bible says the initial seven years went by quickly to Jacob because his love for Rachel was exceedingly strong—"

"That settles things. The Bible says it, so we should believe it." Zack throws his hands up in the air then lets them fall onto the table. His tone and manner are unmistakably sarcastic.

A moment of complete silence passes. We're all taking in Zack's behavior. I consider asking him what's his problem, then Cashmere's voice cuts through the thick silence.

"Have you?" she says, her eyes on Brice.

"Have I what?" he asks.

"Loved a woman the way Jacob loved Rachel?"

Brice studies her with keen eyes that are careful not to drift to her right, lest they land on me. I'm directly across from him, yet all I've seen of his face since we sat at the table is his determined profile. Cashmere's focused on Brice alone, like no one else exists while I sit there, reminded of her one-time crush on him. The crush she said she quickly got over and that he didn't reciprocate; however, everything about this moment contests that.

A dull ache starts in the pit of my stomach and crawls up to my heart, watching them. I was wrong about Brice; I was wrong about Cashmere too. I turn away from the scene, absolutely heartsick. I end up concentrating on the family a few tables away—a mom, a dad, and a son, the only other patrons of the restaurant.

"I had a fiancé once."

Brice's far-away and sullen voice draws me back in. I wasn't expecting him to talk about Seriyah; she's a difficult subject for him. As far as I know, he couldn't remember their best memories without breaking down. What's changed?

"She was my heart. I loved her completely, partly because I had to earn the chance to fall in love with her. She challenged me to be worth her time, and I'm a better man for it. I would have regretted it all my life if I hadn't fought to get close to her because she was the catalyst for a better me."

I don't mean to look at him. I mean to keep my eyes on the family, but it's hard to ignore the palpable love in his voice. I didn't imagine he'd be staring at me first, somberly too. Is he looking for emotional support? Before now, I was the only one of the castmates he confided in about Seriyah. I was there for him then. Is he looking for the same now?

69

"You might be right, Aiden. Maybe I am into a woman who's not that into me," he mutters. "What do you think, Leah? Do I have a chance with her?"

I turn my head slightly in Cashmere's direction. She's biting back a smile. Her eyes meet mine, then very deliberately move in Brice's direction. I think she wants me to answer him, which only causes me more confusion.

"Leahz," Aiden says, "does Brice have a shot or what?"

"I don't know."

"That's cold," a laughing Zack says.

Corey lifts his glass of water high above his head. "Here's to hoping it doesn't take fourteen years for your girl to warm up to you."

The paper ball Zack threw at him goes flying out of Brice's hands in my direction. It's too wide, and I wasn't expecting it; it's going to fall. It doesn't. I catch it with the tips of my fingers.

"Nice save," Aiden says. "Next time we play basketball, you're on my team. You can take Zack's spot. He has trouble passing, catching, and shooting the ball."

"You guys are so immature," Cashmere says, sounding very motherly.

In a voice meant only for me, Brice says, "In case you missed it, that was me shooting my shot. Like I said, I'm not afraid of putting in the work."

Chapter 6

Tell Me the Story of Jesus

O ur waiter, Mateo, returns to the table accompanied by two busboys carrying sizzling hot plates of food. They set to work distributing dishes. Delicious smelling plates beautifully garnished make their way around until arriving at their owner. My mouth salivates in anticipation of the pepper steak and rice in front of me. I'm not the only one eager to dig in. Corey wastes no time putting his fork to use.

"Now that's what I call a meal. This place was a good call—" His forehead creases while his expression changes from delight to bewilderment. "Brice? What are you doing?"

Every head turns in Brice's direction, yet his remains bowed. Corey, a non-believer, has no understanding of what he's witnessing. I'm not sure what Aiden or Zack believe. It never came up, though judging by Zack's frown, he's of a similar outlook as Corey.

Corey looks on the verge of saying something else. I shoot him the same look my mom would give me when we were in public and my behavior was questionable and stop him. I close my eyes and bow my head too. I know I should thank God for every meal. I rarely do, though. I'm going to try to be better about it starting now.

"Amen," I say, lifting up my head from prayer. Brice is done too.

Looking around the table, I notice that although only Brice and I blessed our food, the others haven't touched theirs; they seem afraid. That might be my doing. I didn't mean to scare them into not eating, just not talking.

Laughingly, Brice says, "Thanks for waiting on Leah and me. We're ready to eat now if you are."

He intentionally picks up his knife and fork and takes a bite of his arroz con pollo. That was all anyone needed to see to feel comfortable tearing into their own plate. Minutes of silently savoring our food pass uninterrupted.

"Dude, what were you doing before, when you had your head down?"

Corey's hopelessly tactless. Thankfully, Brice isn't easily offended—not usually anyway.

"I was saying grace," he answers good-naturedly.

"What does that mean?" Aiden asks.

Although Corey posed the question, apparently, the answer's of equal interest to everyone at the table. Realizing that, Brice answers with all the patience and kindness of a devoted teacher.

"I was giving thanks to God for the meal He provided."

"Hey, I know you're into all of that, but I'm not," Zack says, letting his knife and fork clatter noisily onto his plate. He pushes his seat away from the table and folds his arms across his chest.

"What am I into?" Brice asks without condescension.

"The whole church thing and whatever you church people believe."

Zack's visibly worked up—his face is splotchy, and his manner agitated. "Dude, relax." He shakes off Aiden's advice and completely shuts down. This incensed behavior is more like the Zack I first met, who went from zero to one hundred at the drop of a dime—the version of him I didn't care much for.

If Brice is upset, he hides it well. He puts his silverware down, too, and focuses completely on Zack. "I can tell you're really upset—"

"I'm not upset," Zack says. "If you want to believe in that stuff that's on you, just don't force it down my throat."

"What do you think I believe, and how am I forcing it down your throat?"

Zack motions dismissively in the air. "You know, God and stuff."

"It pains me that my faith is offensive to you, Zack. I want to say I understand your anger, but frankly, I don't. And it seems to me that maybe even you don't understand it."

"Don't tell me what I feel," Zack shouts, pointing his finger at Brice.

"I'm not trying to define your feelings to you, but you do clearly have strong emotions about my faith. When I asked you what do you think I believe, you couldn't answer the question. As passionate as you are about your non-belief, I'm even more so about the truth. You can choose not to believe if you want and even get worked up, but at least let me explain to you what it is you don't believe."

Brice is always impressive—that's not a matter of opinion—never quite as much as he is now, though.

Zack crosses his leg over his knee. Without making eye contact with Brice, he says, "I'll pass. I know all I need to."

"I'll bite. Tell me about God," Aiden says. "I'm not making any promises of conversion or anything, but, yeah, I'm down to hear you out." It's hard to say if Aiden's being the peacemaker he always is or if he's genuinely interested.

"Yeah, I'll hear you out too," Corey says, echoing Aiden.

"Hmpf." Zack turns away from the table, pulling out his cell.

"What about you two?" Brice asks, referring to Cashmere and me.

We both nod. Like Aiden, We want to hear more too.

"First, the truth is infallible and unvarying whether or not everyone accepts it as true. It isn't a question of my, your, his, or her truth. The truth is the truth. What is true and without error is that the Earth is the Lord's and everything in it, the world and all who live in it. God is the Creator. All belong to Him—plant life, the cosmos, animals, and mankind.

"Our enemy, the adversary of our soul, the evil one, influenced the first man and woman into sinning; from that time, man was in opposition of God because that's what sin does: It places us outside of relationship with the one true God."

He pauses and looks at us, making sure we're with him. Satisfied, he continues. "Contrary to popular belief, there is such a thing as right and wrong, and it isn't contingent on the era you live in, how a particular thing makes you feel, or what your heart says. Rightness is found in God, not in the reasoning of man. Because we live in a fallen world, we all sin and fall short of God's standard for the way we should live. That's called sin. Sin is offensive to God and separates us from Him. To bring us back to a place of right standing, relationship with Him, there had to be atonement. The justice and righteousness of God mandate payment for sin. Jesus paid the price for us with His blood.

"The Son of God, the second person in the Trinity of God, who was here, in the beginning, stepped into time as a man through the Immaculate Conception. Jesus grew to adulthood. He was baptized and labored for three years in terrestrial ministry. During that time, He called twelve disciples, though many followed Him. At the end of His ministry, Jesus suffered what is commonly called the passion. Jesus was betrayed by one of His disciples to the religious leaders of the time who wanted Him dead.

"Though this came as a surprise to some, it was no surprise to Jesus; it was all part of God's plan of redemption. Jesus told His disciples that He, the Son of Man, would be betrayed, beaten, mocked, flogged, and endure death, but it was necessary. When the appointed time came, everything happened as Jesus said it would. He was crucified on the cross, His hands and feet nailed, and His side pierced because of us. For us.

"We were all convicted criminals—judgment had been pronounced against us because the wages of sin is death. But Jesus, He stood in our place—each and every single one of us—and on the third day, He was resurrected. After walking on the earth for another forty days and being seen by over five hundred people, Jesus ascended to the right hand of the Father. But Jesus sent the Holy Spirit, the third person in the Trinity, to come indwell us.

"This is what it comes down to: 'For God so loved the world, that He gave His only begotten Son, that whosoever believeth in Him should not perish, but have everlasting life.' Not by our own goodness or works but by grace through faith in Jesus Christ. The eternal God was thinking of all of us when His son stood in our place. Our souls are real and can only be saved by accepting the finished work of Jesus on the cross. Jesus is the ransom for your soul, the redeemer of your life, the assurance of your future, and your hope for today. I'd be forever lost without Him. All of humanity would."

None of us speak. We're all still processing. I've never heard the condensed version of the gospel before; it's powerful. I'm becoming more and more aware of all I don't know about my faith. I've been in church my entire life, and I know about as much as Zack does. Brice looks us each in our eyes then stops at Zack who is still turned away from the table but isn't furiously scrolling or texting anymore.

"I really pray something I said sticks with you and causes you to draw near to Christ, or at the very least, makes you curious enough to learn more. Maybe today isn't that day for you, but when you get to that moment in your life where you need fulfillment, and you realize you can't find it in your wealth, career, a spouse, clubbing, or whatever else does it for you today, I pray you remember that Jesus was thinking of you on the cross over two thousand years ago, and He's thinking of you now."

Zack slowly turns back around in his seat and looks at Brice. He's visibly calmer; that's about as much as I know for sure. "Do you really believe that?" he asks.

It's difficult to say whether his question is sincere or an indictment.

"Since God in His wisdom saw to it that the world would never know Him through human wisdom, He has used our foolish preaching to save those who believe.' If you're looking for another answer, an argument made with philosophy, astronomy, or science, I don't have it," Brice matter of factly says.

"That was a great speech, man, but I need proof. Where's the proof?" Zack asks, slapping his hand down on the table, causing our plates to rattle.

"Dude, you have to calm down before you get us thrown out," Aiden says.

"Brice is telling us fairytales, and you're telling me to calm down? Again," he says, staring Brice down, "where is the proof?"

Brice takes a deep breath and lets it out slowly. That he's been able to remain calm with Zack attacking him is proof that regardless of whatever's happening with us, he is the guy I thought he was.

"I could name drop Biblical archaeologists and scientists right now who've made great discoveries backing up the claims of the Bible," Brice says. "Even nonbelieving scientists concede the world is too deliberate in its design to be a result of an accident."

"Wow. I didn't know that," says Corey, who's been very quiet. I wonder what he's thinking.

"Sorry, but I'm not buying it," Zack replies, shrugging.

"The truth isn't hidden, Zack. If you do the research, you'll find out some life-altering things, but even if I could use the things you accept as proof to speak to you about Jesus, you wouldn't believe what I'm saying. You need faith to believe, and faith comes by hearing the good news about Christ."

Zack shakes his head.

"It doesn't make sense to you today. I pray it does someday.

I push my food around the plate, willing it to be gone. My mind is too full for me to eat, regardless of how mouthwatering the meal. Without Aiden, Corey, and Zack's non-stop joking, those thoughts take my appetite away. I'm not alone in being preoccupied either. Everyone has been in their own head since Brice and Zack's back-and-forth.

Brice. I'm still in awe of the authority and passion with which he spoke, the tiniest bit envious, too, of how sure he is of where he stands. I wish I could be a better Christian, the kind who causes the world to ask more about Christ. I'm glad to be right about him. The moment I started thinking Brice isn't the guy I thought he was, he proved he is.

"Two million people and counting around the world are interested in what I have to say about everything. It's exhausting figuring out exactly what I feel and being sure in that feeling before I influence others to feel the same," Cashmere says to Aiden.

In the last minute, they've taken up a lively conversation they're not half as invested in as they pretend to be to cover the heavy silence at the table. They're sweet to try to ease tensions; however, I think pensive minds lead to convicted hearts.

I've never contemplated what it is to be an "influencer" and to have influence. Cashmere has the power to sway the minds of millions of people, especially young adults, on various topics. That's a lot of command for a person to have over a complete stranger's life for no reason other than they're popular and good at talking beauty.

"What are you frowning about?"

If I weren't subconsciously waiting for him to say something to me, I might not have heard him. I move closer to our table to make sure Brice can hear me over Cashmere and Aiden's argument about whether or not being an influencer is a legitimate job.

"Nothing. I was thinking about something."

"What were you thinking about?"

A small smile plays on his lips. It's a new smile, one I'm not used to seeing on him: confident and flirty. I like it. He leans back against his chair, one arm draped around it. He's taken off his suit jacket and rolled up his sleeves. He's trying to play it cool. Inwardly, I smile because he's not as calm as he'd have me think. No one tries to be cool unless they're not. For all that friend talk, I make him nervous, and that puts me at ease, a little.

"I was thinking how fortunate I am to be sitting across from a good friend," I tease, echoing his earlier statement to Ileyana.

"What, we aren't friends?"

"We absolutely are."

"So, what's wrong with what I said?"

"I didn't say anything was wrong with it."

"That's not what your 'I'm pissed at you' face says."

"I didn't know I had one of those too. Thanks for pointing it out. Interesting though how much you know about the faces I make and why I make them."

"It's not that interesting."

"I disagree. Why do you know these things?"

"You know why," he says, his voice soft with emotion.

It's as if my whole body exhales. Brice still cares; he still has feelings for me. I want to shout it to the entire restaurant. Instead, I say, "I wasn't sure that was still the case. I thought maybe your feelings were engaged elsewhere," alluding to that odd moment with Cashmere earlier.

"That's ironic," he says. "I was thinking the same about you."

I see it. I see him let down his guard. His posture changes, and I can tell he isn't whatever he was anymore. He presses into the edge of the table, getting as close to me as possible.

"I got a glimpse of what's between you and Trenton; it didn't feel finished to me. Even if it isn't, you should know by now, you're it for me. There's nobody else."

After what Brice said to Ileyana, I was devastated. I was sure I missed my chance and unsure how I would live in a reality where he no longer feels about me the way he did on our last night in the house. The relief I feel knowing his intentions haven't changed is indescribable. He said there's nobody else; that's all that matters. The rest of it we can handle.

I press my stomach into the table until it hurts. After all these months of being apart and all the misunderstandings, I want to be close to him.

"The thing with Trent was nothing. I only went with him to prevent a bigger scene. I didn't even speak to him."

"You didn't?"

"No, I didn't. He asked if we could talk. I said no, end of story."

"For my heart's sake, I hope so," he says.

"Are you kidding me?"

After practically whispering an entire conversation, Cashmere's voice sounds shrill to my ears. She isn't speaking to Aiden like I thought she was; she's isn't speaking to Brice and me either. She's looking past us. I follow her gaze to the couple who's just arrived.

I struggle to remain calm as I take in Trent and Beverly's matching outfits, linked hands, and the smirk on her face. How dare she show up here with him, how dare he show up with her, and how dare they stand near me?

"Mr. EP, what are you doing here?" Zack asks, standing and walking around the table to shake Trent's hand.

Without letting go of Beverly, Trent clasps hands with Zack. He nods to her and says, "Bev invited me."

Zack's smile falters without completely slipping away as the surprise wears off, and he begins to assess the situation. He's doing the math in his head. Maybe my comment about the show being rigged wasn't simply a clapback. Maybe I was speaking the truth.

Following Zack's lead, Corey and Aiden shake Trent's hand without any of their usual liveliness. They're fun-loving, not fools. They've made the same

79

calculations Zack has. They too know they were cheated out of a fair shot at winning *Star Quality,* and it doesn't sit well with them. Trent and Beverly have made an already weird dinner weirder.

Brice and I lock eyes, realizing what needs to happen next. "I'm *sorry you're in this awkward situation,*" I say with my eyes.

"It's *okay. I can handle it,*" Brice says back with his.

Like a brave soldier meeting a dangerous foe on the battlefield, he rises from his seat and faces Trent. They're two stoic mutes, clasping hands a little longer, a little firmer than need be. Silently, they size each other up. To my knowledge, they've never had a conversation. Trent was never interested in getting to know the guys in the competition.

Side by side, they've never been in this position before. My mind can't resist the urge to take stock of the many ways they're different. Trent is slightly shorter than Brice, and his skin is a deeper brown. His face is angular; Brice's is squarer. Trent has sharp cheekbones and a full, neatly trimmed beard connecting to his sideburns, while Brice usually opts for clean-shaven.

They're both in good physical shape, though Brice, a former college basketball player, looks the part. He's all lean muscle, whereas Trent's broader through the shoulders and chest. He looks older than Brice too. There's a three-year age gap, but that's not what accounts for the difference. Trent looks like he's lived while Brice's appearance is youthful and innocent.

They're unlike the other in most ways, but they're similar in that both are devastatingly handsome. Trent might be prettier, but Brice's beauty is easier to enjoy. As tense as Brice is right now, there's an inwardly pleasing quality to his face Trent simply doesn't have. He's too aware of his attractiveness to ever be unassuming, and that makes all the difference.

The dislike between Trent and Brice is mutual, palpable even to those who don't know what they're witnessing. Corey says something to Aiden that I can't hear; Aiden shakes his head and focuses on Trent and Brice. I can't imagine how confused they are about what's going on.

"Let me handle this," Cashmere whispers.

"Bev," she says in a too bright voice, "we saved you a seat next to Corey. We didn't know about our guest, but I'm sure we can add a chair."

"No need," Brice interrupts. At some point when I wasn't looking, he and Trent released each other from their mutual vice grip, but the staring contest wages on.

"They can take our seats," Brice says. "Leah and I are leaving." For all the authority with which he spoke, he looks to me for approval. His eyes waver, wondering if he did the right thing. I smile, letting Brice know I'm with him all the way.

Trent's eyes, cold and hard, dart to me, the veins in his neck pulsing. The urge to run seizes me. I don't want to be anywhere near him right now. I stand and start collecting my things.

"Are you guys really leaving? The night's still young," Corey says, pouting.

"Leave them alone. It's about time these two got together," Cashmere says, grinning.

I completely misread that moment with Brice earlier. She wasn't asking the question with herself in mind. She was thinking of me.

Aiden raises his glass of water to the table. "To Brice and Leah. It's been a long time coming."

"I knew something was going on. I picked up on a vibe between you," Zack adds. He hasn't spoken to any of us since before Trent and Beverly showed up, but he seems pleased to have his suspicions confirmed.

"Hey, man. You alright?" Aiden asks Trent.

When I turn to him, he looks fine. I wonder what Aiden saw.

"Yeah. I'm good. Continue with your conversation," he says with a smile that doesn't reach his eyes. "I can't tell you how it makes me feel knowing two of the people I put together on my show fell in love."

"Yup. We owe it all to you, Trenton," I reply.

"*Awww.* What's a reality show competition without a real-life hookup?" Corey says, not picking up on the tension. "Just do me one small favor: Name your firstborn son Corey Jr."

"No," Brice and I say in unison.

"But Leah and Brice aren't the only two involved in the show who found each other. Right, Trenton?" Cashmere asks, nodding to Beverly.

Trent narrows his eyes at her. He looks on the verge of snapping. Suddenly he holds up his phone. "Sorry. I gotta take this." He steps away, answering the phone as he does.

"I thought so," she says to his retreating back.

"I hate to break up this little love fest," Beverly says, addressing Brice and me, "except actually, I don't. If you're leaving, hurry up. Bae and I need to sit."

"We're going right now," Brice replies, reading my mind.

It's sweet that everyone's making a big fuss over us. I might've been able to appreciate it if Trent weren't here. I couldn't care less that Beverly's annoyed, but I do feel kind of bad for him.

I don't want anything to do with Trent. I don't want to intentionally hurt him either. This whole conversation about Brice and me colliding into each other is obviously upsetting to him. I don't blame Beverly for wanting us gone.

"Is everything alright?"

A tiny waitress I don't recall seeing before now steps out from behind Cashmere's long, willowy shadow to address us. "Is everything okay?" she asks again just as Trent returns from his call.

"They don't have seats," I say, motioning to Trent and Beverly offhandedly, "but he and I—" I look to Brice— "are leaving, so they can take ours. Problem solved."

The waitress peers intently into my face then into the faces of my companions, both seated and standing, her face changing from curious to excited.

"Oh my gosh," she squeals. "You're them, aren't you, the cast of *Star Quality*? Except for you," she says to Trent. "I'm not sure who you are, but you definitely have movie-star good looks." That gets her a rare chuckle from him.

"I love the show so much. Can I please get a picture for the 'gram?"

"*Ummm.* Yeah," Aiden says, answering for the group. "Can we do it after we're done, though?"

"Of course," she answers, sounding more like she did before she recognized us as pseudo-celebrities. "If there's anything you need, please let me know."

"As long as they're still leaving, everything's fine." Beverly makes a point of cutting her eyes at me then looping her arms around Trent's neck. She's hanging on to him like a monkey swinging from a vine, and he lets her. I've had enough of them. I put my arms in my coat, signaling Brice that I'm ready to go.

When I straighten up, I find the waitress looking between Brice and me; her mouth soundlessly forms the word *oh* as comprehension gradually comes on.

"Brice," she says familiarly, "you're my favorite. You're so handsome and nice." She pauses and, to my surprise, shoots me a sidelong look. "Don't you think you should be with someone...sweeter, like Cashmere or Beverly?"

"Beverly?" Zack, Corey, Aiden, and Cashmere question in unison.

If I weren't shocked, embarrassed, and hurt, I might have joined them in their surprise or laughed. As it is, I can barely keep from crying.

It's been this way since the show premiered two weeks ago. Random strangers commenting on everything about me. I disabled the comments on all my social media, but that doesn't stop them from leaving their opinions on every forum they can. This is the first time it's happened to my face, though. It stings even more.

I quickly wipe the tears pooling in the corners of my eyes before anyone notices. For now, the waitress has their full attention. The only thing that could make this moment any worse is Beverly catching me crying. If I stay here any longer, she just might.

"I'm going now," I declare to one specifically.

"Wait for me. I'm coming with you," Brice says. "I need to do something first."

I hear in his voice how offended he is for me, I appreciate it, but I don't want him defending me. It won't change anything. He faces the waitress, who has wisely moved nearer to Beverly and Trent. She must sense she has an ally in the pair.

"Brice." He doesn't answer me. He's determined.

"Editing has been unfair to Leah. She's not only beautiful and talented, but she's also genuine and, contrary to your opinion, kind. There isn't a man who wouldn't be blessed to have her in his life or regret losing her." Leaving the waitress red-faced with shame, Brice crosses to me.

"Are you okay?" he asks, looking me over.

I grab Brice's hand between mine. Looking into his eyes, I say, "Thank you for what you said." It's the most I can say without collapsing into tears.

"I meant every single word." He turns his hand, interlocking our fingers. "Come on. Let's go."

Keeping a firm grip on my hand, Brice single-handedly retrieves his wallet from his pocket. He pulls out a few bills and hands them to Aiden. "That should cover us." He leads me to the exit, past the hostess, out the door without a goodbye to our friends or foes.

Chapter 7

The Long Good Night

After that chivalrous display back there, I thought I would follow Brice's lead as he whisked me away somewhere, but here he is giving me a choice. When I was with Trent, he always dictated what we did. At the time, I thought it was romantic. Now, I get that he was controlling me. I appreciate Brice being strong enough to lead but follow at times.

I pull my jacket tighter around me against the brisk wind and harsh cold. Behind us is the restaurant we stormed out of. Up and down the block are coffee shops, tearooms, and bakeries. We're in the city, the options are endless. The thing is, I can't handle being recognized again right now. What I need is to go somewhere private, just Brice and me.

"If you want, we can go to your place." I hear how wrong the words sound as they come out of my mouth and rush to clarify. "*Whoa.* That did not come out right. What I meant to say is, I would rather avoid another situation like the one we just left behind."

"No. We can't go to my place," he says without a trace of friendliness in his voice or expression.

"Okay. That's cool," I reply, looking up and down the block for the nearest train station. "I'm feeling tired anyway. I'm going to call it a night. We can have that talk another time."

Brice steps directly into my line of vision, commanding my attention. "Why are you upset?" he asks.

"I'm not upset. I told you, I'm tired," I say, still looking for the nearest subway line. He lifts an eyebrow and cocks his head to the side. "What?" I say without looking at him. "I'm not angry. I really am just tired."

"I know your angry face, remember?"

"And I told you, I don't have an angry face, remember?"

"So, why are you afraid to look at me?" he asks, daring me to do just that.

His hands come down on my crossed arms as a gentle prod back in his direction emotionally. I keep the attitude, but I do look at him.

"See? I'm not afraid."

"I do see...that you're upset. Tell me why so we can work it out."

How can I continue to be mad if he won't let me? Sometimes I really hate how sensible he is and persuasive.

"I'm not upset—I'm not that upset," I confess.

"Thank you for admitting that to me. Now, will you please tell me why?"

"You know why."

"I do, but I want you to tell me."

I pick a spot above his head and ask, "Are you involved with someone?"

"What? No," Brice exclaims.

"If it's not a girlfriend, what are you hiding? Why can't I go to your apartment?" I don't actually believe he has a girlfriend, but I want to know why he doesn't want me in his space. I stare defiantly into his steady brown eyes, demanding an answer.

"Do you remember when I told you Seriyah and I were abstinent?"

I nod though confused about the connection of one thing to another. My intentions are entirely innocent.

"Remember me telling you we were successful because we set boundaries?" I nod again. "With you, I don't know what those boundaries are yet. One thing I do know is we won't learn them alone in my apartment with you looking so beautiful I have to remind myself to breathe."

I look away from him so he doesn't see me blush. I'm really trying to remain angry, but who am I kidding? I'm way too flattered to be upset.

"Okay, so as far as excuses go, that's a pretty good one. I get your point about boundaries, but nothing's ever happened between us before. Why should tonight be any different?"

"We've shared a bed and a couch, but the predominant emotion in those moments was never romantic, and for the record, we've always had boundaries."

"What boundaries?"

"The five other people we lived with, not including camera crews and the cameras themselves. Everything we did was recorded. And you," he says, pointing at me, "were in a relationship."

I try to push his finger away, but he grabs my hand and holds it.

"If I take you to my place tonight, there'd be nothing to stop us—only us." He stares deep into my eyes, "Frankly, I can't say with certainty that right now I could be that strong. I won't willingly put myself in the position to fall prey to temptation."

I didn't think I could respect Brice any more than I already did. I was wrong. I feel how much he doesn't want the night to end, but he'll let it if it means he gets to continue to walk faithfully with Christ. Brice will not compromise on what he knows to be correct. I have resolved to stay away from compromising situations, yet it took Brice's resoluteness for it to occur to me that I was working against my own interest.

"You know, I do recollect that conversation," I say, taking a step away from him. "I've thought about it a lot, especially lately."

"Why?"

The slight strain around his mouth gives away how nervous he is about what I'm going to say. He'll have to be anxious a bit longer, though I'm not about to have this conversation outside on a cold street corner.

"I want to continue talking to you, but I'm freezing," I say through chattering teeth.

Brice unbuttons his navy wool coat and pulls me into his jacket. My hands stay in my pockets, my arms close to my sides while Brice holds the coat closed around us.

"Can we please continue this in the warmth somewhere?" I murmur from inside his coat.

"Alright. Name the place," he says in a shaky voice.

"My house." I purposely leave out the part about me living with my mom. I like teasing him.

"I can't—"

"I promise we'll have a chaperone," I interrupt.

"Yeah? Who's that?"

"It's a surprise."

"Thank you, Mrs. Albanese," Brice says, accepting the offered cup of tea. "This is exactly what I needed."

"Is it alright? Would you like another cube of sugar?" My mom's already halfway to the kitchen, prepared to get Brice whatever he asks for.

"No. Really, it's perfect. Thank you for this."

I hide a smile behind my own mug of the ginger cinnamon brew. It's cute how much one wants to please the other. Brice is extra polite, and my mother overly hospitable. He blows on the hot liquid, cooling it with his breath, then brings the teacup to his lips. It's a spicy, pungent mix. While I enjoy it, I'm not sure Brice does, though he nods appreciatively. I get it; it's his one shot at making a good first impression on my mom. If I were him, I'd be as agreeable as possible too.

"I'm sorry to have put you out," he says to her while setting his cup on its saucer then down on the rustic wooden coffee table. "You looked so comfortable when we came in."

If I didn't know my mom as well as I do, I would have thought she was relaxing too. In actuality, what she was doing was waiting up for me. I called ahead and told her I was on my way home. I mentioned I'd be bringing a guest, someone she didn't know, but I'm sure she'd like. So far, I think I was right.

Introducing my mom to...anyone is terrifying. She's not critical per se;. She just has high expectations of the people I surround myself with and me. Brice meeting her is completely impulsive and nerve-wracking; however, it's something I wanted to happen almost from the moment we met. I want to know what she thinks of him—is he the real deal, or is my vision still obscured?

Mom's a good judge of character, which is why she and Trent were never acquainted. She saw straight through him without ever meeting face-to-face. She warned me about Trent. That didn't stop me from getting involved with him, though. I like to believe I've grown since then. This is my litmus test.

"Can I get you anything else?" She's fussing over Brice like an overzealous waitress.

"You could take a seat," he says with a smile. "I'd love to get to know you."

"I'll sit," she says, lowering herself onto the light gray loveseat, "but I'd much rather get to know you." She perches on the edge of the sofa, body turned toward Brice. "Tell me about yourself."

He lets out something between a sigh, a groan, and a shaky laugh all at once. "Where should I start?"

It was meant to be a rhetorical question, a figure of speech. To his surprise and mine, Brice receives an answer.

"Talk to me as if you were in my place. Tell me whatever would ease your anxieties if you were a single parent of two beautiful young women, the younger of which has had difficulty finding their footing in life as of late.

Though now an adult, you want your child to be happy, loved, and successful, but there's little you can do, so you pray and pray. Then one night, she calls you and says she's bringing home a man. Now you're sitting in front of this man wondering, *Is he worth my daughter or another mistake?* Whatever you'd want to know about him to put you at ease is what you should tell me."

I've never heard my mom speak like this, especially not to a stranger and absolutely not to me. She's been carrying around this maternal fear while I've been none the wiser. I want to hug her, tell her I'm fine, and I'll be okay. Instead, I remain seated in my tufted chair, afraid to say something that isn't true.

Brice places a hand over hers and looks her straight in the eyes. "I'm not a perfect man," he begins, "but I am a man who strives to always live in God's light. I'm not a rich man, but I believe in hard work. With these," he says, lifting his large hands to her, "and the sweat of my brow, I will provide for the family I will one day have. They will be well fed, naturally as well as spiritually. I'm not the most intelligent man, but I pray daily for wisdom and the presence of the Holy Spirit to lead me in all my decision-making. I may be a tall and physically strong man, but all my fighting is done on my knees before the Most High.

"What I'm trying to say is Jesus is at the head of my life. I walk by the direction of the Holy Spirit, and I desire most of all to honor God with all that I am and will be. I will not do anything to compromise my faith, diminish it, or cause others to scoff at it."

He turns his gaze from my mother to me then just as quickly turns it back. "That amazing young woman sitting over there isn't simply your daughter. She's a prized possession of God. I wouldn't do anything to hurt or derail a princess of the King of Kings because then I'd have Him to answer to. You can trust Leah with me, Mrs. Albanese. I promise."

She looks at him for a long time, nods her head curtly, then she's back to normal. She's not fussing or pouring out her feelings; she's her usual, reserved self again. Between sips of tea, she asks Brice how we met.

"We were costars."

"Oh. You two were in a situation where you were thrust together and bonded," she says, setting down her tea, her lips pressing into a fine line. She thinks our connection is fickle, a product of happenstance. We did bond under unusual circumstances though it's not why we bonded.

"I can't say if it was mutual; however, I felt we were friends from the time Leah and I met."

Brice shifts closer to my mom so that his knees are nearly touching hers. At six foot three, he's a whole foot taller than her, yet somehow you don't notice the height difference.

"God is the Redeemer. He can redeem anything, including our choices, and work them together for our good. I'm not sure how or when, but I know Leah and I were always going to meet and stay in each other's lives. With or without *Star Quality*," Brice says, "we were both in the same place at the same time, in need of friendship and able to give that to the other. I opened up to Leah about the hardest time in my life. In turn, she trusted me with the things that kept her up at night."

Brice is vague in his account of the night we were both 'in need of friendship.' I'd woken up from the first of my recurring nightmares, and he was missing Seriyah. That was the night I learned I could trust him, yet if my mom asked me, I would have said we became friends before then. But he's right; that was the first night that changed us.

I feel kind of weird about Brice telling my mom all this. She and I haven't ever discussed the specifics of my life during my time away. She took me back, no questions asked, which I'm grateful for. I expected her to ask. When she didn't, I thought she didn't want to know. I certainly didn't want to share. I guess she was waiting on me to open up.

"If things would have played out differently," Brice continues, "and Leah and I never met on the set of a reality competition, our paths would have crossed eventually because she is the answer to my prayer. This isn't a casual fling, Mrs. Albanese. I know what I want to become of my friendship with Leah. I think you do too."

Something passes between them, a silent agreement. Although the conversation is about me, I'm an outsider watching a profound moment without understanding the full scoop of what's happening in front of me.

As if suddenly coming to a conclusion, my mom rises from her seat. Brice quickly gets to his feet as well. Not knowing what else to do, I stand too.

"It's been a pleasure," she says. "I hope to see more of you."

"I hope so too."

My mom smiles at Brice. He did it. She likes him.

"I'm going to bed," she announces. "Brice, you're welcome to stay and spend some time with Leah—talking."

He chuckles, and surprisingly, my mom laughs. I can't believe it. I can barely get her to crack a smile, and Brice makes her laugh? He walks her to the doorway of the living room. "Sleep well, and thank you for having me."

I watch them with a broad smile, touched by their relationship and his attentiveness toward her. I've always wanted that—someone who loves my mom. She's fond of him, and so am I. "I like your mom," Brice says, sitting back down on the sofa.

"Thank you for handling her with care." I pause, not trusting myself to speak without crying. "It was a really raw conversation and a lot to ask of you, especially since you both admitted things to each other you've never told me. I didn't know my mom was carrying all of that," I say, recalling how honest she was with Brice about her fears. "So, thank you for what you said."

I want to tell him how full I felt—of respect and admiration—for him listening to all he said. He promised my mom she could trust me with him because his intentions are good. He promised to seek God daily for guidance, to work hard, and to see me as God's daughter. Before now, it never even occurred to me to want those things from someone I'm involved with.

Trent promised me fame, fortune, success, big houses, fancy things, and passion. At the time, I thought he was everything, and he gave me everything, but the things don't matter. It's how you get them, who you share them with, what they value.

"You don't need to thank me for that. As your covering, your mom was doing her job."

"What do you mean by covering?"

"I mean, your mom is your leader, protector, and provider."

I shake my head. "No, I've been working since I was a teen, and now I'm a full-blown adult. I'm grown and my own leader."

His eyes soften and crinkle at the corners as he laughs. "I don't get the punchline. I wasn't joking."

He stops laughing and fixes his face into a frown, but then he breaks down into more soft laughter. I cross my arms and angle my body away from him. I hear rather than see him get up, then I feel him sitting beside me. He wraps his arms around my own.

"I'm sorry. I didn't mean to upset you, and I promise I wasn't laughing at you. I was laughing at how fiery you sometimes are. I don't know if you know this," he says in a singsong voice, "but you have a bit of a temper."

"I do not have a temper," I snap.

He looks at me with a wry smile as if to say, *See, I told you.* I have to bite my inner cheek to keep from laughing.

"When I say your mom is your provider and leader, I mean that as her unmarried daughter, she's spiritually responsible for you. Even if you are...how'd you put it," he says smiling, "a full-blown adult."

He hugs me a little tighter, letting me know he isn't mocking; he's being playful. "It's your mother's right to find out what kind of man I am and what my intentions are toward you. I didn't mind talking to your mom. In fact," he says, making eye contact with me, "I liked it. I got to tell her the things I've wanted to say to you."

He lets me go and shifts in the armchair we're sharing to look me in the eyes. "What's uncomfortable for me is the ache I get in my chest every time I see you."

He gently unfolds my arms from around my chest and holds my hands in his. He looks deep and steadfastly into my eyes. I wonder what he sees when he looks at me that way. Does he feel as electrified as I do?

"You never responded to me, Leah. I poured out my soul to you, then I never heard from you again, until today."

I let my head drop, ashamed of how careless I've been with him. Brice lets go of my hand and lifts my head, forcing me to meet his eyes.

"I've tried convincing myself what I thought was between us was in my head. I've tried forgetting about you, being indifferent, even upset. None of it worked. Try as I may, I can't get you out of my head, my heart, or my hopes. I want you in my life, Leah. I choose you. Do you choose me?"

"I—"

There's a pop then the room grows dim. Brice and I are both on our feet searching for the source.

"I think the lightbulb blew out," he says.

I go over to the lamp, turn the tiny knob on the base, hear the click, but the light doesn't come on.

"I think you're right," I say, turning the knob again. "Stay here. I'm going to get a new bulb." I walk the short distance from the living room to the linen closet, where we keep the extra lightbulbs and scented candles. As soon as I pick up the carton, I know it's empty. It's too light. "How do you feel about candles," I yell.

"I'm a fan," he calls back.

"Great."

I come back into the living room, lit candles in hand. Brice watches me as I set one down on both end tables. I go back out to get the third candle and place it on the coffee table. The room's not as well lit as before, but it reminds me of the night Brice told my mom about.

"Does this remind you of anything?" I ask Brice, sitting on the sofa facing him.

He isn't thinking long before he says, "The first night in the cast house."

"Yup." I smile at how in sync we are. "What do you remember about that night?"

"I remember having a bad night. I felt a lot of guilt about Seriyah." He pauses. "That was a hard day for me."

"Why?" I ask, staring into his wistful eyes.

He clears his throat. "I was starting a new journey, and more than that, I was attracted to someone for the first time since her death. And yes, before you ask, I'm talking about you," he says with a sad smile. "I realized I had started living again. At the time, that felt like a betrayal to her."

"You know what I remember?" I ask in an overly cheery voice.

"What?"

"Staying up all night talking. That was one of the most honest, uninhibited conversations I've ever had. It's weird. I didn't know anything about you at the time, but I trusted you implicitly." I take a deep breath, summoning the courage to say what I should've told him nine months ago.

"I admire you, Brice. I admire your commitment to Christ and your ability to inspire others to answer God's call in their own lives. You were a lifeline for me at a time when my relationship with God was on life support. You reminded me to look for His hand in every situation and to listen for His voice in the stillest moments."

I fight the urge to duck my head or run and hide. Part of me wants to tell Brice I choose him too; the other part of me screams to leave well enough alone. What if I'm wrong about Brice? What if I'm right about him?

"Leah, please, finish what you were saying," Brice says with eyes that seem to glow in the candlelight.

"When the producers led you off set for the last time, I broke down. I couldn't stop crying. I cried the whole way back to the cast house. I was still crying when I found the letter you left in my dresser. I read it through tears, and it gave me the strength I needed to confront some hard truths, like how I felt about you, and most importantly, what was happening in my life. God had been speaking to me for weeks. I wouldn't hear Him, though. I refused to let go of Trent, my fool's gold. But God used you to reach me."

I take a deep breath quelling the storm brewing within me. "When I got to the brownstone Trent and I were supposed to move into after we were married," I continue, "he wasn't there at first. I knew they had history. Trent and Beverly had a fling a while back. There might have been a time or two when I thought there was something still there, but I never seriously considered it. There might have been a time or two when I thought there was something still there, but I never seriously considered it. I should have trusted my instincts."

I tell Brice every last detail of Trent's betrayal while he rubs my back.

"He gave her my rehearsal footage, told her about my panic attacks, and even gave her the part in the movie he not only promised me but wrote about me. Who does that? He said he did it because he loved me and didn't want to lose me," I say, chuckling. "Funny, right?"

He doesn't respond. He doesn't tell me how much of an idiot I am to have gotten involved with Trent. Brice just keeps rubbing my back.

"The truth is," I continue unprompted, "he did it because he enjoyed dangling my dreams in front of me. Trent knew how much I wanted to be a working actress and how discouraged I'd grown about that ever coming to fruition. He promised he'd make it happen for me; I believed him because of his success. Trent has three reality shows on television right now and his own production company. He could have helped me if he wanted. Instead, he preferred putting out bait, watching me reach for it, then snatching it back right when it was almost in my hands."

He's diabolical.

A surge of anger courses through me. I'm getting worked up all over again. Seeing them together today and now talking about what happened makes it feel brand new. The cheating doesn't bother me nearly as much as the conspiring against me.

Brice's arm curls around my shoulders. "We don't have to talk about this if you don't want to."

"Yes, I do," I snap. "You asked me a question. Let me answer it." He nods, agreeing I should continue.

"I confronted Trent. Beverly left after I told her if she loved her life, she should go. Standing in the most beautiful house I've ever been in, across from the most handsome man I'd ever known—except you maybe—I finally understood. It was a mistake. Trent, the show, the engagement...all of it was a mistake. I had been blind, but finally, I saw what I needed to do." It was a perfect moment of clarity.

Unfortunately, nothing has been as clear since.

"I've been trying to do better, trying to make up for my past mistakes. Some days I'm fine—I think I've turned a corner. Other days I'm convinced it doesn't matter how hard I try, nothing will change for me. On the worst days, I'm sure I've missed my destiny, and I'll never be more than what I am right then."

I wipe madly at my tears. I didn't plan on saying that much. I haven't admitted those feelings aloud. Then again, talking to Brice has always been easy. I trust him with my fears. I look at him through wet lashes just able to make out his blurry form.

"Is it too late? Is there a way back for me?"

Brice wraps me up in his arms and lets me cry all over his crisp white shirt. He holds me tight until my tears slow. "What do you believe in, Leah?"

"What?" I ask, pulling back but not breaking away. I heard him, only I don't understand what he's asking.

Brice lets me go, nudging me back into my own space. "I said, what do you believe in?" he repeats.

I focus, consider his meaning and the answer. What do I believe in? "God. I know I believe in God, Jesus, and the Holy Spirit."

"Great. So when you say you believe in the God the Father, God the Son, and God the Holy Spirit, what is it exactly you believe?"

Again, I have to search deeply for an answer. Nothing comes to mind. I have no real conception of what it is I believe. Angry tears burn my eyes, threatening to fall.

"Would it be okay if I told you some of the things I know?" Brice asks. I nod. "If you know some of those same things, too, let me know." I nod, communicating my willingness.

"God so loved the world, He gave His only begotten son, so that whoever believes in Him shall not perish but have eternal life. Do you know that to be true?"

I nod again more enthusiastically this time. I do know Jesus came into the world to atone for all sins.

"Some of the most notable followers of Christ were previously notable sinners, however, those who have a greater debt forgiven are the more grateful for His grace. Peter, Mary Magdalene, Zacchaeus, the Samaritan woman, Paul are just a few. Do you know that too?"

I shake my head. Some of the names I know, but I've never considered how any of their stories coincide with mine.

"Do you know right before the time had come for Jesus to be arrested, beaten, and crucified, He told His disciples they would fall away? Knowing they would abandon Him, Jesus still loved them to the cross. He encouraged and prayed for them because Jesus knew they would come back. Did you know that?"

I didn't know all the disciples abandoned Jesus in His hour or that Jesus knew they would, yet kept them near Him anyway. What a love.

"If Jesus accepted them back, if He loved you specifically because He died for all sins and sinners ever, enough to leave His majesty in heaven, why would He give up on you?"

Brice is a patient teacher, reinforcing the building blocks before adding new levels. Can it truly be as simple as God hasn't given up on me?

"I know how it feels to be convicted of your iniquities—every sinner turned believer does. It's the necessary sorrow that leads to genuine repentance and ultimately to Christ. The blood of Jesus was shed for this specific reason, the forgiveness of sins, including yours, Leah." I look away.

"Yes, God still has a plan for your life, a plan of redemption. No, it's not too late for you. And there is a way back. It's also the only way. Jesus Christ is the way, the truth, and the life. None go to the Father except through Him. Believe in Him and receive His cleansing and pardon. Stop defeating yourself, start trusting in the work of Christ on the cross at Calvary."

My eyes are red, mascara's running, and my eyeliner's smeared all over my face. I back away from the mirror to get a more complete picture of myself and back into the wall of my small, narrow room.

I'm a weepy mess. I can't believe I let Brice see me this way. I meant to tell him how much I like him and instead ended up confessing the anguish of my mind. I haven't cried that hard since I was a child. Brice, he held on to me tight while I sobbed into his beautiful shirt. He didn't even get upset when I got makeup on it; he just held me deeper into the crook of his neck until I was all cried out. Today's been a lot. Being in the same vicinity as Trent was a low point. Understanding it's not too late for me makes it all worth it.

Face wiped clean of makeup, still coiffed hair tied with a satin scarf, and dressed in sweats and an oversized tee, I plop down on the couch. Brice smiles at my more relaxed look, making me blush. He's seen me this way more times than I can remember, a testament to how comfortable I am with him, yet he makes me feel like a runway model in couture every single time.

"Sorry to have kept you waiting."

"Are you referring to the twenty minutes it took you to pull on sweats or the whole nine months I've known you?"

Brice isn't usually this direct. On the few occasions when we have been, I've put up a wall or redirected, mostly because I was in a relationship but also because it's Brice. I spent weeks dreaming of him before I realized he is literally the man of my dreams. We have a connection, which cannot be explained by physical attraction or shared experience.

The same way I knew all along I shouldn't have been with Trent or in any of the relationships I had before him is the same way I know that Brice is the one who scares me. Though missing out on what is meant for me scares me more. With that in mind, I reply, "The whole nine months."

He tips his head back while lifting a fist above his head. "Thank You, God. I was beginning to think it would actually take fourteen years."

"Hey," I protest. "In my defense, I didn't know you were waiting on me. I've thought of your feelings as a more recent development."

"Really? I thought you knew."

"Nope. I didn't."

Between one second and the next, Brice goes from elated playfulness to solemn.

"I liked you instantly, Leah. I didn't want to accept it; I fought it because that meant I was moving on from Seriyah. I didn't think I'd ever do that. It never crossed my mind to pray for love again or to even want it, then you showed up and turned my world on its axis."

The candles burn low. By their dying light, I watch Brice's face closely for the normal distress it holds at her name. I don't find it. For the first time since I've known him, Brice mentioned Seriyah without despairing. He'll always love her, but it's incredible that he can love again. That it may be me is humbling.

Brice holds out his hand to me palm up. Carefully, I put mine in his. He rolls my fingers into a fist covered by his. In that small gesture, I feel more secure with him than I ever did with Trent.

"You're worth the wait, Leah. You're it for me. I know it. I've known that as long as I've known you, and that's not going to change."

If we were in a cartoon, an animated heart would be thumping exaggeratedly out of my chest. From the time we first locked eyes, I've felt this thing between us, and I haven't stopped feeling it yet.

"Earlier before I spilled my guts," I say, looking up at him through my lashes, "then proceeded to blubber all over your dress shirt, there was something I wanted to say to you."

"Okay," he says, obviously caught off guard by my lack of response to his declaration and change of subject.

"I like you, Brice. I like you very much. I like that you like me, and I don't want you to like anyone else."

"I like you, too, Leah, very much. Possibly, probably, definitely more than that. Truth be told, I like you enough to give you what you need most...although it'll hurt me to."

My heart plummets to the pit of my stomach. What can I need that will hurt him to give me?

"Wh–What do you think I need?"

"Time," he says. "To heal from your last relationship and to grow in the most important one you have."

"Are you...breaking up with me?" I try to pull my hand out of his, but he holds on tight.

"Will you just hear me out a minute before you lose your cool?"

"I'm sorry. Should I not lose my cool when someone I'm not even dating dumps me? That's what you're doing, right, letting me down gently?"

"What you should do is listen, then you would know you weren't dumped. You were loved." I look away, touched by the sentiment, though not understanding how loving me equates to hurting me.

I refuse to look at him. I keep my eyes on the melted candle wax.

"It broke my heart seeing you cry," he says. "If someone cares for a person the way I care for you, their natural reaction is to want to protect them from hurt. I want you to be okay, and you will be; however, it won't happen if you're focused on me and not Christ. What you need most—to feel loved and forgiven—you can't receive from any man."

As much as I hate to admit it, he's right. I'm not ready for another relationship right now. I could start dating someone, even someone as amazing as Brice, but after the newness of it wore off, I'd still be dealing with everything I was beforehand. As much as I like him, being with Brice isn't a remedy for my troubles. Eventually, I'd realize I still have the same questions and unquiet in my spirit as I do now. I have work to do on myself before I can be with anyone, including him.

I sigh deeply. "For something that isn't a breakup," I say, "it sure does feel a lot like it." I try to sound breezy. I'm not sure I've pulled it off. How ironic it is sitting as we are, decided on not pursuing romance, that I would feel connected to Brice more fiercely now than ever before.

"We're not breaking up," he says. "We're just beginning. I fully intend on courting you...when the time is right."

"I thought we just agreed I need time to heal, grow, et cetera, et cetera."

"Yes. Which is why I won't court you immediately, And when I do, it'll be slowly."

I bury my head in his chest and smile. I like the idea of being courted. From there, I hear Brice say, "I asked you to let me love you once. If you give me a chance, I'll show you that godly love restores."

I wrap my arms around him and tip my head back to meet his eyes. "How do you plan on doing that?" I ask. Brice's arms wrap around my torso as he returns my embrace. *I wish we could stay entangled in each other forever.*

With a gentle touch, he caresses my face. "Wait and see."

Chapter 8

When It Rains, It's a Media Downpour

We're startled awake by a crude noise. I jolt upright, dazed and confused; within seconds, the pulsing blue light on my phone clears up the mystery. I don't bother checking it. It's probably Cashmere asking how things went with Brice. Since I'm still with him, it's not a conversation I can have right now.

I don't remember falling asleep or feeling tired. Last I remember, Brice and I were talking about our favorites: books, movies, music, singers, food. We must have dozed off between one word and the next.

Brice fell asleep sitting up with the wall as a headrest. He's a good sleeper—no snoring, drooling, or thrashing. He just rests.

"What?"

My head jerks back at the sound of his voice. I thought he was still asleep. "What, what?" I ask.

"You're staring at me."

"How would you know I was staring at you? Your eyes are closed."

His lips spread into an amused smile. "Okay, Leah." I lean over and hold his eyelids open. I get right up in his face and say, "This is staring."

"Okay. Okay. You weren't staring at me." Brice swats my hands away, laughing. "By the way, what was that noise?"

"My phone. I got a text. Thanks for coming to my rescue," I say, narrowing my eyes at him.

"You didn't need rescuing."

"But you didn't know that."

"Yes, I did," he says, sitting up. "I've been awake the whole time. You fell asleep in the middle of a very incoherent sentence about term papers. I thought about waking you, but I missed watching you sleep. After a while, I started feeling sleepy myself. I closed my eyes then your phone vibrated on a heavy wooden table, waking you. The rest, you know."

Brice gets up from the sofa in one smooth movement. I feel safe with him, not because of his stature, but because of the way he's looking at me this very second. Without question, I matter to him.

"Are you still upset with me?" he asks.

"Why don't you tell me? You're the facial expression reading expert." I jut my chin forward exaggeratedly, inviting closer inspection. "Tell me," I say. "Am I upset?"

Brice peers over my every facial feature, clinically at first. "Mouth," he says, "hard set. Eyes—sharp. Brows—arched. Face...arresting."

The atmosphere shifts, and we're not joking anymore. Space around and between us is alive and stirring, pushing him and me closer together.

"I, *ummm,* should get going," he says, ending the spell. "It's late, and we're both tired."

The moment passes as suddenly as it came.

I don't want him to go, but it is late, and I highly doubt my mom would appreciate him spending the night.

"I get it now why you didn't want us going back to your place." I step to the side to avoid being hit by Brice's long arms filling out his coat sleeves. "If

I didn't know my mom would kill us if she woke up and found us asleep together on the couch, I'd let you stay."

"I absolutely believe with my whole heart your mom would kill me." He laughs softly. "You know, restraint is only one of the reasons I didn't want to take you back to my place. There's another."

"Yeah? What is it?" I ask, doing his top button. His hand covers mine, stilling it from its task.

"I believe in setting the expectations for a relationship. Any man who takes a woman to his house on the first date lets her know what he wants from their situation. I wouldn't take any woman to my apartment when we're just beginning to get to know each other, especially not you. I want you to stick around for more than a season."

"Can I plant a field of you and repopulate the male species?"

Seriously, Brice is everything I never knew I needed. He's a good man, a man after God's own heart, and a straight-up anomaly. I've never met anyone like him.

"I'm not a farmer; however, I'm thinking that's not how it works," he jests. "If it's any consolation, you can have me."

"You said I couldn't."

"No. I said I'd wait for you while you take the time you need. It hurt hearing you talk like that... While we're back on the subject, I think you should read the book of John."

"John?"

"One of the four gospels in the Bible."

"Oh, that John."

"I only bring it up because when I started my faith walk, it was the first book in the Bible it was suggested I read. I didn't grow up in a Christian household. I didn't know much about Jesus. John really helped me believe in and understand the work of Christ. I think it'll help you too. Try reading one chapter a day. I promise it'll help keep the doubt away."

Hand and hand, we walk a short distance to the front door. Brice glances down at his phone then back up at me. "Five minutes away," he says of his Uber.

Five minutes isn't nearly long enough to say good night. No amount of time is when I don't know when I'll see him again. I throw caution to the wind, break all sorts of slow courting rules, and hug him.

Brice doesn't hesitate to hug me back. His chin digs into my shoulder. I don't mind; it reassures me he's real and here with me, if only for another four minutes. I breathe in his familiar musky cologne and breathe out all the anger, doubt, and negativity of the day. I wish this night didn't have to end.

"Are you working in the morning?"

"Work? That's what you want to talk about when we have less than four minutes left with each other?" I balk. I don't want to talk about my job. After the debacle at the reunion when Ileyana asked what I was working on, I feel even less inclined to talk about my job.

"I was actually making small talk to distract me from how much I don't want to say good night but now, yes, I want to talk about work."

"Well, I don't. I am onboard with the not saying good night thing though. Let's run with that."

"Leah."

"What?"

"Why don't you want to talk about work?"

"I just don't."

Brice, perceptive as always, pulls away from our entangled arms to meet my eyes. "Okay then," he says. "We won't talk about the what; we'll focus on the where. You quit your job at thelist.com before filming *Star Quality,* right?" I nod. "Where are you working now?"

"I don't get why you're making a big deal of this," I say, cheeks burning. "Fine. I work at a small boutique in the village. I'm a sales associate. Happy now?"

I'm not ashamed of an honest living, but compared to what everyone else has going on—movies, beauty deals, modeling campaigns, sponsorships—it doesn't feel worth mentioning.

"Leah, look at me."

I keep my gaze steady out the window. I don't feel like looking at him right now, but Brice is relentless. He takes the few steps separating us and joins me at the window.

"You have nothing to be embarrassed about. You may not be where you want, but where you are is a step on the path to where you're going."

How is it that he always knows the right thing to say? I must've applied to a million jobs and went on as many interviews. Jolie is the only place that would hire me. It must be where God wants me right now. I just have to trust Him to move me when He's ready.

It suddenly occurs to me that I don't know anything about Brice's life in New York.

"What about you?" I ask. "Why did you move to New York City? What are you doing here?" I can't believe we haven't talked about this stuff. I guess with everything else going on, we forgot.

Laughingly he says, "That's the New York attitude everyone back home warned me about."

"I guess I did come off a little brash, huh?" I shrug and smile at his wide, unoffended grin. "What I meant to ask is why did you relocate."

"I moved to New York mostly for work, but I did have another incentive." I try not to blush too much as I take in the implication that I'm his other incentive.

"I could tell you all about my new job," he continues, "though I'd much rather show you. What do you think about meeting me Saturday morning at ten?"

"I think...I'll see you Saturday."

Brice's Uber is well out of my line of vision by the time I shut the door. Saying good night was hard. Thankfully, we'll see each other soon. I miss him already. The house feels empty without him. Maybe I should call him, keep him company on his ride home. I spot my phone on the coffee table, blue light still pulsating from the unread text. I pick it up and read the message.

He's just a friend, right? I guess you and that clown are friends like Beverly and I are.

I'm dragging this morning. Two cups of black coffee later, I still can barely keep my eyes open. In hindsight, I really should have requested today off. I'm way too emotionally spent and physically exhausted to be productive at work, fill Cashmere in on what happened between Brice and me, and the message I got from Trent late last night.

Are you telling me I endured hours of Beverly fawning over Trent so you and Brice could decide to be friends?

Not friends exactly. We're very slowly working our way to more. It's actually super sweet.

I don't tell her why we want to take it slow. I can't talk about that with her. She sees me as some kind of authority on Christianity. I broke down in front of her once, which is maybe understandable, but twice? She looks to me to keep her accountable. How convicted can Cashmere remain if the person she's looking to isn't that steady herself? No, it's best that much remain between Brice and me. I won't be responsible for her apostasy. The phone buzzes again.

Of course it is. Brice is sweet. I wouldn't imagine him treating you any other way.

I read the text over, trying to discern the tone. Am I detecting shade or overanalyzing? I've never actually asked Cashmere if she would be okay with Brice and me. Her unwavering belief in his feelings, coupled with what she said last night, made it seem unnecessary. Does giving her blessing mean she doesn't have her own feelings about Brice to contend with? We spent the first part of our acquaintance at odds over a boy. I don't want our friendship to end in the same way.

I want to ask you something, and I want you to be very honest in your response.

OK.

Are you OK with Brice and me getting together?

I put my phone down on a shelf behind the cash register and walk out from behind it. I'm afraid of her reply because I don't know what that would mean for our friendship if she weren't okay with it.

A stinging breeze sweeps through the store. A woman not much older than me stands in the open door inside and out.

"Excuse me, miss. Can you tell me where I can find the jacket in the window? "

I smile at my new customer. "Absolutely. It's right back here." I motion her toward the rear of the store, temporarily putting my questions about Cashmere out of my mind.

While helping the woman with the jacket, foot traffic picks up. The small boutique crowds with shoppers, each one wanting my attention. Shouts of "miss," "excuse me," and "I need some help" overwhelm me. Between pulling sizes, tracking down shoes, checking stock, putting clothes back, and ringing up sales, I don't' have a moment to breathe, let alone to check my phone. When things finally slow down, I read through my messages.

Girl, bye. I had a slight crush on Brice for all of three seconds, and that was only because I appreciated that he saw there was more to me than how gorgeous I am ;) Seriously, it's OK. I'm happy for you two.

With immense relief, I read the rest of the messages from Cashmere.

I'm excited about Sunday. You're still going with me, right?

Ten minutes later: *What are you going to do about Trent? You do know the only reason he came to our dinner was that you were there.*

"Yeah, I do," I mutter aloud to myself. There's nothing to be done, though. We're over.

Have you been on Instagram today?

Why would she ask that? She knows I try to stay off social media.

Why she asked remains a mystery for as long as it takes to scroll to the following text, a screenshot. It's only my profile, and it's kind of a blurry picture, but it's definitely me today.

Don't even trip. I can't tell you how many times I've been the butt of an internet joke since I gained a social media following. People are mean with short attention spans. Pretend it's no big deal, and it'll blow over. Just don't read the comments.

How many times has someone snapped a photo of you at work—not glamorous work, by the way—and shared it on a celebrity gossip Instagram page? Oh yeah, then caption the pic, I guess we know who isn't Star Quality? I'll wait.

At least the pic's flattering. I love that blouse, by the way. You're going to have to let me borrow it.

I don't respond. I appreciate her trying to downplay the situation, but I'm the one who's been publicly humiliated. I can't pretend it's no big deal. I log on to Instagram and go to the original post. In just over two hours, my picture has garnered hundreds of comments.

She's walking around that house like she somebody; meanwhile, she's out here folding clothes for a few coins.

That could not be me. She looks cute though.

No shade, but who is she, and why do we care?

My vision is too blurred with tears to get through the rest of the comments. My throat aches with the effort of fighting back sobs. My knees buckle, and I have to lean against the wall for support. Why? Why is this happening to me?

I'm trying God, I am, but why is everything so difficult for me?

I can't be here right now. I have to go home.

Cara., Not feeling well. Really need to go home. Can you get someone to cover the rest of my shift, please?

112

The door swings open noisily, letting in a blast of cold air that jolts me back into professional mode. I turn away from the door, wiping my eyes and face clean of tears. I wouldn't want a customer to catch me crying.

"Excuse me, salesgirl." The woman's voice is sharp and acidic. "Can I get some help over here?"

I really can't deal with a nasty privileged woman right now. I'm this close to going off on someone. If this lady doesn't adjust her attitude accordingly, it'll be her. I take a deep breath and turn around. "I'll be with you in a—" The words die on my lips.

"Beverly?"

Because she's the one person who can make any bad situation infinitely worse, Beverly's here and not alone. Trent's with her. He's checking out jewelry he would never buy on the table closest to the exit. A precautionary measure, I think. If I were him, I'd stay away from me too. I'm as angry as I've ever been.

They've done the impossible: They've gotten my mind off the post. What I don't get is how one minute Trent's proclaiming his undying devotion; the next, he's showing up at my job with Beverly to further humiliate me.

Lord, help me, please. I want to put my hands on them, especially him.

I stare from her to him, too upset to speak.

"Is this it?" she asks, checking out the dresses on the nearest clothing rack.

"What do you want?"

"Isn't it obvious?" She smirks. "To shop."

"We're closed."

"That's fine," she says, practically skipping from one area of the boutique to another. "There's nothing worth buying in here anyways."

"Listen to me very clearly." I pronounce every word with painstaking control. "Leave. Right now. Of your own volition. If I have to make you leave…" I force myself to let the rest go unsaid. Doesn't she understand she's one more snide comment away from the beatdown she deserves?

"What? If you have to make me leave, what are you going to do? Hit me?" she jeers. "You're pathetic. No wonder he left you."

"Beverly," Trent shouts. He speaks more forcefully to her than he's ever talked to me. "That's enough," he says. "We're leaving, now."

That he would stop her from doing the very thing he's been allowing and enabling her to do from the time she and I met to this very moment sets me off. Without reserve, I want to say to him every horrible thing my mind has conceived of these last seven months.

"Don't try to pretend this wasn't your plan from the get-go," I scream at him. "You want to jump in now and what, defend me? If you care so much, why would you bring her here in the first place? What did I do to you to warrant this kind of disrespect?"

Trent flies across the room in two seconds flat. Yesterday, backstage, he kept a respectful distance; now, he disregards all spatial boundaries. We're closer to each other than we've been in months, separated by a mere inch or two. It's temporarily disorienting. The momentary glint I see in his eyes says while I'm uncomfortable, he's enjoying this.

"What, this doesn't feel familiar to you?" he asks in a harsh, breathy whisper. For a moment, I think Trent means his nearness. He smiles a little, and I know he's teasing me. Showing up at my job with Beverly is revenge for what he believes is me flaunting my relationship with Brice.

"That was different, and you know it," I spit. "Nothing happened between Brice and me while we were together, and even if it did, what right do you have to be angry about it? You were with her—" I point at Beverly— "the whole time. Oh, and let us not forget everything else you did."

"It wasn't the whole time," he argues. "It began after I found out about what you were doing."

"Wh–What I was doing?" I stammer. How Trent could accuse me of being disloyal to him is beyond me. He's sicker than I thought. "No. You betrayed me the moment you decided to plot against me. You betrayed my every trust."

"I had to do it, to protect us," he says, eyes feverish.

I throw my hands up in the air, at my wit's end. "Do you hear yourself? You had to sabotage and conspire against me for us?" It boggles my mind how effortlessly he can lie to my face. I need him—Beverly too—away from me before I do something I'll regret.

"Whatever. Just get out and take her with you." He doesn't move an inch. "If I have to ask a second time, I promise you won't like it."

Do I imagine it, or do flames flicker in his eyes? He's enjoying this. This is what he wanted, why he came here, to get a reaction out of me. I back away from him much too late. I played right into his hands. He's got what he came for: proof that I still care.

"Come on, Bev." He speaks to her, but his focus is on me. Trent used Beverly to hurt me again, and she happily obliged—again. With a satisfied smirk, she walks straight out the door, leaving Trent and me alone.

"It was good seeing you, L." The endearment that once made me smile now makes my skin crawl.

"Store it up in your memory because it'll be the last time," I spit.

"Doubtful. We have more press scheduled for the show: as a final-three contestant, you must be present. If you decide to skip an event..." He takes a step closer to me, eliminating the already scant space between us, "the network will sue you for breach of contract."

Trent's lips linger perilously near mine, a hair's breadth away. Heat radiates off him in waves, engulfing me in his flames.

"I hate you." My voice is shaky, without conviction.

"You love me."

Alarms go off in my head, indicating danger. My brain screams at my body to back away, back away, but it protests. My lips want the kiss the moment promises.

"What is going on here?"

Chapter 9

Wading in the Middle

Cara, my boss. I forgot I texted her. As her ice-blue eyes take in the scene, they grow from surprised to upset. I don't blame her. I can only imagine what this must look like to her. I open and close my mouth several times without finding the words to explain what's going on. It probably doesn't help that Trent's still here, still so close to me that we're sharing the same breath.

"Go. Please." I look at his self-satisfied grin through the tears welling in my eyes, and all the fight goes out of me. He broke my resolve, and we both know it. If Cara hadn't interrupted us when she did, we both know what would have happened. We would've kissed. How did I let things get that far? Wordlessly, Trent backs away from me, past Cara, out the door.

"We need to talk."

Cara leans against the edge of the same jewelry table Trent stood at minutes prior, silently examining me. I shrink beneath her gaze, afraid of what she's going to say. She's been a good boss. I hate that I have to disappoint her like this.

"Cara, I'm so sorry." She holds up her hand, cutting off my apology.

"You've always been a great employee, Leah. I've had no complaints where you're concerned—until today," Cara says, sighing heavily. "About an hour ago, my phone started going berserk with texts and from social media notifications. I thought, *'Great. The boutique must've got a huge shout-out from an influencer.'* Nope."

I duck my head, unable to meet her fiery eyes. Cara's right to be angry. I never thought about what that post would mean for Jolie, the boutique. I didn't realize Cara could be hurt by it too.

"The company I built with my blood, sweat, and tears is being lambasted all over the internet. Why? Because it turns out my most trusted associate is a reality television star and neglected to tell me that. Not cool."

"I had nothing to do with the post. I don't know who took the picture. And if you think about it, they were insulting me, not the boutique."

"To make matters worse," she continues as if I haven't spoken, "I walk into my business and find you making out with some guy—albeit a very attractive guy—in the middle of the store. Under other circumstances, I'd applaud you, but not while you're at work and not on the sales floor."

"I know it looks bad, Cara, but really, we weren't doing anything." Strictly speaking, that's true though not wholly. We weren't kissing. He was threatening me, but that didn't stop the inferno raging between us. I wanted to kiss him as much as I wanted him gone.

"You're absolutely correct. It looks bad. I don't care that you weren't. I care that it looks like you were. Can you imagine a customer walking in on that? But that's not even the point. The point is your personal life is spilling over into my business."

It's my fault Jolie is getting negative press, but so am I. I didn't ask for this. I didn't want the world to know that all the promise I showed as a younger woman has amounted to nothing. I did plays and commercials. I was Miss Black New York, and I almost won *Star Quality*. Now, I'm nobody, and social media thinks it's funny. They're laughing at me, not Jolie. Doesn't Cara get that? Jolie might be a far cry from Trent's beautiful loft, his brownstone, and the cast house. It's not a pilot on a major network, a beauty influencer deal, a recurring role on an Emmy-winning show, but it's all I have. I don't want to get fired.

"I'm sorry," I say because I sincerely am. "Really, it's not what it looked like. I'll make sure my personal life stays personal."

I trip over my words, trying to reassure Cara that this was a one-time mishap and won't happen again. I can tell she doesn't believe me. The cold, stern expression on her face injures more than any comment I've read today. I was wrong to not tell her about my short-lived time as a reality television participant. I honestly didn't think it would make a difference in her decision to hire me either way, so I didn't say anything; still, I should have told her.

"Maybe, maybe we can use all the press to your advantage somehow. Why don't we call your marketing guy? He'll know how to capitalize on the moment."

"I'm sorry to do it, Leah, but I have to let you go." Her voice cracks, and I know she is sincerely sorry. "I like you, but I don't want the kind of publicity you're getting. I should disassociate with you before your employment here ruins my business. I've worked too hard to build and sustain my brand to lose it on account of an employee's antics."

"Antics?" I whisper numbly.

Working at Jolie is not what I wanted for my life. I took the job out of necessity, but over time, I've accepted that maybe this is where God wants me to be. What am I supposed to do now? No Jolie, no job, no prospects.

I curl up in the fetal position with the heavy comforter wrapped tightly around my body. Inside my cocoon, I rock back and forth, trying to soothe myself to sleep, my only refuge from reality. It's no use. In the stillness of my bedroom, my ex-boss, Cara's words scream to be heard. "I have to let you go. I've worked too hard to build and sustain my brand to lose it on account of an employee's antics," she'd said.

What antics? I did everything right this time, and I still ended up losing. God, why is my life like this? Why did You want me to quit the show if nothing better was waiting for me?

Fresh tears fall onto my soaked pillow. I should switch out the wet pillow with a dry one, but what's the point? It'll only be soaked through in minutes too. I wouldn't have won the competition if I stayed with Trent, but at least I wouldn't be broke. Trent has plenty of money, and he was generous. I stop rocking. My body goes as stiff as a board.

"Where did that come from?" I ask myself aloud. "Get a grip."

Minutes later, I'm rocking back and forth again, determined to fall asleep. My eyelids droop close with fatigue. I'm almost asleep when my phone chimes. I push the covers off my head. Without getting up, I reach for my phone, grab it, and bring it into my cocoon. I hit the home button and smile

Brice: *Hey.*

Me: *Is this allowed?*

I waste no time texting Brice back. I didn't expect to speak to him until tomorrow.

Brice: *?*

Me: *Talking. I'd think we were breaking some kind of slow courting rule.*

Brice: *Luckily for you, this is a friendly hello, no courting involved.*

Me: *None?*

Brice: *Not with intention.*

Me: *I'm not sure how I feel about that.*

Brice: *Behave.*

Me*: I'll try my best.*

Brice: *How was your day?*

Should I tell him I've been in bed crying my eyes out since I got home from my last day of work? Should I tell him about my viral humiliation? Odds are he doesn't know. All he has is an Instagram page he never interacts with. He's maybe seen the photo but not likely. Should I tell him why I was fired?

Me: *It was a day. How was yours?*

My fingers come to a decision for me. For now, it'll be my cross to bear.

Brice: *Good. Got a lot of work done.*

Me: *The work you still won't tell me about until tomorrow?*

Brice: *Yes. That work. Did you start reading yet?*

Me: I haven't gotten around to it yet. I will.

I completely forgot I promised Brice I'd read a chapter of the book of John daily.

Me: *Soon.*

Me: *Promise.*

Brice: *Don't do it for me. Do it for you because it answers the questions that are holding back your peace.*

Tones and intents are difficult to decipher in texts, but this feels like a stinging reproach. It's difficult for me to open up to people about the things that matter. Antonia, Amanda, and Cashmere understand this reserve I have, even with them. With Brice, it's always been different.

Maybe it's because our friendship began one vulnerable night when we were in no state to hold anything back. Brice saw me at a very low moment and vice versa. Since then, I've trusted him with the truths about me other people have to beg for. He's never thrown anything back in my face or used privileged information to make presumptions about me, but it feels like that's what he just did. Then again, it's been an emotional day. I might be seeing something that's not there.

ME: *Right… I'm super tired. Going to bed. TTYL.*

Instead of reacting, I'm going to cut the conversation short and re-evaluate in the morning. Everything looks better in the light of a new day.

His reply comes quickly: *Are you OK?* I ignore the impulse to respond and turn over in my bed.

Brice: *I hope you're not wearing your mad face right now.* The following text comes a few seconds later. *See you tomorrow morning?*

We'll see, I think as I drift asleep.

"Onward Christian Soldiers Ministries."

I read the awning on the small building in the very residential neighborhood my Uber dropped me off in front of. The driver assured me he'd taken me to the correct address.

"If you're not where you thought you were going, the address is wrong."

I'm definitely at the address Brice texted me, but it's definitely wrong. I dial his number. He doesn't answer. I hang up without leaving a message. As cold and frustrated as I am, no good could come from anything I say right now. I'm not exactly dressed for standing around outside, although I should have considered that as a possibility.

I'm in a green tweed miniskirt, voluminous sleeve blouse, sky-high stiletto booties, and Moto leather jacket. Good thing I had the foresight to wear thick opaque stockings; otherwise, I'd be frozen to death by now.

I redial Brice's number. It goes straight to voicemail.

"Ugh."

Why am I calling him? Why hasn't he called me? Who invites someone somewhere then becomes unavailable at the time they should be meeting that person? I call him. Straight to voicemail again.

"Hey, so I'm standing outside of the address you gave me, but I think you messed up because it's a church. I've called you three times already. If I don't hear from you in the next minute, I'm getting in an Ub—"

A song I vaguely recall from childhood flows out from the church. The melody is clear and familiar, though the words are lost to me from where I stand. Spurred by instinct, I walk the short recess to the entrance of the church. Through the front doors, no longer listening from a distance, words I forgot I knew escape my mouth.

"Just a closer walk with thee, grant it, Jesus is my plea."

My feet carry me through the lobby without any conscious thought. I hardly register a thing, not even the color of the walls. I enter the sanctum and walk down the aisle separating the left and right sides of the room. I'm nearly at the pulpit by the time I realize what I'm doing. Quickly, I take the nearest available seat.

In an ivory suit and church hat, a lone woman—beautiful, middle-aged— leads worship while most people sing along with closed eyes and upraised hands to God.

"I am weak, but thou art strong. Jesus, keep me from all wrong. I'll be satisfied as long as I walk, let me walk, close to thee."

Silent tears flow from what feels like my soul as words pour out of me. I long to walk close to Jesus to be fed by the strength of our relationship, but every time I take a step forward, I always end up two steps backward.

"Just a closer walk with thee," I cry, begging the Lord to grant my plea.

When we've sung both verses and the chorus, we go back to the beginning. People are on their feet, some on their knees, singing the words of the song as an earnest prayer. Almost reluctantly, we sing the last note.

In the quiet, I feel the spirit of the Lord moving in the midst of us. I've never had this feeling before now, yet I know the warmth, the electric current running through me is the presence of the Holy Spirit. With my eyes closed, still, in wonder of what I'm feeling, the worship leader continues service with prayer.

"Glory to the Father, the Son, and the Holy Spirit. Our Lord in heaven, we come before You at this moment in worship of You and Your goodness. Lord, You are good and righteous, most worthy to be praised. Thank You for blessing us with the fullness of Your Spirit and choosing us to experience Your faithfulness. Lord, all that we are is by Your grace because You chose to love us unto the cross. Please help us as we live our lives every day to be in constant remembrance of Your love; The love that caused You to come into the world, the Son of God as the Son of Man. You suffered persecution, crucifixion on the cross, and resurrection on the third day. All this You overcame for the forgiveness of our sins."

"Thank You, Jesus," says the woman seated next to me. Her eyes are closed tight, hands clasped in prayer beneath her chin. In those three words, I hear her heart for Jesus.

"Thank You, Jesus, for setting us free from the power of sin, brokenness, disease, death, and even from ourselves. Thank You, Lord, that those whom the Son has set free are free indeed. Thank You, Jesus, for deliverance, from everything that would prevent us from coming into the fullness of a relationship with You. Help us, Lord, to walk closer with You today, tomorrow, and always."

The entire sanctuary seems to vibrate with the hum of electricity. At first, I think it's feedback from the piano, then I realize I'm not hearing something. I'm feeling Someone, the Holy Spirit.

"We give this day to You, Lord. Although all days are Yours, we ask You to please bless this one as we have set it aside to approach Your throne of grace in unity. Please, Lord, continue to bless us with the presence of Your Holy Spirit and lead us throughout the service as we draw nearer to You. We thank

You, Lord, for the name Jesus, that breaks every chain and in which we pray. Amen."

"Church, you may be seated." In nearly perfect unison, the congregation sits. "Welcome, brothers and sisters, back into the house of the Lord. Before we continue, we have a few quick announcements," the worship leader says.

I shift uncomfortably in my seat, beginning to feel how accidental my being here is. I don't have a Bible, and I'm not dressed for church. Nothing's exposed, but I do feel the want of a longer skirt.

"Will all the first-time visitors please rise and greet the congregation?"

Slowly I rise, attempting to discreetly pull my skirt down. I try not to look at anyone while I wait for the microphone, but my eyes rest on the modest altar where the pastor sits alone.

He's a bald, middle-aged, deep brown skin man with kind eyes. I know you're not supposed to judge a book by its cover, but I like him instantly. He's like Brice; he radiates light. The usher, a young man, hands me the microphone. I take it with trembling hands and a fast-beating heart.

"Good morning, church."

"Good morning," they respond.

"My name is Leah. I didn't plan on being here today, but I'm happy I am. Thank you for welcoming me into the house of the Lord. May He continue to bless you all."

I hand back the mic to the usher. He returns it to the worship leader.

She looks at me and says, "Many are the plans in a person's heart, but it is the Lord's purpose that prevails."

She continues on to more announcements as if her comment were only a general statement without any intended target though clearly aimed at me. It was obviously a response to my admission that I did not plan on being here; however, it resonates with me deeper still. I've had many grand plans. None have worked out. Actually, they've all pretty much ended in disaster.

Secretly, I've sometimes felt it was the Lord frustrating my plans. I planned on being rich, famous, married, and successful at this point in my life. Seven months ago, I planned on winning *Star Quality* and marrying Trent. Instead, here I am, unemployed, broke, still living at home, single, and randomly visiting a church. If this is God's plan for my life, I don't get it.

"Before we give the service over to Pastor Charles, I want to tell our parents the great work our new youth ministry director, Brother Brice Young, is doing. If your child is not yet involved, encourage them to attend the meetings every Friday night. There, they're free to ask the questions they don't feel comfortable asking at home. They're taught and encouraged in Christ. And in a few short weeks..." She pauses, looking excited, "they'll be putting on an original play written by Brother Young. Brother Young, stand up so everyone can see you."

My head swivels in every direction looking for Brice. I spot him upfront in the second row, standing tall. Brice's new job is youth ministry director at Onward Christian Soldiers Ministry.

"Turn around, Brother Young. Let the congregation get a good look at you," she says.

He turns around, facing the congregation. His eyes land immediately on me. They ask, am I upset. I have questions—a lot of them—but I'm not upset. In response, I clap, participating in the loud applause he's inspired. He smiles and takes his seat.

"Church, go with me to Matthew chapter four. Let us begin at verse thirty-five," Pastor Charles says. He gives the congregation a minute to get there then begins. *"That day when evening came, He said to His disciples, 'Let us go over to the other side.' Leaving the crowd behind, they took Him along, just as He was, in the boat. There were also other boats with Him. A furious squall came up, and the waves broke over the boat, so that it was nearly*

swamped. Jesus was in the stern, sleeping on a cushion. The disciples woke Him and said to Him, Teacher, don't you care if we drown?'"

Pastor Charles looks up from the passage, out at the congregation. "Today, little children, I'll be speaking about wading through the middle." He pauses for a beat then continues. "The middle is the densest part of our lives. It is when we face trials, tribulations, and temptations of every kind. I propose that to make it through the middle, we must wade, that is persevere through what's restricting our forward motion.

We're all journeying through life, commencing at birth, concluding with eternity. For the faithful, the promised end is reigning forever with Christ. In between the beginning and the end is the middle. We are in the middle this very second." He opens his arms wide, emphasizing the here and now.

"This is the middle, the longest part, the most challenging part, the part when your faith is weighed in the balance. Will yours be enough to get you over to the other side?

"Jesus said to the disciples, *'let us cross over to the other side.'* The disciples, following Jesus's command, got into the boat and began to indeed cross over. They were obediently traveling with Jesus. It probably never occurred to them that the voyage from here to there," he says, taking a large side step demonstrating here and there, "would have trouble."

"While in the boat, a mighty wind arose. At the realization of the water-filling boat, fear and panic seized the disciples. They woke Jesus saying, 'Teacher, don't you care if we drown?'

"What a question," Pastor Charles says. "'Don't you care if we drown?' he repeats, taking his time.

"How many of you have ever been in the middle of obedience to God's will, doing just fine then suddenly, a furious wind rose against you?"

"Amen" and *"mmm-hmm"* are heard all around the church. I remain silent though inwardly shout right along with everyone else.

Pastor Charles waits for the assembly to quiet before asking, "What did you do in those moments when the winds rattled and beat against you uncontrollably? Did you cry out, 'Jesus, do you not care if I drown?' You see, the middle is where you sink or swim. Either you will trust Jesus to rebuke the winds, or the currents will overtake you.

"At the beginning of this chapter, Jesus tells the people gathered to witness him a parable, the parable of the sower. I don't believe it's a coincidence Jesus explains this to His disciples before they encounter tumultuous winds while crossing over 'to the other side.' Let us look at what Jesus had to say about the fruitful and unfruitful ground. Stay in Mark four, beginning at verse three. *Some people are like seed along the path, where the Word is sown. As soon as they hear it, Satan comes and takes away the Word that was sown in them. Others, like seed sown on rocky places, hear the Word and at once receive it with joy. But since they have no root, they last only a short time. When trouble or persecution comes because of the Word, they quickly fall away. Still others, like seed among thorns, hear the Word; but the worries of this life, the deceitfulness of wealth, and the desires for other things come in and choke the Word, making it unfruitful. Others, like seed sown on good soil, hear the Word, accept it, and produce a crop—some thirty, sixty, some a hundred times what was sown.*

"The seed is the Word. We are the ground. Each instance of unviable ground—the seed that fell along the path, in rocky places, and among the thorns—the Word is taken from the believer. In the first case, the liar took it. The second, trouble or persecution. And the third, life's worries, the deceitfulness of wealth, and the desire for other things. Simply put, the middle has so much white noise that many of us forget Jesus is always present. We stop looking to Him, focusing our gaze on the raging winds instead. Preoccupied with things that feel pressing at the time but are ultimately trivial, we overlook Jesus, who can calm the opposition of our lives with a word.

"*He got up, rebuked the wind, and said to the waves, 'Quiet! Be Still.' Then the wind died down, and it was completely calm.*"

The assembly stills to complete silence, the power of the words of Jesus setting us at peace, truly stilling our spirits.

"Why are you so afraid?" Pastor Charles continues. *"Do you still have no faith?"* The disciples asked Jesus, doesn't He care if they drown? Jesus, in turn, asks the disciples, *"Why are you afraid? Do you still have no faith?"* What is happening right now in your middle that has caused your ground to become unviable? What do you fear: poverty, loneliness, lack of success? Do you not know that all things are possible with God?

"The seed that fell among the good ground heard the Word, accepted it, and produced a crop. How do you think that seed grew to produce a crop, thirty, sixty, one hundred times what was sown? Patience. Faithfulness in adversity. The middle is your growth period. The very rains that make you fall away are the rains meant to cause your growth.

"Friends, you are not alone. Our Savior, the Lord Jesus Christ, is with you in the difficult moments and the uncertain ones, too, ready and capable of quieting the winds. Do not fall away burdened by what you see. Trust in He who is faithful and true. The disciples called Jesus and learned He is God who calms the storms of our lives.

"Check your motives. Why are you following Christ? Is it for relationship or for things? If the latter, you won't make it to 'the other side.' You will fall away like the seed in the rocky place and among the thorns because you have no roots yet desire for other things. When trouble comes because of the Word, you will not stand. God rewards those who seek Him, not those who insincerely follow Him. *But seek first the kingdom of God, and His righteousness and all else shall be added unto you.* May the fruit of the Spirit, which identifies you as a child of Christ, be multiplied in you some one hundred times as you wade through the middle."

Chapter 10

Looks Can Be Spot-on

"We were happy to have you with us today, Leah. Visit us again soon," Sister Carol says, pulling me in for an embrace.

"Thank you. I enjoyed service very much. The sermon was convicting, and you..." I shake my head, thinking about the worship service she led. "The worship was filled with the presence of God."

"I can't take any of the credit. That was the work of the Holy Spirit. I was simply the vessel."

"Amen," I respond, letting go of her. Sister Carol hangs on.

"One day at a time," she says. She doesn't wait for a response before ushering me out the double doors.

"Hello."

"Are you upset with me?" To make him sweat, I wait ten seconds before answering.

"Not really."

"Not really? So you are upset?"

"No. I'm not upset. I'm processing."

"Processing?"

I have never felt as spiritually connected at a service as I did today. The worship was equal parts genuine praise of the Lord and conversation with

Him. I didn't just sing; I sang to the living God. He was present and received it. And the message, it hit home.

I had been like the seed that fell among the thorns. I spent the entirety of my life attending church, but I had no roots. I was quickly scattered by the strong winds. I spent my days looking to what I wanted, then dissolving into panic attacks the farther they slipped away from me. Jesus was my afterthought, not my forethought. Small wonder I made the decisions I did.

"How about we discontinue Twenty-one Questions for now and take cover, preferably somewhere warm and serving hot buttermilk pancakes?"

I can tell Brice's laughing though I don't hear it over the wailing sirens of the fire truck speeding down the street.

"Are you still there?" I ask, once the truck's far enough away for me to hear him again.

"Turn around. I'm right behind you."

Seeing Brice is a rush every single time. It's not the heat I have with Trent. It's sweeter but more satisfying.

"How did you know where to find me?" I ask.

"I followed you outside after service. I would have caught up with you earlier, but I got pulled into conversation with the mother of one of the girls in youth ministry. I kept my eye on you though. I saw you walk in this direction. I nearly ran to catch you once I was able to get away."

"*Awww.* I feel so special."

"You are. To me." Our eyes meet again, and I'm reminded we have plenty of sparks, too, even when we're doing an awkward shuffle.

"So," Brice says, casting about for a topic of conversation.

"So."

I'm fifteen again, trying and failing miserably to have a conversation with my first real crush. Brice and I have never had trouble talking. Then again, we've also never had the weight of our mutual feelings between us.

"I dressed myself today," he blurts out. "No stylist. How do I look?"

Brice must really be nervous if he's asking how he looks. I'd like some normalcy, though, so I play along. I make a big show of looking him over like I really need to think about the answer.

"You look alright." I'm joking. Of course, Brice looks better than alright. His suit isn't custom like all Trent's are, but he looks just as handsome. He's gorgeous and doesn't care one bit. I love that about him.

"Yeah, I look alright?" he questions, sounding more like himself. "You look alright too."

"Don't be funny. I look fantastic, though completely wrong for church." I frown. "Thank you for that, by the way. You gave me zero guidance. I'm surprised the saints didn't kick me out. I almost didn't go inside. You're lucky the Spirit was moving."

I fold my arms across my chest and look away, this time out of anger, not nerves. Apparently, I am a little upset with him after all.

"I'm sorry, Leah. In hindsight, I see that I should have told you. It's a lot to spring on someone without warning. I should have given you all the details and allowed you to decide. Again, I'm sorry. I hope you can forgive me."

My face is still turned away from him, but I don't pull away when he begins rubbing warmth back into my shivering arms. It doesn't do much against the forty-degree weather; however, I'm thawing toward him.

"Secondly," he continues, "our mandate is to 'welcome one another as Christ has welcomed us, for the glory of God.' If you wore shoes and nothing else, you wouldn't have been turned away, the ushers may have had to get you a blanket, but all are welcome in God's house." He wraps his arms around me.

"Also, you were never in danger of wearing the wrong thing. You're Leah Albanese. You look amazing to throw out the trash."

I duck my head, hiding my smile.

"Lastly," Brice continues, "I don't believe in luck. I believe in God's providence. Chance had nothing to do with you walking into the church this morning. You were led by the Holy Spirit."

"Lord, we thank You for providing this meal we are about to receive. We ask that You please allow it to nourish our bodies as You, Lord, nourish our souls. Please bless those who are less fortunate, who don't know where their next meal is coming from, as well as those without friends and family to share a meal with. Please bless the hands that prepared this meal and those that provided for it, that neither their hands nor their stomach ever goes empty. We thank You, Lord, and in Jesus Christ's holy name, we pray."

I join Brice in saying, "Amen."

I take a bite of my omelet. My eyes close against the delicate balance of flavor. It's so good. Not the usual bland eggs with toppings. It's actually seasoned and delicious.

"What'd I tell you? Good, right?"

I nod and keep chewing, my mouth full. Brice laughs and digs into his own plate.

"I owe you an apology. The whole time you were parking the car, I'm thinking to myself, what kind of rinky-dink place is this?" He chuckles softly. "I was getting ready to tell you about yourself."

"That's nothing new. You tell me about myself on a pretty regular basis," he jokes.

"Because you deserve it. I don't just go around giving tongue lashings unless the person has earned it."

"Noted," he says, eyes twinkling with laughter. "I'll have to be on my best behavior around you."

"Can I get you folks anything else?"

"No. We're good for now. Thanks." Brice smiles at her, and the waitress blushes.

"It's weird seeing you outside of the cast house."

He tilts his head to the side. "What do you mean it's weird seeing me outside the cast house? It's not weird for me seeing you outside of the cast house."

"Not a bad weird. Weird, in the sense that I got to know you in a controlled environment. It's different seeing you in your element."

He's still Brice. What's different is getting to see how people respond to him. I'm not the only one who sees how special he is.

He nods. "I see what you're saying. Personally, I'm excited about getting to know you outside of *Star Quality* and all the other stuff."

I put my hand on top of his and look him in the eyes. "Me too. Speaking of which, I have a question for you."

He sits rod straight in his seat. "I'm listening."

"Going from coaching high school basketball to acting isn't a huge leap. They're both in the realm of entertainment. What I don't understand is how you ended up leading a youth ministry or how you ended up on *Star Quality*, for that matter."

"That's a funny story," he says.

It must be. Everything about Brice just got a little brighter. I find myself sitting at the edge of my seat, not wanting to miss a word of this story. "Lay it on me," I say. "I'm always down for a good laugh."

"It's not funny, haha," he warns.

"That's fine. I still want to hear it."

"Okay," Brice says. "I didn't submit myself for the show."

"Then who—"

"My brother," Brice says, smiling.

"I didn't know you have a brother. What's his name? Is he older, younger, single?"

"Ha," Brice laughs. "His name is Jordan. He's five years older than me, and whether he's single is a moot point because you won't be for too much longer."

"Touché," I reply, fanning myself. *The flirty side of Brice is exhilarating.* Brice shakes his head. "You're crazy," he says, a grin on his face.

"In the best possible way. Continue with your story."

With the trace of laughter still on his lips, Brice continues. "I'm checking my emails one day and see an email from Stephanie Piscano. Fortunately, I read it instead of deleting it like I normally do with emails I think are spam. In it, Stephanie said, she received my audition footage on Vimeo and enjoyed the scenes from my play. Then she asked when I could fly to New York for a screen test. Obviously, I didn't know who she was at the time, and I hadn't auditioned for anything. I wrote her off as a scam artist and forgot about it until a few days later when Stephanie sent me a follow-up email. That's when I Googled her and found her IMDB credits. I realized she was legit, but I had no idea what *Star Quality* was or how she got footage from my work in a play."

"What play?"

"An original I wrote. My brother and I produced plays at my church home in Charlotte a few times."

"Is Jordan an actor too?"

"No. He was the youth ministry director. I had my full-time job at the high school coaching basketball, but I also helped him out. Jordan's not a creative person. He realized though, many of the young people in the church were. He enlisted my help in creating outlets for the youth members to utilize their talents for God."

"It's amazing that he catered to the gifts of the youth ministry in that way."

"Jordan is amazing." Brice nods. "He's the best big brother a person could ask for. It's his gift for noticing and nurturing other people's talent that led to me ending up on *Star Quality*. After I read Stephanie's letter, I knew Jordan had something to do with it. I asked him if he knew anything about the emails, and he said yes. Jordan said he knew I enjoyed acting and that I was good at it, that at some point, I had to move from grieving Seriyah to living. Jordan said pursuing something I enjoyed on this grand of a level would force me out of complacency into the new territory God had for me."

"Wow. Jordan sounds about as bossy as my older sister, Antonia."

"I think bossiness is a requirement of being an older sibling," he says. "No. But I'm glad he did it. You know I struggled with allowing myself to be happy again." I nod, remembering finding him on the roof of the cast house. Brice was grieved over moving on.

Wow. I thought he was talking about Cashmere when he told me he was conflicted over having feelings for someone. He wasn't though. Brice was talking about me.

"I was beyond upset with Jordan for submitting me for the show. Then I prayed about it. I got this sense of peace. I figured maybe this was a door God opened—the best-case scenario I win, and worst case, I go back to the life I like and am comfortable with. God had better in store for me, though."

He doesn't say it, but everything from his wistful smile to his hand on top of mine says I'm the better God had in store for him.

How ironic is that? I thought Trent was my Godsend. He obviously wasn't. I didn't consider I could be that for someone, though—or better yet, that we could be that for each other.

"So," I say, "you helped your brother with the youth ministry in your old church, and that's how you ended up directing the youth ministry at Onward Christian Soldiers?"

"Yeah. I helped my brother with the youth ministry for two years until he started leading the men's ministry. After that, I moved into the role of youth ministry director. I did it for a year until I went to shoot *Star Quality*."

"I had no idea... Makes a lot of sense, though."

"What does?"

"You. Us. Your friendship with Cashmere. You're used to helping troubled young people."

Brice is a helper. It's one of his many gifts. I've known that for a while, although I'm seeing it in a very different light at the moment. His penchant for guiding lost souls back to the right path does make me wonder: Is what he's feeling genuine or a strong delusion steeped in empathy?

"Stop thinking what you're thinking."

"What? I'm not thinking anything."

"Yeah, right. I know you, Leah. Right now, your mind's racing to the wrong conclusion."

I raise my right eyebrow in challenge. If Brice thinks he knows what I'm thinking, he'll have to prove it.

"Right in here." He reaches across our small table and gently touches my right temple. "You've worked it all out that I'm confused. I've got my feelings all mixed up. What I really want is to counsel you like I do the kids in the youth ministry. No?" he asks tenderly.

I shrug like I couldn't care less either way. In truth, I couldn't care more.

"Have you always been skeptical and untrusting, or did *he* do this to you?"

Brice isn't trying to be cutting. There's no malice behind his words, only observation. Unfortunately, something being truthful has never stopped it from also being hurtful.

He fixes me with a fond stare that goes a long way in quieting my pesky doubts. "What's happening here," Brice continues, "isn't displacement. The instant I saw you…" He shakes his head. "Fireworks. All I wanted was to know you." An unexpected grin splits his face. "Do you remember when I came to your room right after we moved in?"

Now I'm smiling, too, because what stands out most in my memory is how out of touch Brice was with pop culture. He was seriously behind culturally relevant references, like at least a decade.

"You were super awkward the whole time, and I couldn't figure out why you were there."

"I wasn't super awkward," Brice contests. "I was nervous."

"How cute," I tease. "I make you nervous."

"Occasionally."

He leans back in his chair, staring long and hard enough to make me blush. Is it his intention to make me nervous? If so, he's succeeding.

"You know..." The inflection in his voice carries a note of uncertainty. He's debating whether or not to say what he's about to.

"I could tell you were questioning why I was at your door. I questioned it too. We were already a minute into our conversation before it hit me I left my room to find you. It was impulsive, unlike me, and I didn't know why I did it. Thanks, by the way, for not calling me out on that."

I did want to know what brought Brice to my room, but we fell into such easy conversation that I forgot he was uninvited.

"When Cashmere barged in and made that comment about you working quickly, I was bothered because I thought she meant something was going on between you and me. That upset me. I didn't want her or anyone else thinking I was interested in you."

Before I can do more than fix my face to protest, Brice is explaining. "I did like you—I do like you," he corrects. "I...wasn't ready to let her go," he says with a sad smile.

I return it with one of my own.

"Later that night, when the EP of the show randomly showed up and joined our game, I thought maybe he was friendly, but he wasn't friendly at all. He was borderline hostile, only to you. The rest of us he ignored. It didn't take long for me to figure out the two of you were dating. I didn't like it." He considers for a moment. "Actually, I was pissed."

This is news to me. I knew Brice pieced things together fairly quickly, not as early as our first night in the house, though, or that he was upset about it. What I remember is the disagreement we had after he confirmed that he knew about my relationship with Trent.

"You were upset because you thought I had an unfair advantage in the competition."

Brice looks at me, shaking his head. "You haven't been paying attention, have you? What I was feeling had nothing to do with the competition. I was upset because I was moving on without my mind's approval, that it was settled on you of all people made things worse. You were dating my boss— my rich, good-looking boss. How could I compete with that?"

"That's ironic," I say, more to myself than him.

"Why's that?"

"Because. He was concerned about competing with you."

Brice nods thoughtfully but otherwise makes no reply. As threatened as Trent felt by Brice, I'm surprised Trent didn't find a way to kick him out of the competition earlier.

"I feel sorry for him."

"Don't. He doesn't feel sorry for himself," I reply.

Brice's compassions are wasted on Trent. He's a lot of things. A sympathetic figure isn't one of them.

"That's exactly why I do." I shake my head, unable to keep up with Brice's circular logic.

"Trenton believes in the influence of his success, the power of his charm, and the might of his money more than anything else. He considers himself the god of his life. In his mind, it was intelligence, hard work, and appeal that established him."

That's true. Trent is very proud of himself, how hard he's worked, and how far he's come because of it.

"He disregards God because he doesn't see the point in seeking God when he's already obtained for himself everything he could have wanted, which is the greatest tragedy. What holds the greatest value to him can be purchased. But what we have in Christ can't be bought with money or earned by hard work. Grace can only be received."

"Yeah, but he doesn't want grace. He doesn't think he needs it," I say.

"And that's the tragedy. Everyone needs grace, Leah, especially those who don't realize they do. We're all sinful. We all make mistakes. Grace gives us forgiveness, but that comes through Christ alone. He is the only way. Either Trenton doesn't know this, or he doesn't believe it, and that makes me feel very sorry for him."

I stare across the table at Brice, not knowing what to say because it's true. Trent believes only in himself. He wanted me to believe in him too. Constantly, he made remarks about what he could and would do for me if I ignored what he liked to call "an antiquated book with unevolved ideals."

I eventually agreed to do things on his terms, not because I thought he was right. I gave in because I wanted what I wanted, which makes me no better than him. Worse even, Trent doesn't know better. I do.

"Leah," Brice says with concern.

"Yeah," I respond as normally as I can.

"Are you alright?"

I sigh deeply, disturbed within myself. "I don't know what I saw in him." In a haze of self-pity, I miss Brice's reply. "What'd you say? I didn't hear you."

"I said..." He pauses. "Lust. That was what was between you two." He shifts in his seat as color rises in his cheeks.

"Excuse me?"

"Before you tell me about myself, hear me out," he says. "We make a lot of decisions with our eyes. Something looks good, therefore, we eat it, buy it, date it. People love beautiful things simply because they're beautiful, even if it's bad for them."

I want to tell him he's wrong. I open my mouth to, but I can't. I can't even meet his eyes.

"I've seen you guys together. You have heat. You're obviously wildly attracted to each other." He shrugs. "Physical attraction can be a powerful temptation."

Brice leans across our table, reaching for my hands. His trustworthy eyes say *I'm not judging you*, then his mouth says it too. "We've all done things we're not proud of. We can't take any of it back. All we can do is strive to walk in His light."

"What about you? Do you have regrets?"

"Hmmm..." He casts his gaze upward in thought. At long last, he says, "It's hard to say."

"Figures." I try not to sound bitter, a tricky feat, seeing as how I have a list of regrets a mile long.

"What do you mean by that?"

"I mean, you're Brice Young. You're pretty perfect."

"You think so?" he asks, voice neutral.

"Yeah, I do."

He shakes his head. "I'm not proud of the man I was before God got ahold of me or comfortable with everything I've done. I am, however, aware of God's grace."

"Uh-uh." I nod. "No way do I believe you."

"You should believe me. I'm telling the complete truth. B.C.—before Christ." He looks away, Let's just say I was out here."

"You? No," I say. "I can't see it."

"Seriously, I'm as much a sinner as anyone else. There are moments, especially when I first began my walk, that I feel incredibly guilty. That's why I love Romans eight, verse one so much. I had to constantly walk around reminding myself there is, therefore, no condemnation for those who are in Jesus."

"Did it work? Did you stop feeling guilty?"

"It was difficult, but yes. I've learned to let go of the old man along with his works to enjoy newness of life in Christ. I choose to thank God for the blood of Jesus and His plan that drew me near, not dwell on what was."

"Anything specific you weren't proud of?"

"You're not going to let this go, are you?" he asks with a wry smile. I shake my head.

"I'm not a naturally humble guy. Seriously, Leah," he says to my incredulous expression. "I used to be ignorantly proud of being proud. I was a decent ballplayer my entire life. I enjoyed the game, but not more than the admiration I received from excelling at it. Being adored is a seductive feeling."

Brice gets a faraway look in his eyes. He's physically present though somewhere else entirely. "The people knowing my name, shouting it on the court, on the streets, through the halls..." He shakes his head and fixes his stare on me. "It's intoxicating. I liked the attention too much. I was blinded by it. Then I met Seriyah. I didn't impress her the way I did everyone else. Popularity, success, those things didn't matter to her. She didn't care how handsome the girls said I was. The only way to get to know her was to get to know Christ. He's the only man she was ever interested in following."

This part of his story Brice has shared with me before. Seriyah was the one who first introduced him to Christ. She didn't insist he become a Christian like her; she just made a decision to live her life uncompromisingly. Either Brice was going to be okay with that or not. Her commitment to Christ was a convicting testimony.

"I was walking a destructive path without knowing it. I was enjoying being young, wild, and free. I didn't think I needed to change. Why would I when everyone loved me? If the Holy Spirit hadn't done His work within me, I'd still be that clueless slave to the world. Gradually, God has broken me of the biggest temptation of my faith: pride. I'm not a finished work; I struggle every day. It's a process. What I've learned is to trust God to meet me where I fall short."

"Is there anything else I could get you, folks," the waitress asks.

"No. We're still fine. Thank you," I answer with a smile.

The waitress's smile doesn't quite reach her eyes.

"Okay. That's the third time the waitress has been by in fifteen minutes. She wants us out of here."

"I know," he says. "I feel badly, but I'm not ready to go."

"Me either."

Hanging out with Brice in this way, unrestricted by time or propriety, is amazing.

"Heads up, she's coming back around." Brice heads her off before she can say a word. "Thank you for your awesome service. We'll be out your hair soon, and I promise to take care of you."

"It's been my pleasure," she says with a smile.

"You know, you can be pretty charming when you want to be," I say.

"Only when I have the right incentive. I'm not ready to say goodbye."

Brice is giving me all the feels.

"Does moving all the way to New York for this job as a youth minister mean you've given up your acting aspirations?" I ask, changing the subject.

During the competition, the judges acknowledged his talent while questioning his passion and desire. I wonder if being in ministry is where Brice's passions truly lie. In contrast to Brice, I wanted fame too much. Maybe stardom, like power, is better suited for people like Brice, those with the talent without the ego.

"Not at all," he says, drumming his fingers on the table. "I enjoy the stage, but I think my true gift is writing." He chuckles at my accusatory expression. "Yeah, we have that in common too."

Makes sense. Avid readers tend to be writers too. Why he didn't tell me this after I shared my writing with him is a question for later.

"Before I left home for the competition, I was working on a story. When I got back, it morphed into something almost completely different, but it was the story I needed to tell. I completed it—quickly." Brice's eyes shine bright, and his grin is wide as he tells me about his manuscript.

"I couldn't sleep until I got the story down. I sent seventeen query letters: eight went unanswered, six were rejections, one bounced back, one was no longer an agent, but the last said yes."

"What's a query letter?"

"Oh, sorry." He laughs. "A query is a letter writers send to agents, introducing themselves and their manuscript. The hope is they'll find your story compelling and profitable. If so, they make you an offer of representation. It then becomes their job to shop your book and represent your literary interests."

"I learn something new every single day. Go ahead. Continue with your story. One agent said yes."

"Right," Brice says, getting back into the story. "My agent, Jael, worked at a major publishing house here in New York until she went out on her own. I'm her first client. I think that'll change soon. She's brilliant," he says, voice full of warmth.

"When my pastor told me our sister church in New York needed a youth leader and asked if I would be willing to go help out, it seemed that God was aligning everything in my favor. I want to continue acting. Right now though, I think it's important I produce Christ-centered content."

I ignore the uncertainty I felt at the mention of this Jael person and marvel at what he's been able to accomplish. "I'm happy for you, Brice. I can't wait to buy my copy of your book. What's it about?" He tilts his head to the side the way he does sometimes when he's thinking something through. "It's okay," I say. "You don't have to tell me. I don't even want to know. I only asked to be polite."

I wait for him to get upset. Instead, he picks up a white napkin from the table, holds it between us, and waves it. I bite my bottom lip to keep from smiling at his act of surrender.

"It's a Christian fiction novel," he says, "about a young woman who tries to leave God, but He refuses to give up on her."

I swallow the lump forming in my throat. I'm all too familiar with that story.

"How does it end?" I ask in a small, tremulous voice.

"With grace."

Grace sounds nice, but what does that even look like?

Chapter 11

Hallelujah but First Can I Get a Picture for the 'Gram?

Brice parks his five-year-old Camry in front of my house. It's not as fancy as Trent's...anything. He has a car for every day of the week—beautiful ones, fancy ones, sporty ones, and expensive ones—but none I've felt half as comfortable in as I do in Brice's modest car.

"Are you working tomorrow?"

Seven hours, yet the right time to tell him about my job didn't present itself once. I can't put it off anymore. It's one thing to avoid the topic. It's an entirely different thing to lie straight to his face. I have to tell him I lost my job and how.

Brice undoes his seatbelt, reaches across the small space, and hugs me. It's the kind of hug that stops time, dwarfs reality, and convinces you everything will be okay.

"I'm sorry, L."

I stiffen at the endearment and push him away. "Don't." Answering the hurt in his expression, I try to explain. "I'm sorry. It's not you. I just don't like to be called L."

Comprehension chases away hurt. Without me saying so, Brice understands my reaction to being called L is tied to Trent.

"So what am I allowed to call you?" Brice asks, glossing over the awkwardness of the last minute.

"I can't tell you what to call me. You have to think of a cute nickname for me, which I will veto if I disapprove."

His face lights up. "How do you feel about Leahz?"

"I feel...that's what Corey and Aiden call me."

I don't mind them calling me Leahz. It's playful like my relationship with them, but that doesn't feel appropriate for what Brice and I have.

"L. Dot?"

"L. Dot?" I shake my head. "That's a hard no. I'd prefer a nickname that doesn't sound like the newest release in a line of sneakers."

I don't think I've ever seen Brice laugh this hard. It makes me smile. I like being able to bring that out of him. Laughter still on his lips, he takes my hand. With his finger, he traces a pattern on my palm. At first, I think he's messing around, then I realize he's tracing the same pattern over and over.

"What are you writing?"

"Focus," he says, lifting his gaze to me.

He repeats it, slower this time. His index finger moves vertically, top to bottom, at the base. He makes another line, this one horizontal.

"L," I say with excitement.

He smiles then bends his head, returning to the task at hand. He makes two diagonal lines going in opposite directions, kissing at the tips. In the middle is a smaller horizontal line.

"A." He nods. "LA?" He nods again.

"What do you think about that?"

LA. Leah Albanese. "I like it, except doesn't it make me sound Hollywood when I'm so Brooklyn?"

We laugh at my corny joke until the mood turns from playful to electric like it did the other night. And just like then, Brice shuts down the moment. He deposits my hand back into my lap, leaving me frustrated.

"I'm not sure if you heard or not," he says, ignoring the last minute. "I'm getting all the kids in the youth ministry together to put on a play. It'll be my directorial debut. The show is in six weeks. I have way too much to do to possibly get it done alone. If you're willing, I could really use the help. There's no pay, but dinner's on me after every rehearsal. You'll be helping young people and...I'll be there."

I raise an eyebrow wordlessly, asking the significance of the second statement.

"If that in any way motivates you," he quickly adds.

I nod, though I make no comment on whether his presence sways my decision in either direction.

On the one hand, I have nothing else going on, and I think I would enjoy being on the opposite side of the stage. On the other hand, I'm not sure I'm the best person for the job. Brice isn't just directing the church's play, he's the youth ministry leader. If I'm his assistant, I become an extension of him. Right now, anything I could say to these young people would be hypocritical. I'm only a few months removed from some of the worst decisions of my life. Some days I question precisely how removed I am. What do I have to offer them?

"You think I would be a good fit?" It's less of a question, more of a statement, a reminder to Brice of my shortcomings.

"I know you would." My eyes meet his, hopeful beyond reason, at the certitude in his voice that I'll be contradicted. "You have a perspective that I don't."

My heart sinks. The difference in our perspectives is indeed great—Brice, committed and loyal; me, feeble and struggling. I scoot away from him, pressing myself up against the door and turning my sight out the window.

"I'd actually prefer not to be the cautionary tale used into scaring rebellious teens straight."

It's not my intention to be mean and sardonic. I can only shake the feelings of unworthiness, shame, and guilt for so long until they come rushing back like a sucker punch to the gut. When that happens, in my mind, I feel I'm wearing a bright scarlet A, sins visible for the whole world to judge.

"Why are you so hard on yourself?"

"I'm not. I'm realistic. You should really stop looking at me through rose-colored lenses."

I keep my gaze out the window, watching as the sun sets over Brooklyn. The timing of the streetlights is perfect. They come on precisely as the last rays of the sun fade into evening. The harsh streetlight floods the passenger window, making me squint and turn the other way, back toward Brice.

He's wearing an expression I've never seen on him before. Maybe it's the spots of light dotting my vision, making it hard to read him. I blink a few times, trying to rid myself of the glare.

"I can't make you receive God's forgiveness even though it's yours for the taking." The anger in his voice demands I look at him. "The things you're beating yourself up over, Jesus has already atoned for. What you have to do is believe that." His eyes bore into mine. "There's such a thing as godly convicting sorrow, and then there's condemnation. The former leads to repentance and right living, the latter to further straying and spiritual death. Stop doing this to yourself. It doesn't glorify God." Brice sighs heavily, his righteous anger morphing into something less angry though just as righteous.

"I would love your help on this. You're talented, and you have a testimony, whether or not you realize it. When you're given grace, it's your responsibility to now be a steward of it." Despite the former fire in his tone, his voice is gentle. "I pray you get to know Jesus and as a result who you are. I pray you understand the breadth, width, height, and length of His love and stop doing the devil's work for him. Nothing you've done is unforgiveable. Your life isn't over."

He cups the side of my face, asking me to believe him. I want to. I want to so much.

"The most difficult battles of your life happen when you decide to forego your former ways. A war ensues. The enemy of your soul understands that you're teetering, capable of going either way. He will attempt to bring you back under his grasp through lies and accusations, but those the Son has set free are free indeed. Our first practice is Wednesday at five. I really hope to see you there."

In the Garden Christian Assembly is enormous. I'd heard of its popularity and size, but my wildest imaginations failed me. The building spans an entire Manhattan square block. I crane my head back as far as I can as Cashmere and I walk toward the front doors, wanting to see how high up it goes. It's no skyscraper, but it dwarfs Onward Christian Soldiers and my mom's church too. It's as large as any of the many cathedrals nearby. I agreed to go to Sunday service at In the Garden Christian Assembly with Cashmere because she asked me to. She's still looking for a church home. I want to support her in that, however as we walk through the glass doors, I have a strong feeling this won't be it.

The floor in the atrium is white ceramic tile. I imagine it takes constant maintenance to keep it white—the walls too. They're white as well. The only color in the lobby is the three closed-circuit televisions broadcasting the service and the mahogany information desk. Our heels click-clack against the floor all the way from the revolving doors there. Greeters welcome us with broad smiles and point Cashmere and me to the assembly hall.

"It's like an airport terminal in here," Cashmere whispers.

You can't help whispering in a place so large, so white, and so quiet.

"Yeah, it does, but a really nice one. Definitely not like anything we have in New York," I whisper back. "Cash, you're going the wrong way. She said go right at the row of ATMs, not left. I'd hate to end up at the restaurant and have to walk all the way back. We're already twenty minutes late."

Cashmere cracks a broad smile, which causes me to laugh. There aren't too many places where a statement like that would be bizarre. We just so happen to be standing in one of the few exceptions.

"Come on. This way," I say, dragging her along behind me.

In the same neon t-shirts that read *In the Garden Christian Assembly*, ushers flank either side of the open sanctuary doors. They're momentarily forgotten as I take in the endless sea of people. It's amazing. I've never experienced a gathering of people this large at one time, except maybe at a concert. It sort of feels like I'm at a concert. The low lights, loud music, packed seating, all of it reminds me of being at a show.

An usher leads Cashmere and me deeper into the theatre, past cameras and rows upon rows of filled seats. When we're much closer than I would have thought possible, being as late as we are, I ask if he's sure there's available seating this close to the front.

"Yes. We have a celebrity seating area near the pulpit."

I stop dead in my tracks. When did the church get a VIP section and why? Secondly, I'm not a celebrity. Cashmere's a successful social media influencer, though. I'm her beneficiary if I can call celebrity seating in church a benefit. I grab Cashmere's arm. She wobbles in her heels and has to hold on tightly to my arm to prevent a fall.

"What?" she says.

"I don't feel comfortable with this celebrity seating thing. I don't think it's fair to everyone else. Why should we have better seats than the people who were here on time? Because you have a million followers?"

Behind her, the usher notices we're no longer following him. "Ladies, are you coming?" Impatience fights through his cheery tone.

"No," I say at the same time Cashmere says, "Yes."

"Well, which one is it?" he asks, no longer trying to hide his irritation.

"Listen," Cashmere says, "it's not that big of a deal."

"If it's not a big deal, then let's sit with everyone else."

"Fine," she agrees. "Let's sit with the masses."

"I just loved your *Wolf of Your Wall Street*. After I saw you as Jordan Belfort, I watched the movie again...twice," says Fangirl with stars in her eyes and a toothy smile.

She hasn't stopped talking to us since we were ushered to our seats in the row behind her. She and practically everyone else seated in our section in the back of the sanctuary have made it their duty to express how much they love us.

Cashmere's spent the last half hour posing for selfies and hopping on IG stories. I can understand if we were anywhere else but church. Jesus is the star of today's show, not us. That should go without saying.

I purposefully look past Fangirl to the colossal monitor positioned high above the pulpit, emphasizing my preoccupation with the reason I hope we're all in attendance, to praise God.

Worship's led by a male and female duo, both young people, early twenties maybe. The accompaniment is fantastic, and the song is catchy. Still, I feel nothing, not even an ounce of the warmth that filled me at Onward Christian Soldiers. The words of the song, an original, are up on the screen for following along. I read them, searching for meaning in the ambiguous phrases and find none. Cashmere's no longer taking pictures with fans, but she isn't singing along either. Maybe she feels as disconnected as I do.

"Can I have a picture with you for IG?" Fangirl's relentless.

"Okay. Let's take it quickly," I tell her. "I don't want to miss any more of the service."

"I bet you wish you were in the celebrity seating area now, don't you?" Cashmere whispers.

I roll my eyes at her. I hate that she's right.

"Let's give our fantastic worship leaders a round of applause," Pastor Jackson, head pastor of In the Garden Christian Assembly, says in a booming voice. The crowd obeys, breaking into loud, enthusiastic clapping. I join in, slightly less enthused than everyone else.

"What'd you think?" Cashmere asks. She hasn't said as much, but I can tell she really liked In the Garden. She's beaming, exploding with excitement. For her sake, I wish I could say the same. I cast about for an answer that won't deflate her while we slowly make our way toward the bridge.

"The building's beautiful," I say, keeping my response brief and positive.

"That's it? You thought the building was beautiful?" she asks while holding on to the back of our Uber driver's headrest. I silently thank New York City potholes for the extra ten seconds of thinking time.

"The worship was extremely professional," I add.

"You didn't like it."

"*Ummm*...It's not that I didn't like it. It just wasn't what I was expecting."

"What do you mean?"

I feel ridiculous tip-toeing around the truth. I can tell her how I feel without asking she feel the same way.

"After all the time you spent obliging fans, I get why VIP seating might be necessary," I admit. "I still don't like it, though. It feels wrong and more in line with society's views about fame and fortune, not at all what the church should be."

"I think you're making too much of that," she says, waving off my concern. "You're just not used to the star treatment yet. If *Star Quality* continues trending, you'll have to work on that."

"O-kay," I respond, drawing out every syllable. "But then there's the worship service."

"It was like being at a concert, right?" Cashmere asks. I nod. "I had to remind myself a few times I was actually listening to gospel. I need to talk to the lighting crew because the stage was on point. I've evolved so much from when I first started on YouTube, but I can still use some pointers on lighting—" Cashmere stops short in the middle of her thought. "What?"

"Nothing," I say, looking out the window.

"You didn't like the worship, did you?"

"I didn't say that."

"So, did you?"

"The music was beautifully arranged," I say, sighing, "but it didn't impact me—not one direct reference to Jesus or scripture the whole song." I shrug. "It might be that I'm more traditional in worship than I realized."

Maybe I am partial to the old hymns. Still, I didn't feel anything in the music. Not like I did at Onward Christian Soldiers.

"I could overlook the VIP seating area and the superficial worship if the message was good, which it was."

"It was good," Cashmere agrees.

"It was also incomplete. It's irresponsible to speak about the blessing without talking about He who bestows the blessing. It was an extremely one-dimensional sermon. Preaching on wealth and prosperity without cautioning that it should never become your god is reckless."

I've lived the dangers of having a skewed perspective. I don't want that for anyone else.

"I don't know," she says, sounding controlled and guarded. "I liked that he encouraged everyone to believe they, too, could be blessed and prosperous. Some people need to hear that," Cashmere counters.

"I agree. We all need to be reminded God has better for us. I still feel it was incomplete. I know from first-hand experience that you can have a full belly yet still hunger… When you got the huge beauty deal," I cautiously begin, hating that I'm even bringing it up.

"It was a good thing, right?" She nods despite her darkening expression. "But it was also hollow, right?" She nods again. "And that hollow feeling…it led to a dark time?"

I let my tone say what I won't—the hollow feeling that led her to attempt to take her life. Cashmere nods again, understanding what I'm truly asking.

"What I'm getting at is this: All the fortune in the world can't satisfy a thirsty soul."

"Just to make sure I understand you…" I brace myself. Whenever someone attempts to sum up what you said in their own words, they usually completely mangle your point. "You think it's wrong to preach about prosperity?"

Laughing, I ask, "When did I say that?"

"You said—"

"I believe the Lord does want us to be blessed and prosperous, but He also wants us to prioritize a relationship with Him first. Everything else will come as a result of that relationship."

It took weeks' worth of recurring nightmares to understand that's what God was saying to me.

"Pastor Jackson should have reminded the congregation that having a relationship with Christ is the greatest blessing, and everything else stems from that, and not as a postscript, as the point."

Pastor Charles said that in his sermon. It's stuck with me, and it feels appropriate.

"I get it. I think I even agree with you. We probably just missed that sermon. I'm going to keep going for a little while, at least. You're welcome to accompany me."

I decide not to point out that having a relationship with Christ isn't something that should only be preached occasionally. That much I do know, and I answer her question. "Thanks for the offer," I say. "I'm going to have to pass though. I think I may have found my own church home."

"Would it happen to be Brice's church?"

"He doesn't own Onward Christian Soldiers. He's a congregant and the youth ministry leader. That's all." Feeling the need to defend myself against Cashmere's smirk, I add, "I'm not going because of him, you know. I'm going because I felt the Spirit of the Lord."

"*Umm-hmm.* If you say so."

Chapter 12

Act One,
Scene One, Take One

"Hey, Mom. How was your day?"

I scoop the bags of groceries out of her arms into mine and help her inside. I thought at twenty-seven, I'd be bringing groceries to the big, beautiful house I bought her. I didn't expect my mom to still be feeding me. Times like this, I almost wish I married Trent. Though little good that would have done. She would have never accepted his money or anything his money purchased. I wrench my mind back from some of the very thoughts that led to my detour in the first place and decide to be grateful that we have a roof over our heads, food on the table, and health. Everything else will come in time.

"Thanks for your help."

"No problem."

"How was your day?" she asks, stopping to looking at me.

"Alright. I found some promising leads. Hopefully, I hear something back soon." My optimism is purely for my mom's benefit. She worries about me. Truthfully, today was a hard day. Pouring over job boards again searching for retail and administrative positions was soul crushing. It was all I could do not to give in to despair. Hardly a minute passed without me questioning my life.

When I was all but decided on giving up, I remembered Pastor Charles's sermon. Good ground makes it over to the other side.

There was a moment when I thought how much more powerful it felt hearing that message sitting in church. Then I recalled that the seed that fell on the rock received the Word enthusiastically until the wind came. Because it had no roots, it was scattered. I think God's telling me it's time I start growing some roots.

"Don't get discouraged," my mom urges. "The right thing—the opportunity from the Lord—will present itself in due time. I know things are hard. Hold on, be of good courage. It's those who cannot wait on God who give birth to pain."

I don't have to think too hard to riddle that one out or find a real-life example of its validity. My life is enough.

"You should look at Romans five, verses three through five for perspective."

"Perspective?" I repeat, flashing back to the last time I heard that word.

"Yes, perspective," my mom replies. This is the second time in a few days that I was spoken to about my perspective. I've long stopped believing in coincidences. Maybe I will check out Romans, for perspective.

Not only so, but we also glory in our sufferings, because we know that suffering produces perseverance; perseverance character; and character, hope. And hope does not put us to shame, because God's love has been poured into our hearts through the Holy Spirit, who has been given to us.

The Word is so satisfying, a refreshing glass of cool water on a hot day in the arid sun. I have to read on past where my mom suggested.

You see, at just the right time, when we were still powerless, Christ died for the ungodly. Very rarely will anyone die for a righteous person, though for a good person someone might possibly dare to die. But God demonstrates His own love for us in this: While we were still sinners, Christ died for us.

I sit at the kitchen table, mulling over what I've read, especially verse six. It's true, no one would volunteer their life for the life of another, maybe for a loved one or a particularly good person. Who would die for a bad man? I definitely wouldn't.

My thoughts turn self-reflective. I'm not a murderer or a thief. There was that comb I took from Walmart that one time when I was five. I don't lie...much.

I try to be kind, though I fail at it more often than I'm comfortable admitting. I love my neighbor like I love myself. Although, I do have the tendency to be self-absorbed, unable to see past my own afflictions. I'm not a particularly good woman, not the type you die for anyway, but Jesus did. Jesus died for me. Why?

I turn to the book of John, which Brice recommended I read it. I've been putting it off. I don't know why. I only go there now because I need to understand why Jesus would die for me. John starts off by explaining Jesus is and always was. He is the Word of God made flesh. The Son come as the Lamb of God to take away the sin of the world. Ferociously, feeling thirstier and hungrier, I consume John. I don't stop until I've read the last line of chapter twenty-one.

Jesus did many other things as well. If every one of them were written down, I suppose that even the whole world would not have room for the books that would be written.

I go back to chapter one, verse one, and reread, this time more slowly, savoring every word.

For God so loved the world that He gave His one and only Son, that whoever believes in Him shall not perish but have eternal life. For God did not send His Son into the world to condemn the world, but to save the world through Him.

I stop at the end of chapter three, verse seventeen, amazed and in awe of such a love. Jesus died for me because I needed Him to, and it is the Father's will that the Son save humanity. I go to bed feeling better than I have in some time. Understanding the sacrifice of Jesus on my behalf has put my present circumstances in perspective: If Jesus endured the cross for me, He wouldn't forsake me. I get a sure feeling in my spirit I'm not in this alone. I think it might be the beginning of faith.

"I didn't think you were coming."

"Neither did I." My words come out shaky.

"Since you're here, why don't you follow me? I want to introduce you to the youth we'll be working with."

"Okay," I say, following Brice to the front of the church where a small group of young people—twenty or so—sit waiting for him. All day I had a nagging feeling there was somewhere I needed to be. I got dressed, rode the subway, transferred, then got off the train without ever deciding to be here. I kind of just ended up here, at Onward Christian Soldiers Ministry, at the first rehearsal.

"Good afternoon, soldiers."

I'm taken aback by the greeting though no one else is. They respond, "Good afternoon, soldier."

"This here," Brice says, briefly turning my way, "is my friend Leah. She will be helping me—us—out with the play. She's a very talented actress doing me a favor. Don't scare her off, got it?"

"Brother Young, I have a question," says a girl sitting in the front row directly in front of Brice.

She looks up at him with adoration and something else, something mischievous. He smiles at her, flatteringly coloring her chestnut complexion. She's too artful in her movements to be as innocent as she's aiming to appear. I have a hunch she's about to prove that.

"What's your question, Ella?" Brice asks.

"Yes," the girl, Ella, replies. "Brother Young, is Leah your girlfriend?"

It's a rare thing to stump both Brice and me. We hem and haw until she saves us the trouble of responding.

"If she is, my mom won't approve of me participating in the play."

I hear the snickers all around me though all I see is Ella's smug smirk. Every clique has a queen bee, even a church youth ministry, and the little tyrant just made a power play. I risk peeking over at Brice. I want to see if he's as upset as I am. He wears a passive expression and takes a step forward, closer to the first row of occupied seats. Ella's encouraged by this and smiles more broadly.

"Really?" Brice asks her in a surprised tone. "Your mom wouldn't approve of a young couple using their time to serve God's purpose together? I'd just have to ask her if that were the case. But as I said before, Leah is my friend, not my girlfriend."

She looks to me, her smile impossibly broader, then back at Brice. She raises her hand and begins speaking without being given permission.

"My mom wouldn't have an issue with your hypothetical girlfriend helping you out with the play. She has an issue with her specifically," she says, gesturing to me with her chin. "We've watched you on that show. Her too. She has a bad temper, and she came to church dressed like she was looking for attention."

Ella leans forward in her seat, teetering on edge. She covers the right side of her mouth with a cupped hand. She says, "My mom disapproves of her behavior. She said if she were her child, she would have straightened her out a long time ago."

Everyone hears the exchange because she meant them to. I stand around, mortified, watching as teenagers laugh at me.

"Soldiers." With a word, Brice brings everyone to silence, his face no longer passive.

It registers how disappointed he is in Ella and her performance.

"Why do I call you soldiers?" he asks.

The response comes swiftly and in unison, "Because that's what we are, soldiers."

"In whose army?"

"In the army of the Lord."

He paces, hands behind his back, never taking his eyes off them. "Who is our enemy?"

"The opposer of our souls, the accuser of the brethren."

"Again. Who is our enemy?"

"The opposer of our souls, the accuser of the brethren."

"Who accuses the brethren?"

"The opposer of our souls."

"If you, a soldier in the army of the Lord, accuse one of your brethren, what does that make you?"

They turn to one another, asking the answer to the question posed by their leader. Brice must not have taught them the response to that one. He looks at them, each allowing them to feel the weight of his displeasure.

"It's hard enough for Christians, especially young Christians, without the added distress of being attacked by other believers. We're meant to be shining lights in this dark, lost world. How can we do that if we behave just as they do, tearing other Christians down with malice? Even if you need to exhort, do it with love."

This speech, delivered with audible hurt and disappointment, is more effective than any other forms of punishment I could think up, except maybe a whooping. Some kids—Ella—need that from time to time. If she makes another snarky comment, I might have to give her one.

"We don't tolerate gossip, innuendos, and accusations in the church. If you have a question, ask. This is a safe space to discuss things, but it will be done respectfully or not at all." Brice addresses himself to the group in general now. He takes a knee in front of Ella and speaks to her specifically.

"You're a smart girl, which means you know the church isn't exclusively for perfect people. It's for people who know they need Jesus, those who have found Him, and as a result, want to walk in close fellowship with the Lord. I'm pretty sure if your life was recorded twenty-four hours a day for weeks on end, then edited, there'd be some hard-to-explain moments too. You know better, Ella, Do better." He holds her gaze until she drops hers, then gets up and walks away.

I study Ella as Brice turns his back to her, unsure if what he said made any difference at all. When she sees me looking at her and smirks, I know it didn't. I turn away and accidentally catch Brice's eye in the process. He seems to be communicating something to me. Before I can get a read on what he's thinking, my phone chimes loudly in my purse. My focus briefly shifts to the purse still on my shoulder. I look back at Brice, but he's already returned to the kids.

"That brings me to our first rule," Brice says. "Cell phones are to be off for the duration of rehearsals."

I think better of asking if I'm also subject to that rule when I notice how hard he's staring at me. I clutch my pocketbook a little tighter. I don't dare reach for my phone.

"Leah, would you please pass these out?"

Brice takes a few quick strides to the stairs leading up to the pulpit, where a brown leather messenger bag lays on the steps. He reaches inside and pulls out a massive stack of papers. He separates a stack from the bunch marked off by a blue paperclip and puts the rest back in the bag. He walks over to me and hands me the pile. I take the handouts and distribute them to each kid.

"In your hands, you hold the list of rules for participation in the play. I expect you each to follow them," Brice says. "Ella, would you be so kind as to read the second rule aloud for us, please?"

"Sure," she says with a flirty smile that explains much.

She has a crush on Brice. That's why she attacked me. I don't blame her. I have the exact same crush. Personally, I think he's too young and good-looking to be in charge of a primarily female group of teens, which is probably another reason he asked for my help. I guess he's not as unaware of his charms as he seems.

"All soldiers are required to complete at least twenty hours of community service?" Ella asks more than states.

"Yes, all of us. Leah and I included."

I try to keep my face neutral. I don't want the kids to know I share their outrage. I did not sign up for volunteering beyond this room, a point I plan on reminding Brice of privately.

"We will be completing community service hours weekly. By the end of the six weeks, we should have eighteen hours. The show, which will be free and open to the community, will count as another two hours for a total of twenty community service hours. I've already planned our projects. They're once a week, three hours a day, starting next week."

"That's not fair," one of the few guys in attendance says.

"Yeah. I already have a lot going on. I don't have time for anything else," Ella says.

"Soldiers," Brice calls, putting an end to all murmuring and regaining the attention of the room, "it's great you want to be part of the play. It would be better for you to want to help others. We all have to get in the habit of thinking beyond ourselves. That isn't a suggestion but a command from Jesus. Love your neighbor as you love yourself. Remember when you give whether it be your time, talents, or finances, it shall be given back to you in 'good measure, pressed down, shaken together, and running over.'"

That shames us all into quiet. In the thoughtful silence, Brice walks back to his bag, retrieves the remaining papers, and hands them to me.

"Leah's coming back around with a calendar. Once you have the calendar, study it. You will find the tentative date of our performance, rehearsal schedules, as well as community service project dates, time, and locations. Additionally, my number and email address are at the top right corner. If, for any reason, you cannot make it to any of these events, please contact me beforehand. If there are no questions, you are dismissed for today. Our next meeting is next Friday."

Brice extends his hand to me, holding yet another stack of printouts. He's like a magician pulling papers out of a hat.

"On your way out, be sure to grab sides, which are the audition pieces, from Leah. Come prepared. There will be no favoritism. The person who deserves the role will get the role."

He smiles at the small group of teens who feel like his younger brothers and sisters and instructs them to stand, form a circle, and join hands for prayer before we go.

"Bye, Leah."

Smiling, I give sides to the sweet girl I noticed sitting alone during the meeting while everyone else sat with a friend. She looks a little younger than the others, fifteen maybe. I'm not sure if it's shyness or her age that keep her apart, but I feel an instant kinship to her—I'm feeling kind of out of place myself. I follow her out the doors to the lobby with my gaze then turn to Ella and Brice. She's got him cornered. She stands close to him, leans into him even, pointing to something on her calendar.

I get the whole crush on an older guy thing, but she's too brazen with her attempts. When I was her age, I wouldn't have—that's not strictly true. I've been attracted to an older guy or two, but what happened to subtly? I wonder what her mom, who she was quick to point out disapproves of me, would say about her daughter throwing herself at the youth ministry director? The idea keeps a smile on my face while I busy myself collecting forgotten garbage.

She detaches herself from Brice and walks to the door. "Oh yeah, I almost forgot." She turns, makes eye contact with me, and tilts her head to the side. "Bye, Lola."

Brice shakes his head. "Ella?"

"Yes, Brother Young?"

"You've just tacked on an extra five hours of community service."

She pushes open the doors with more strength than needed and stomps her way out.

"Serves her right," I mutter.

Brice takes a seat on the steps of the pulpit. I would join him, but I can tell him off much better from here.

"You know," he begins, beating me to the punch, "community service isn't a punishment."

"About that," I say, "you should have told me beforehand. I appreciate what you're doing with the kids, but I'm an adult. You can't make decisions for me without consulting me. At the very least, do me the courtesy of telling me before you tell them."

"I didn't think it would bother you."

"It doesn't bother me," I snap. "What bothers me is being disrespected by little girls with big girl crushes, being rejected in front of a group of teenagers, commentary on my life, and paper cuts."

Although I'm frustrated, I keep my voice level, not wanting to somehow desecrate this place of worship by yelling. I stop Brice's response with a finger over my lips and one pointing to the doors; I don't want to talk about this in the church. We can talk outside. He demonstrates he understands my half-cocked sign language by nodding.

Silently, I collect my purse and put on my coat. As I do so, I get the feeling I'm being watched. I look up and catch Brice staring at me the way he sometimes does. I ignore the butterflies in my stomach and walk out of the church with him trailing behind.

Brice locks the doors and chains the gate as I stand off to the side waiting for him. Done, he faces me with a rueful smile. "What were you yelling at me about before?"

Unable to dredge up even a little bit of my former anger, I say, "I didn't yell. I spoke passionately."

Brice is laughing before I finish my sentence. I try to school my features into annoyance, which only makes him laugh harder. I start laughing too. We walk to his car, both of us hysterical.

"If you hadn't stepped in earlier, I would have had to send your girlfriend to time-out."

"Whoa." Brice stops dead in his tracks in the middle of the sidewalk, his expression drained of all amusement. "Don't play like that. All of those kids are like my younger brothers and sisters. I would never be inappropriate with them."

"I wasn't suggesting you would be. I was making a joke about Ella's obvious crush on you. I didn't mean to imply anything improper on your part."

With no actual acknowledgment of my apology, Brice starts walking again. I follow silently behind him; I guess the joke was in poor taste. I pat him on the back as he begins to cough. He grabs hold of my hand, twisting away to face me. He wasn't coughing at all; he was clearing his throat.

"I'm sorry." Brice puts the full weight of those two words into the way he squeezes my hands. "I know you were only joking and meant nothing by it. It's just that I take my role in the lives of those young people very seriously. I've been entrusted with their development; the possibility of somehow derailing their spiritual progress keeps me up at night."

Feeling worse, I accept his apology and offer one of my own. "It's okay, I shouldn't joke around like that," even if it's true. I don't say that to him, though. Looking much lighter, he laces his fingers through mine and resumes walking.

"I figured she had a crush on me," Brice says, reopening the topic. "I would call it innocent, but she's made a point of telling me she's 'not so innocent,'" he says with air quotes.

We arrive at his parked car in the nick of time. Not having to respond is the best way I can think of to not offend him again. Brice opens my door first,

169

waits for me to get in, then closes it. He gets in the driver's seat and buckles his seatbelt. "You're not going to say anything?"

I shrug. "Depends. Are you going to bite my head off?" He looks like he's on the verge of apologizing again, and honestly, there's no need for it. I get why what I said was upsetting to him. To show him all is forgiven, I say, "It's not unusual for a younger girl to like her attractive, handsome, older instructor. She's what, eighteen?"

"She said she's eighteen. I think she's probably seventeen."

"Makes complete sense. Ella thinks she's an adult. She wants adult freedoms and to be seen as a woman, not a child. Unfortunately, her fast attitude won't wear down until she gets a rude awakening. I don't wish it on her, but I know the realities of being an attractive young girl eager to be a woman."

The engine roars to life. "I wish I could help her. Frankly, Ella's one of the main reasons I initiated this community service program."

"Really?"

Brice drapes a hand around the back of my headrest as he pulls out of the parking space. "Yeah," he says, sounding a bit taut, straining, as he is to see behind him. "I've noticed how mean she is."

"Have you?" I ask. "After her performance in there, I wasn't sure."

Keeping his eyes on the road, he sighs. "I handled it the best way I know how. I don't think embarrassing her will help. Teaching her humility, that's the key. She's the only child from divorced parents willing to show how much they each adore her. By adore, I mean spoil. She's social media famous, I'm told. You know how much I pay attention to those platforms, and she's self-assured."

I nod along with him.

"None of those things by themselves are inherently bad, but she's also arrogant and a bully. Worst of all is, everyone's her willing victim. I'm not unaware of what's happening, but sometimes you have to meet people where they are to take them higher. She can only be taught the lesson if she sticks around long enough to learn it."

I was ready to throttle Ella and Brice with her for tolerating her disrespect, but his trying to help her is commendable.

"Do you really think she's in for a—what'd you call it? A rude awakening?"

"It sounds ominous when you say it like that."

"It isn't? Ominous is definitely the vibe I got from what you said."

I contemplate the question, do I think Ella's in for a rude awakening. I don't know her, although I know her type—bark louder than her bite, eager to assert her independence.

"Yes," I say. "Yes, I do."

"Would you be willing to work with her?"

"What do you mean work with her?" Brice takes his eyes off the road for a second. "I think she would benefit from your mentorship."

"Mentoring?"

How can I mentor her? My general dislike of the brat to the side, how am I to be her mentor? I'm unemployed. I can't help guide her on a career path. I'm not like Brice, sure and certain about all things Christianity, and as Ella was so kind to mention, she's already watched me make some of the biggest mistakes of my life. Even if I could find something of merit to say to her, would she listen to me?

"No. I can't be anyone's mentor," I decide.

"I beg to differ. Like I said before, you have a testimony that a girl not unlike Ella would greatly benefit from. You can't change what's happened, but you can affect the choices someone else makes. We all have the responsibility to witness about Christ so that the same grace you've been given they, too, can experience. She may be a little callous at times—"

"A little," I interrupt.

"Fine. Sometimes she's malicious," he agrees, "but this isn't the end of her story. How would you feel if you knew you had the ability and opportunity to impact someone's life, but you didn't take it because they offended you one time?" Encouraged by my thoughtful silence, Brice presses his advantage. "Think about it for a second: Isn't there anything you know now you wish someone would have told you when you were younger?"

I don't have to think hard. There are plenty of things I wish I knew before, things if told by the right person I might have actually taken heed to. I have to try with Ella, even if I feel it futile.

"I'm not making any promises," I say resignedly, "but I'll give it a shot."

"Thank you."

"Yeah...well, don't thank me yet. I'm willing to attempt this whole mentor thing. That doesn't mean she's willing."

A slow smile spreads across his face. "Actually...that extra five hours community service I assigned her will be forgiven if she agrees to an hour a week with you."

I turn my gaze out the window. "An hour a week with Ella sounds likes fun."

"I was hoping you'd feel that way."

Chapter 13

Is That Opportunity Knocking?

Dear Miss Albanese,

My name is Brian Lafferty, producer at TS Productions, an up-and-coming, cutting-edge production company. We've recently secured a partnership with a top-rated streaming app to develop an original talk show, tentatively named Clapback. Unlike other programs of its kind, Clapback has the voices people genuinely want to hear. We aren't assembling a cast of the usual suspects; our panelists are the personalities everyone already knows and loves. They have the follows to prove it. We've pegged various influencers from around the country to come together to discuss the things that matter: music, celebrity gossip, other influencers, beauty, et cetera. We've got a great cast lined up, and we'd love to add you to the roster.

We've been following you on Star Quality. You're hands down the most exciting player. You inspire conversation, which is exactly the kind of presence we're looking for. If this is something you're interested in (I hope you are, this is going to be epic), please respond immediately. We have to move fast. I look forward to hearing from you soon.

There are only so many times and so many ways you can read eleven sentences. The email says what it says. My mom did say the right opportunity would present itself. Is it possible it has? I would be great as a commentator, host, or whatever you call them. I'm never without an opinion. But before jumping all in, I have questions. First, who is TS Productions?

A quick Google search brings up nothing more than what Brian already mentioned in the email. I Google Brian Lafferty instead. All I'm able to find are LinkedIn, Twitter, Facebook, and Instagram pages. I check out his LinkedIn first. The TS Productions hyperlink in Brian's profile leads to very little new information. I'm only able to find the address.

A reverse search brings up a building in midtown, home to multiple media companies; among them, I recognize an online beauty magazine. TS Productions must be legit if they share an address with reputable companies. It isn't surprising I can't find much information on a new production company. I find plenty of information about Brian, though.

He's twenty-nine, originally from Kalamazoo, graduated from the University of Michigan, loves tacos from the taco truck that parks right outside his office, he's been seeing his girlfriend for over a year, they met at a baseball game, and before his current job, he worked for three cable television networks in seven years. I may not know much about TS Productions. However, I know Brian Lafferty enough to want to learn more about the opportunity with *Clapback*. A conversation can't hurt. Besides, what else do I have going on?

Brian wasn't exaggerating when he said they'd be moving quickly. The morning of the casting comes too fast and too early. I can't believe I'm doing this. I wasn't trying to test for anyone's anything. I also don't want to let the right opportunity pass me by.

"Hi."

I wave to the girls in the waiting room as I walk in. They're chatting familiarly among themselves. They probably all know each other to some degree from social media—even I recognize a few of them, though only by their user handles and the hashtags they've inspired. It feels like I'm in the makings of a hashtag myself. I bob and weave my way to a lone chair out of the epicenter of activity. I'm not trying to be caught in anyone's Live.

The last casting I went to was for *Star Quality,* and it was disastrous. I should've known then that it wasn't going to work out well for me. This feels different from that experience, though. Brian patiently answered all my questions. And I got the opportunity on my own, making this already infinitely better than my last project, although there are some notoriously loud and boisterous personalities present.

Dread hits me like a ton of bricks. What if I'm repeating my mistakes? *Clapback* is my first offer since I left *Star Quality.* What if I turn it down, but another opportunity never comes? I close my eyes, cutting off the chatter and lights. I can't tell anymore. Did I make the correct choice or a mistake?

"I'm pretty sure it's her," a hushed voice close by proclaims.

I think I might be the "her" in question.

"Looks like it, but I'm not sure," a voice distinctly different from the first responds. "Should we wake her up first or just go live?"

I'm absolutely positive they're talking about me though I don't know who "they" are with my eyes closed.

"I wouldn't do that if I were you," I say, opening my eyes.

Across from me, sitting on the black leather sofa, are two young women in colorful wigs, looking caught. I sit up and stretch my hand across the table between us, extending my hand to each girl in turn.

"I'm Leah."

"We know who you are," the girl in the periwinkle wig and lipstick says.

Actually, I know her too.

"You're Alexis, right?" She nods. "You dated Lil—"

"*Uh.* No," she interjects, palm sticking straight up at me. "I don't speak that man's name. He's dead to me. I'm simply Alexis, a'ight?"

"*Ummm.* Yeah. A'ight."

If I caught my superstar boyfriend in the direct messages of another Instagram model, then went through an ugly breakup that played out on social media, I'd be upset at any mention of prior association with him too.

"Sorry," I offer. "I didn't mean to stir anything up in you."

She gives me a sidelong look. "It's cool."

"Tori," the other girl says, breaking the tension of the moment. "Please excuse Alexis. She's still feeling a type of way about the situation."

"Best believe I'm still feeling a type of way. Wouldn't you if your man…" Alexis stops, considers something, then says, "You know what? He ain't even worth it."

"Anyways," Tori says. "Sorry. We didn't mean to wake you. We weren't really gonna put you on Live without your permission."

"It's fine. I wasn't sleeping, just relaxing."

Tori and Alexis exchange what I think is meant to be a covert look though completely obvious.

"What?" I ask.

"Nothing." Tori's reply comes too quickly for it to be truthful.

Alexis nudges her in the side with her elbow, fixing her with a meaningful look.

"I don't know why Tori's playin'," Alexis says, rolling her eyes at her friend, "but she wanted to know if Brice was your man because she's been crushing on him—hard."

Tori's eyes go wide. "Why would you tell her that?" she says, addressing Alexis.

"What?" Alexis replies, looking Tori up and down. "It's not true?"

"You know what," Tori says, shaking her head. She turns to me. "Since Alexis put it out there, yeah, it's true. I'm trynna see what's up with Brice. Can you pass him the digits? I mean, if he's not your man or anything."

I laugh aloud. I can't help it. Of course, complete strangers know the details of my personal life and feel entitled to the right to ask for clarity on the status of my relationship. It's so ridiculous I can't help but laugh. What's even funnier is Tori's request. There is no circumstance ever where I would be a go-between for Brice and a potential love interest.

"What's the joke?" Alexis asks.

She's ready to pounce. According to the stories about her online, she's never met a fight she backed down from.

"Please don't be offended," I say. "I'm still getting used to how much of my personal life is now public knowledge. Laughing is how I deal with how surreal it is."

Tori and Alexis both nod.

"You know," I say to Tori, "you're not the first person to ask about Brice." I smile to ease the tensions. "Ninety percent of the questions I'm asked are about him. I've never had anyone ask me to slip him their number, though."

Satisfied I'm not laughing at them, Tori and Alexis laugh along with me.

"No disrespect, Leah, truly, but that man is beautiful," Tori says.

"Which man is beautiful?" I'm not sure who asked.

Seven sets of eyes stare excitedly in our direction. Not wanting Brice and me to become a topic of conversation among women whose life's work is to give their opinions, I say, "Girl, there're too many to name."

"I know that's right," Tori agrees, erupting the room into loud boy-crazed chatter.

Grown women, yet the mention of good-looking men undo us. Whatever. Let them talk about any guy, every guy, except Brice. He's off-limits.

"Ladies."

All talking immediately ceases. We give our attention to the youngish male addressing us from the doorway; he's probably a producer or production assistant. I think I recognize him from a group photo on Brian's Instagram page.

"We're ready for you. We'll begin with a group of four. Afterward, you'll be switched out at the producer's discretion." He looks down at his clipboard. "Traci, Tori, Brooklyn, and Leah, follow me, please."

Mechanically, I rise from my seat. I feel the eyes of every other person in this room on us four who were, depending on how you look at it, lucky or unlucky to be called first. Talking to the girls distracted me from my nerves. With only seconds between the casting room and me, all the fear and uncertainty rushes back. Is this the right opportunity for me? What if I don't do well? My legs aren't working as quickly as they usually do. I lag behind the three other girls nearest Tori. She slows down a bit and hooks her arm through mine. Maybe she's nervous too. Whatever the reason, I'm grateful for it. Together we bring up the rear.

Two hours. That's how long it takes for me to finally be switched out. All the nerves I felt walking into the room dissipated when I saw where we'd be testing. It wasn't anything like what I was expecting. I anticipated a small room with fold-out chairs. What we get is a set. Four director-style chairs are placed in a semi-circle around a high table, shot by cameras I can barely see because of the bright set lights.

I came alive under those lights, steering the conversation about any topic thrown our way by producers. Tori and I work well together while Brooklyn and Traci are quickly replaced with Camille and Cali who have great energy, but it's impossible to get Cali to stay on topic. I verbally nudge her at least a dozen times in half as many minutes. Camille is sweet but without any strong opinions. She's replaced with Anna almost as soon as she sits down.

Anna's that fine line between passionate and aggressive. She toes it for a few minutes then clears it by a mile when she jumps in Tori's face over her dislike of a certain female rapper. Anna is escorted out of the building after that, and Tori is swapped with Alexis.

Thanks to her ex-boyfriend, Alexis personally knows many of the names and the stories being discussed. When she isn't strongly insinuating in word or look, she out and out says. She stays on set a while too. I wind up working with every single girl in almost every combination before I'm rotated out with Cecile, a well-intentioned loudmouth.

"You did really well today," the production assistant, walking me back to the green room, says.

"You think so?" I ask, slowing my pace to get as much insight from him as possible.

"I'm only a production assistant," he says, glancing my way. "My primary responsibility today is escorting talent back and forth from the set." I drop my head. "But," he continues, "I overheard a lot of the feedback from the casting directors and producers." I hold my breath, waiting for the rest of his sentence. "They loved you." I exhale. "They'll be in touch very soon," he says, smiling as we arrive back at the waiting room where I left my jacket.

"You're free to go. You're all done for the day. Take your time. Leave when you're ready. I'm headed back to set."

"Okay. Thanks for today."

"You're welcome," he says, walking out of the room.

A slow smile spreads across my face. "I did it," I say to myself, laughing.

I can't wait to tell Brice. I didn't want to mention it to him or anyone until I knew for sure it was real and that I had a shot. After all these months, things are finally looking up for me.

"Hey."

My body stills. Slowly, afraid of what I'll see when I do, I turn around and face the voice. I gape at him, mouth open, unable to comprehend what I'm seeing. Trent's leaning against the doorframe, stalking me with his eyes like a bird of prey.

"Wh–What are you doing here?" I stammer.

A flip switches inside me. Before he can answer that question, I'm barreling toward him, ready to attack. I knock away his open arms and get in his face. Does he really think I'd hug him after everything he's done? All possibility of us ever meeting as friendly acquaintances went the same way as my job at Jolie. I ignore the familiarity of his scent and the part of my heart that breaks every time I see him and jab my finger into his chest.

"Are you listening?" I ask, fingernail digging into his chest. "Leave me alone. Don't call me, text me, messenger me letters, or show up anywhere you know I'll be. Stop it. Stop all of this," I yell.

With hands upraised in surrender, Trent takes a weary step around me and walks farther into the green room. He stands off to the side, a safe distance away.

"L—"

"*Shhh.* I don't want..."

My thought trails as it's replaced by another. This doesn't make sense. How did he know?

"Wait a minute," I say, eyes narrowing, "How'd you know where I was? And don't say coincidence because it's clearly not."

He stares at me with his magic eyes, their power being the ability to mesmerize the looker into forgetfulness, but they don't work on me anymore. I want answers.

"Are you having me followed?"

Trent says something I don't hear. The wheels of my mind are turning again. "T...TS Productions."

My mind spins with returned bits of forgotten conversations. Before we broke up, Trent was getting his production company off the ground, securing distribution deals. I don't recall the name, although I have a good guess.

"Trenton Shaw Productions?" I ask, already knowing the truth. "Answer me," I shout.

Trent didn't follow me; he didn't need to. He already knew where I would be because he arranged for me to be here.

I back away from Trent, feeling light-headed. I collapse onto the couch and close my eyes. When I open them again, I'll have woken up from this nightmare.

"Is everything okay here?" I take a peek at the owner of the voice, a man not too much older than myself and obviously an employee. He looks between Trent and me, assessing the situation.

Trent steps in front of him, blocking his view to me.

"Everything's fine," he says.

"The lady doesn't look fine," he counters. "Ma'am, are you okay?" He cranes his head around Trent to look at me.

I shrug because I don't know.

"You don't talk to her. You talk to me. Got it?" Trent's hands are balled fists at his sides.

The other guy hesitates a bit, then says, "I need to hear it from her that she's okay."

"What you need to do is know that this right here," Trent says, motioning to the office, "is mine. I run this. Next time you want to act like a hero, don't."

"Leave him alone." My voice is feeble, but they hear me. "You're acting like a predator. What's he supposed to think?" I turn my eyes on the employee. "Thank you for coming to my aid." He nods and leaves.

Trent stares after him, looking murderous. I'm not sure that man will have a job tomorrow. "He's lucky you were here."

"Luck had nothing to do with this. You arranged it, remember?"

Slowly, the way you'd approach a wild animal with an unpredictable nature, Trent walks my way. I watch him like a hawk, unsure if I'm going to attack him or not. He doesn't get as close as I'm sure he would like to. He satisfies himself by sitting in front of me on the edge of the table that held snacks two hours ago. I thought something was different about his appearance earlier. I was too upset to realize it's his beard. It's gone.

"Did you give Brian the direct order to get me onboard? How did this whole thing go down?" I ask, tears building behind my eyes.

I stare at the beautiful face that at one time captivated me, waiting for an explanation. I'd forgotten the fleck of lighter brown in his dark eyes and the curl of his lashes. My hands itch to explore the things about his face previously hidden now revealed by his clean-shaven face. Brice said what I had with Trent was lust. What if he's wrong? What if it's love?

"Yes, I did tell Brian to cast you," he says, "but not for the reasons you think."

Our eyes lock, and time moves in weird ways—backward instead of forward. Our first dance, first kiss all replay in my mind's eye, and I feel my resolve weaken. I know there are reasons I should stay away from him, but they don't seem to matter at the moment.

"I did have Brian reach out to you not because I want you back— obviously I do, but that's not why. I told you I'd make you famous. I still want to do that."

His mouth moves even after I've stopped listening. It's always the same thing with him: He targets my most carnal part. Trent's Pavlov holding a juicy steak in front of me to get me to obey him. And like a fool, I was close to letting him do it again.

"My mom," I say, recollecting her voice months ago, cautioning me, "she warned me about you. She said, 'beware of wolves in sheep's clothing.' Without ever laying eyes on you, she knew. And she was right, of course. You are..." I look for words big enough to completely convey my sentiments, "the biggest regret of my life," I finish.

Trent flinches away from me as if I'd hit him. "Don't," he pleads, "don't say that."

"Why shouldn't I? It's true. From the moment I got involved with you, my life has been a hot mess."

Trent's eyes, leeched of all traces of light brown, widen. "You weren't saying that when I put that diamond on your finger," he says, "or when you were spending my money. Or when..." He lets his gaze explore.

"Watch your mouth," I spit. "After all you've done, you would take it one step further and disrespect me?"

Trent gets up savagely from the table. I follow right behind him, hot on his heels. He wanted a confrontation, a confrontation he'll get.

"What do you want from me?" I yell when I've got him backed into a corner of the room.

"For you to let me make things better," he yells back, "and to stop making me the villain of your story.

Is that what I'm doing, absolving myself scapegoating Trent? He's no angel, and getting involved with him was, without doubt, a mistake, but the mistake I made. No one forced me. I was a willing victim.

"I want you to stop hating me," he whispers with a vulnerability I haven't seen from him ever. It's hard to ignore.

"I don't. I don't hate you," I say. I wish I did hate him. "I'm sorry if I've made you feel like the villain of my story, but you do know you're not the hero either, right?"

"Yeah, because that's Brice."

I bite back the scathing retort on the tip of my tongue. "No," I reply. "Brice isn't the hero either. Jesus is."

That wasn't the answer he was expecting. Still, it's true. I couldn't see how far away I had gotten from the Lord and the damage my relationship with Trent was doing to my soul. God showed me my destruction if I stayed with Trent and called me to walk in the good way until I eventually listened. That's the reason we broke up, not Brice.

I step aside, letting Trent out of the corner I backed him into; whatever anger previously fueled me is gone. He walks to the bank of windows lining the west wall of the room. With his back to me, he says, "I–I went to church recently."

"What were you doing there?"

He chuckles. "I imagine I was doing the same thing you do when you go," he replies.

From where I stand, I see him only in profile, the personification of every bad boy heartthrob I've ever crushed on. This isn't a movie though. Trent doesn't have a heart of gold, and the good guy should get the girl. I've already given him way too much of my time and energy. I need to walk away now before I'm too weak to. I turn my back on him and return to the seating area to collect my things.

"I might have arranged for you to be here, but they loved you," he says. "You did that all on your own. The spot is yours if you want it."

"Where have I heard that before?"

"It was true then." He shrugs. "It's true now."

"Nah. I'm going to pass."

"Don't be stupid, L. An opportunity like this may never come knocking at your door again."

Laughing, I say, "I've learned to look out the door before answering opportunity because it might just be the devil looking to see who's home."

I readjust the strap of my purse on my shoulder, ready to go. Try as I do to leave, I can't. Seconds tick away. I stand rigidly in the same exact spot, not moving a muscle. Trent doesn't budge either, nor does he ask me to stay, but I can't leave him like this. Every interaction we've had since we broke up, he's been obnoxious, never heartbroken, not until now, and I'm not unmoved.

I cup his smooth cheek. His eyes close against my touch. Maybe if his mom hadn't died when he was a child, maybe if she'd passed her faith on to him, Trent would be different, less broken. Possibly other things would be different too. But she did die, he is broken, and I can't fix him.

My hand moves to where I feel his heart beating rapidly in his chest. His eyes fly open and hold mine. I shake my head, answering the hope in his eyes. I don't want to reconcile. The hand on his cheek is for me, to quiet my longing. My hand on his heart is for him, to repair some of the damage loss has done to it.

"When I go to church," I say, holding his gaze, "I'm looking for Christ."

I didn't know what I would say to him until I said it, yet I know I said the right thing. Trent needs saving as much I do. There's only one person who can do that.

"You're not my villain, Trent, but you're not good for me either. I'm happy you went to church. I pray you encounter Christ and find peace."

"That was so amazing. I hope the producers pick m— Oh."

Startled, I quickly snatch my hands away from Trent.

I recognize Alexis's voice before I turn around. I forgot there was still a group on set. You'd think their jackets and purses would've reminded me, but that's the way it always is when I'm with Trent. I'm entirely consumed by him.

"Sorry. We didn't realize this room was busy," Cali says.

She's obviously curious about the handsome man I've been caught with when there's another handsome man I'm supposed to be dating.

"It's fine," I say. "I'm leaving anyway." I don't offer an explanation. I don't owe them one.

He grabs my hand as I turn to go.

I look down at our connected hands then up at him. "Goodbye, Trenton," I say, feeling the finality of us. I pull away. He lets me, which hurts.

Chapter 14

Helping Hand

I feel the way I do when I have a cold. My chest feels heavy-laden, except instead of phlegm, I'm weighed down by sadness. The instant I walked away from Trent this afternoon, it has hurt to breathe. I did the right thing; I'm absolutely sure I did. Still, it's painful. The ache in my heart makes a strong argument that my feelings for Trent were as strong as I one time professed them to be. I can't escape the look on Trent's face when I told him he was my greatest regret any more than I can forget the pressure of his hand begging me not to leave him.

Hidden in the warmth of my down comforter and flannel pajamas, I try to fall asleep and put this whole day behind me, but rest doesn't come. My mind refuses to quiet. It stirs up my heart leading to the unrest of my body. I kick the blanket off and stare up at the dark ceiling. I guess sleep is out of the question tonight. I sit up and turn on my bedside lamp. Retrieving my Bible from the nightstand, I open it to the bookmarked section and read.

Jesus answered, everyone who drinks this water will be thirsty again, but whoever drinks the water I give them will never thirst. Indeed, the water I give them will become in them a spring of water welling up to eternal life.

My yellow highlighter carefully glides over the verse. I've read it over three times already, each time more potent than the last. I'm not a carbon copy of the woman at the well, yet I see myself in her actions. The woman had many past relationships. Even then, as Jesus spoke to her, she was in an ungodly relationship. It had been her way to unwittingly search for in men, something only Jesus can give. Neither the water from the well or the men she sought solace in could quench her thirst.

What she truly sought was the love that satisfies, makes whole, heals, and alters not. The love found in Christ alone. Part of my sadness is fear I was turning my back on a genuine love, but what I had with Trent falls amazingly short of what love should be. A loud, satisfying yawn escapes my mouth, my eyes are heavy, and suddenly I'm unable to keep them open. Sleep doesn't seem so far-fetched anymore.

I put away my Bible, turn out the lights, and slide down into my bed. Slipping rapidly to sleep, I pray for the spring of water welling up to eternal life. I yawn again. I'm tired of looking for sustenance in things that take too much energy to obtain and never fulfill.

"Stacey, Skylar, Tiffany, Lacy, Clarissa, Ashley, Denise, Jade, Lisa, and—" My gaze meets Brice's briefly before saying, "Ella."

He hides a smile while she ambles over to the rest of our group, looking as thrilled as I am to have her as part of my team. Neither of us particularly fancies the other—at least we share that. I read online, finding common ground is necessary for a successful mentor-mentee relationship. I'm still not sure this will work; however, I promised Brice I'd try. Therefore, I smile at Ella and pretend to be happy about spending the next three hours with her.

"Okay, the rest of you with me," Brice says, leading his team into the galley, leaving my group and me to organize the makeshift shopping area for the food pantry.

"Gather around, ladies." I motion with my hands for the girls to huddle close. "As you know, today is our first community service project. We've partnered with Neighborhood Works and the local supermarkets to distribute food to those in need."

Each girl's eyes are turned to me with rapt attention except Ella. She's studying her cuticles. I fight the urge to call her out, remembering what Brice said about meeting her where she is to take her higher. He owes me big time.

"Before we can distribute the food, we have to first transform the community center gym. There are ten collapsible tables stacked against the wall right outside of this room. They need to be carried in and set up horizontally before we can start unpacking the groceries Brice and his team are carrying. Separate into pairs, then get to work."

The girls team up quickly and scurry off, except for Skylar and Ella. I'm not surprised about Skylar. She's shy and unpopular. Ella, on the other hand, could have had her pick.

Not wanting to embarrass either of them, I say, "I don't want to see anyone carrying a table alone" to the entire group.

"Are you without a partner?" I ask Skylar, noticing she's still standing around. She nods.

"I asked Ella. Normally I wouldn't have, but since neither of us has partners." She shrugs. "Ella said she'd carry all the tables in herself before she works with me."

Skylar tries to pretends it's no big deal. The quiver in her voice gives her away.

"I don't mind working alone," she says. "I'm used to it."

My heart breaks at her downcast eyes. I hate that she's ostracized. I make a mental note to bring it to Brice's attention later. No way he'd let this kind of bullying go in if he knew it was happening. For now, I zero in on Ella.

She's standing a few feet away texting. She looks older with straightened hair and cherry-painted lips. I don't doubt for a second that her makeover is an attempt at getting Brice's notice. I decide now is the perfect time for her first lesson.

"Stay here," I say to Skylar. "I'll be right back."

"Hey," I call when I'm almost upon Ella.

She looks up from her phone. Seeing it's me, she rolls her eyes. I don't care that she doesn't want me speaking to her.

"Where's your partner?" I ask.

She looks exaggeratedly to her left and right. "I obviously don't have one."

Ignoring how blatantly rude she is, I press forward. "Yeah, you do. She's standing right over there," I say, nodding in Skylar's direction, "waiting for you."

"I'm not working with her."

"Yeah, you are," I snap, "and you're going to be nice to her too."

She looks at me defiantly. "Or what?" she questions.

"Nothing," I reply. "You know... Brice believes in you. He thinks you have a lot of potential for goodness. I think he's wrong."

"I don't care what you think." She bristles. "The mystery is what he sees in you."

"For starters, I'm not jailbait." That quiets her. "Brice is a good judge of character—most of the time. He can see through to the reality of a person when others cannot. He hasn't been wrong yet, but there's a first time for everything. I question whether he's right about you."

"Yeah, he is," Ella replies.

"We'll see," I reply, casually walking away.

Ella quickly catches up to me. "Yeah, we will."

I watch with a pleased smile as she approaches Skylar. They exchange a few words then head outside to collect their table. I knew she'd come around. The only person Ella dislikes more than Skylar is me. The only person she respects enough to value their opinion is Brice. Annoying me is a great incentive for getting into Brice's good graces—inspiration. Perhaps I'll be a better mentor than I thought.

"I'm proud of you girls. You've done a wonderful job today."

I smile at Lacey and Tiffany, two of the hardest-working volunteers. They've unloaded box after box of cereal and oats without a single complaint crossing their lips.

"I want to thank you and Brice for making me do this," Lacey says. "Knowing there'll be a few less hungry people tonight feels good. I wish I would have been part of something like this before now."

I don't deserve Lacey's thanks. I wasn't exactly a willing participant—not at first. I'm happy I'm here, though. I'm on the verge of saying as much when I notice Tiffany straighten up all five feet four inches of herself. She nudges Lacey, who looking at me, doesn't see whatever it is Tiffany does. Annoyed, Lacey nudges her back then Tiffany points at something behind me. Lacey smiles and smoothes down her pulled-back hair. The abrupt change in their demeanor can only be caused by one thing: boys. I'm reasonably sure I know which boy specifically.

I turn around, doing my best to keep my face blank. It's hard not to smile at Brice or the effect he has on people.

"Do you need any help?" he asks.

Done carrying in the boxes, he and his team have been helping with setup wherever needed.

"No, we're almost done," Tiffany responds for us all, though I wish she hadn't.

I wouldn't mind a moment with Brice.

"Great," he says, "then I'm going to borrow Leah for a minute, if that's okay."

Tiffany and Lacey snicker and whisper to one another like the sixteen-year-olds they are as Brice leads me away from the table. We end up in a far corner of the gym, not exactly private, although as close to it as we're going to get. Up close, I notice a light layer of sweat covering his forehead.

"Supervising must be hard work," I joke. I dab his forehead with a paper towel from my pocket.

It happens again, whatever's been happening between us every time our eyes meet. We're not in the community center gymnasium surrounded by teens. We're only us. The moment ends too soon with Brice pulling away like he's done every time before.

"I can do that," Brice says, leaning away from my hand while reaching for the napkin. Our hands brush when the paper towel passes from mine to his. In that touch, I return to the cast house, to the night Brice took care of me.

"Do you remember the time I fell and hurt myself? I was a panicked mess, but you talked me down and iced my knee." He nods. "So this is nothing. I owe you one."

"Small gestures make the greatest impacts," he says with a smile.

I return his smile, wondering exactly which gesture is supposed to have impacted whom.

"Thank you," he says. "It's been a long time since someone's taken care of me in this way...feels nice."

I hook my fingers through my belt loops and look down at my sneakers. I can barely meet Brice's eyes. He's been alone for years while he grieved his fiancé. He's finally ready to open up again. I don't want him to get hurt. I don't want to be the one who hurts him.

"So, how are things going with your protégé?" Brice asks, rubbing the back of his neck.

With a subtle nod, I point to Ella's scowling face. "That's how it's going."

"Nothing you can't handle," he says, laughing, seeming less tense than a moment ago.

"I haven't killed her yet, so I guess I can." Brice watches me with such attentiveness and soft expression, my stomach flutters, and my heart races. "I should, *ummm*, get back."

"Alright," he says, feet shuffling. "I'll see you later?"

"*Duh.* We have two hours left unless you're asking something else." Brice shoves his hands into his pockets and fixes his face into a clueless expression. It's just a figure of speech, LA."

"*Ummm-hmmm.* Okay. I'll see you around then," I say, walking away. "By the way," I say, looking back at him, "your poker face is terrible."

His rich laugh follows me to the fresh-fruit table.

"Today, I saw powerful young soldiers in the army of the Lord taking to heart His words. Your presence may have been mandatory, but I thank you for showing up ready to be of service."

Brice is the picture of a proud dad. He beams with pride, taking in the faces of each youth member that made this day a success.

"Skylar," he says, "please lead us in prayer."

Brice closes his eyes and bows his head. Everyone else does the same. I'm not sure that soft-spoken, timid Skylar can do this.

"Father God in heaven," she begins, voice loud and clear, "humbly, we approach before Your throne, overwhelmed by Your grace and mercy. Thank You for today, putting it in Brother Young's spirit to show us the gospel, as You would have us preach it."

"Yes, Lord, teach us the gospel as You would have us practice it," Brice answers in prayer.

"James says, 'Religion that God our Father accepts as pure and faultless is this, to look after orphans and widows in their distress and to keep oneself from being polluted by the world.' Oh Lord, how can a young person keep their ways blameless before you?"

"How indeed, Lord? How indeed?" Jade answers.

"Teach us, Lord, how to keep ourselves from being corrupted by the world. Help us to delight in a spirit of charity and of servitude, being unafraid to take the low seat, always acting in love." Skylar's voice cracks, revealing how heartfelt her prayer is.

"As we ready to leave each other, please let us stay together in spirit, connected by You. Please bless all those who were fed today and those who are hungry. Please bless those who participated and fill us with your presence. We thank You, Lord. We pray to You humbly in the name of Jesus Christ, our Savior. Amen."

Brice is beaming again. So am I. Who would have thought all that eloquence existed in such a shy package? It doesn't last long, though. Skylar's already receding into herself—her head's bowed and shoulders hunched—but I now know she's a force. I'm going to make it my duty not to let her fade again.

"Remind me to call you next time I need prayer," I say to Skylar, saddling up to her on our way out of the community center to the borrowed church van. She ducks her head, hiding the blush on her cheeks.

"Seriously, Brice is going to have to promote you from soldier to warrior."

She ducks her head again, uncomfortable with being noticed. I'd love to give Ella some of her humility and Skylar some of Ella's confidence. I put a sisterly arm around her shoulders, the way my older sister, Antonia, sometimes does to me even now as adults.

"That you're unaware of how awesome you are makes you that much more awesome." She allows herself a small smile. "Come on," I say. "Let's get on the van."

"Thanks, Brother Young. Bye, Leah," Clarissa and Ashley shout in unison as they close the car door. We drop them off at the nursing home where their mother works. They have a standing dinner date with her every Sunday afternoon. They pretend to be annoyed about it because they're sixteen and seventeen, way too cool to hang out with their mom, but I can see how much they secretly enjoy it. They're good girls, still innocent in a lot of ways. I pray the world doesn't change that. We wait for them to get in their mom's car then pull out of the lot.

"Where to next?"

"You tell me," Brice says, quickly glancing my way. "You're my navigator."

I look at the addresses on the sheet in front of me then at the group behind me. Stacey, Joshua, and Jade sit together, chatting in the second row; Skylar and Ella sit in the first row talking to Brice and me. Ella and Brice do most of the talking, actually. Skylar and I hang back but not for want of trying, at least on my behalf. Ella refuses to let Brice and I converse without her.

"LA," Brice says, getting my attention.

"What do you think? What would be easier for you?" I ask Brice.

"Maybe—"

"I think you should drop off Stacey. She lives closest," Ella says.

I'm happy overall with what I saw from her today. I watched Ella closely during the distribution. She was kind to all and downright helpful to most. She lifted heavy bags, rearranged grocery carts to accommodate more goods, made small talk, and smiled. She's making progress, just not with me.

"What's it gonna be, LA?"

As much as I hate to admit it, I think I need more time to work on Ella. "Joshua," I say. "He's next."

"Bye, Sky. See you Wednesday."

Skylar and I share a baffled look. Either Ella's been replaced by a kind robot version of herself, or she's trying to impress Brice by playing nice. She's tenacious, I'll give her that. She keeps up her good-girl routine, waving bye until Skylar's hidden from view behind her front door, leaving the three of us together.

"So," I say, looking at Brice, "how did you enjoy today?"

"It was a great experience," he responds. "I pray it wasn't a one-off for any of us and that even after we've completed our required hours, we continue volunteering."

"Wait. Was this your first time doing charity too?" I ask.

He grins. "Does that surprise you?"

"Yeah, it does, actually."

"Everyone has to start somewhere."

"What about you?" Brice says, looking at Ella through the rearview mirror. "Did you enjoy today?"

"I didn't like the setting up part," she says, looking pointedly at me as if it were a punishment I designed specifically to inflict upon her. "But," she continues, "we did a good thing. I'm looking forward to doing it again."

I focus my gaze outside the window. If Ella sees me smiling, she'll know I approve of something she said and take it back. Today was a success. It impacted even the most self-absorbed of us. Nothing rocks our existence to the core like witnessing people in need.

In no time, we arrive at the attached two-family in East Flatbush Ella calls home.

"Bye, Brice. Thanks for the ride," she says, shutting the car door.

I might as well be invisible for as little as she notices me.

"If this is going to work, one of you is going to have to extend an olive branch to the other."

"Yeah, I was just thinking the same thing." I roll down my window and call out to her. I wait for Ella to turn around. "You did good today," I say. "Our friend might be right about you after all."

Her satisfied grin is just visible in the waning afternoon light. "Was there ever any doubt?" Ella continues to her front door but doesn't go in. Despite the distance and the dying light, I know it's me she looks at. "Bye," she says, "Leah." I smile quietly to myself at progress.

"What gives?" I've been anticipating this portion of the car ride—being alone with Brice—since our talk earlier. I hoped maybe we could talk, but he's quiet. His thoughts are clearly elsewhere.

"Huh?"

"You've been super weird all day. Something's on your mind. What is it?"

Slowly, he lets out a puff of air. "I talked to Jael a few nights ago."

"And?" I cross my arms over my chest. Every mention of Jael drives me crazy. It's ridiculous because she's Brice's literary agent, that's all. There's no need to worry about her.

"I'm in awe of God."

"I don't follow."

"A three-book deal, LA. I have a three-book deal with a major publishing house."

I shriek. "That is fantastic news. It couldn't have happened to a more deserving person."

"Of course it could have," he says. "Nevertheless, by His grace, He designed it for me."

"I guess I can't argue with that."

"There's more." I can't imagine anything being able to top a three-book deal, but I listen. "Jael got me on the guest list of the book release party for a bestselling author on the publisher's roster."

"Check you out, getting invited to exclusive parties," I joke.

"Something like that," he says. "Jael wants me there meeting people and press, something about it being good PR. Anyway, I have a plus one, and I was hoping you'd go...with me...as my *ummm*...date...please."

That's why he's been weird. Brice's been working up the nerve to ask me on a date. The whole thing is so sweet that I'm choking back tears. I lace my fingers through Brice's non-steering hand, the one drumming on his knee. He glances at me, then back to the road. "What's wrong?"

"Nothing," I reply. "Absolutely nothing."

He gives a smile I can only half see and grips my hand a little tighter. "I miss you, LA. Feels like we haven't spoken in days."

"We haven't, thanks to you and your bright ideas about giving me space and time."

"It is a bright idea, also incredibly inconvenient."

"Emphasis on inconvenient."

"Tell me about it," Brice says. "I'm looking forward to spending more time with you, though."

"Yeah?"

"Yeah."

"So, what's new with you?" I ask, disrupting our comfortable silence.

"I told you what's happening with me, remember?" Brice takes his eyes off the road to look at me. "The book deal?"

"Of course I do," I quickly reply. "I meant did anything else wonderful and exciting happen to you?"

"I scored a date with the prettiest girl I know. I'd call that wonderful and exciting." His lips curl up at the corner into a smile. "Aside from that, you're all caught up on my past week. What about you, LA? What's going on with you?"

I should've thought about it before I asked him that question. Now, he wants to know what's new with me. Since we last spoke, I got hoodwinked into testing for a talk show produced by Trent's production company, followed by an explosive run-in with the man himself. I'm not sure how much I should tell him—if I should share anything at all. I'm under no obligation to tell him all that's happened. Not telling him, though, feels like a lie.

"I, *ummm,* went to a casting."

"That's great, LA. How was it?"

This is it. This is the in I hoped for. "It...*ummm...*" I falter. I look down at our interlocked fingers and lose my nerve. I can't do it. I can't tell him. "It didn't go well. I wasn't cast in the project."

From the corner of my eye, I catch Brice sneaking peeks at me every few seconds though he should be watching the road and the crazy New York City drivers.

"LA, you shine brighter than the brightest Hollywood lights. You're ridiculously talented. Someone else noticing or not doesn't change that. Be patient. God has a day for you too."

I wish I hadn't lied to Brice. He's so concerned about me, but if I backtrack now, he'll never trust me again. "You really think there's a special day where God will make all my dreams come true?"

"Yeah, I do," he says, "As long as those dreams are in alignment with His will for your life."

"Well then, I pray it comes soon because I don't know how much more of always being in this same position I can take."

"What position is that?" he asks softly.

Struggling to hang on. I'm always struggling to hang on. To Brice, I say, "I've been reading John."

Silence. Brice, who loves discussing the Bible, doesn't say a word. "Did you hear me?" I ask. "I said, I started reading John."

"I heard you, LA."

"So why didn't you respond?"

"Because," he says, taking his eyes off the road for a second, "I'm not finished with our last topic."

"It's nothing, okay?" My words come out sharper than I intend. "I don't want to talk about it," I say, watching my tone.

"That's fair," Brice replies, not answering my aggression with any of his own. "I won't force you to talk about what you're not ready to, but whenever you do want to talk, I'm here."

"Thank you," My voice is barely above a whisper. *Why did I catch an attitude with Brice? He didn't deserve that. He deserves much better than me.*

"So. You read John," Brice asks, sounding falsely chipper.

"Yeah," I say, happy for the change in subject.

"What are your thoughts? What do you think about all the pictures of grace?"

Chapter 15

Hot and Cold

"Apostle John chose the miracles and encounters he recorded very carefully," Brice says. "His intention wasn't to document every miracle Jesus did."

"I think I read that in the last chapter of John. It said something like, if everything Jesus did was written down, the whole world wouldn't be able to store all the books that would be written."

"Yup. That's John chapter twenty-one, verse twenty-five," he says, looking at me with bright, alert eyes. Brice is never as passionate as he is when he's talking about Jesus. "John meant to witness that Jesus Christ is indeed the Son of God, the Father and the Son are one and that Jesus, as the Son of Man was crucified and resurrected on the third day."

He pauses, momentarily lending all his attention to making the tricky left turn off the traffic-heavy boulevard onto a small residential side street a few blocks away from my street.

When he's made the turn, he continues. "Jesus was miraculous in the signs He chose to do, including healing. He gave sight to the blind and healed lepers."

He pulls up smoothly in front of my house and puts the church van in park. I make no move to exit. Brice doesn't suggest I do either. He's waiting for me to decide whether I stay or go. "Don't stop. Continue with what you were saying."

Brice unbuckles his seatbelt then faces me. Having his full attention makes my stomach flutter. He's so perfect, and I'm so flawed. Sometimes I think he can see through to my every mistake. If he can, he doesn't say anything. He just smiles at me like I'm the best thing in the world.

"First," Brice says, sounding very serious, "let me apologize to you in advance because it's highly probable that I'll geek out and turn into that one professor who goes on and on without stopping. I'm going to try to be as succinct as possible, but I make no promises. When I start talking about Jesus," he says, shaking his head, "I can get carried away."

"Brice, it's okay. I asked you your thoughts on John, and I'd really like to hear them, long-winded and all."

"Okay. Just don't complain when ten minutes from now I'm giving you a geography lesson."

"I won't." I laugh. "Promise."

"So, I've always felt some of the greatest miracles and demonstrations of the nature of Jesus is in who He chose to publicly forgive and those He called to follow Him. Did you get to chapter four yet, the Samaritan Woman?"

"Yeah, I did," I answer, remembering how much of a comfort it was to me a few nights ago.

"Did you find it odd that the disciples were concerned Jesus was talking to a Samaritan woman?"

"I did," I say, thinking back to the passage.

"The story behind that is the Jewish and Samaritan people did not get along. They reviled each other to the point of complete avoidance. Journeying Jewish men and women often took a longer route than necessary to Jerusalem simply to avoid Samaria. There's a long history of why, but I won't get into that right now."

"Promise you will at some point, though."

Brice beams at me. "Girl, you'd better stop before you mess around and become my Bible study partner."

I shake my head. "We'll see about that. Continue. I'm listening."

"So, the reason I brought that up is that Jesus simply traveling through Samaria was radical. Neither coincidence nor fatigue brought Jesus to that well; God had a plan. Jesus could've revealed Himself as the Messiah to a man. One with a better reputation than this woman. Instead Jesus chose her. That to me is a testament of His grace." I hadn't thought about it that way, but it really is remarkable.

"What about the woman caught in adultery?" Brice questions in a loud voice. "Everyone—believers and non-believers alike—correctly quote Jesus as saying, 'Let he who is without sin cast the first stone.' What amazes me is Jesus would have been well within His right to stone her. Instead, He completed the law while giving grace."

"What does that mean?"

"Under the law, the punishment for adultery was death by stoning. When Jesus said, let he who is without sin cast the first stone, He's upholding the law. Here comes grace, though. Jesus said, just let the person who is perfect be the first one to throw a stone."

"That's deep."

Brice nods. "Jesus forced her opponents to face their own unrighteousness. When everyone had turned away feeling their own guilt, Jesus asked the woman where her accusers were. She replied that they left. Jesus then said, neither does He condemn her. Do you get how huge that is?" he exclaims. He doesn't wait for my reply to tell me.

"Jesus didn't condemn her. He said, 'go and sin no more.' I don't know about you, but that blows my mind. Jesus forgives sin, including the most shameful. He sets us free from our old selves. Mary Magdalene, Peter, Paul are all further examples of that though not a complete list, not by a long shot. There are more people than can be named transformed by Christ, myself included." He smiles. "I'm continually awed by who God chooses—sinners in need of His grace. That is our Savior, Jesus Christ, Redeemer of man, who stepped into eternity on your behalf."

My head jerks back, caught off guard by Brice's use of the word *your*. "I thought we were speaking in generalities," I say. "How'd I get dragged into this?"

He raises an eyebrow. "I was still speaking in generalities, LA, but what Jesus did is specific to us all. Christ was crucified for everyone—past and present—without exception, once and for all. Mankind needed the Savior, and He came and did just that. Jesus saved all humanity. He paid the price for our sins that we couldn't. His blood fulfilled the debt. That's very personal. The question is, why does that make you uncomfortable?"

"It doesn't," I say, looking away.

"I'm not sure I believe that, LA," Brice says gently.

Intellectually, I understand Christ was crucified so that I can have forgiveness for my sins. Emotionally, I'm stuck on how guilty I feel.

"Nothing is holding you back from fully enjoying the redemptive freedoms found in Christ alone, LA. Jesus did the hard part. What's left for us to do is receive it."

"What do you mean, receive it?"

"I mean, we have free will. God won't force you to do anything. The door is open. You decide if you walk through it or not, but you can't toe the line. At some point, everyone decides to either surrender their lives to Christ, receiving eternal life, new life, and freedom in exchange or not. And not deciding is the same as deciding."

There has never been a point in my life when I didn't know the name of Jesus or His work on the cross and in the resurrection, but I don't know that I have ever made any decisions about that outside accepting it as truth.

"Is it enough to believe?"

"In Romans chapter ten, verses nine and ten, it says you must confess with your mouth that Jesus is Lord and believe in your heart God raised Him from the dead. 'For it is by believing in your heart that you are made right with

God, and it is by openly declaring your faith that you are saved.' Don't get me wrong," he quickly interjects. "Doing those things doesn't give you carte blanche to continue walking in sin. The man or woman who has sincerely accepted Christ into his or her life is transformed and made anew; they can't go on doing the same things they used to. That person's life will reflect their commitment to a Christ-filled life."

"What's it like?" I ask. "Choosing either way?"

"Liberating and reviving if you chose Christ; fun then hollow, inevitably damning if you don't."

"Do you remember the nightmares I used to have?" I ask Brice, thinking about the house of horrors that plagued my dreams for months. He nods. "I never told you what I dreamt of, did I?"

"No. You didn't."

"Every night, I would come to a fork in the road. To my right was an old house in desperate need of repairs but with good bones. To my left was a gorgeous colonial. I always went left. And every night, that beautiful house would come alive with terrors." I shudder even now thinking about the black hole that tried to swallow me up.

"Are you okay?" Brice asks, eyebrows drawing together.

"Fine," I say, waving off his concern. "Knowing the beautiful house would turn into an ominous wreck where dead hands and frightening agents of torture reached out to drag me in, I still chose that road, every time. I had a choice in my dreams. I could have gone to the other house, the one on the right, for refuge. I chose not to because it wasn't as appealing as the other initially was. So, I understand perfectly what you mean when you say we have a choice."

Neither of us speaks for a while, then Brice says, "Many people think Christianity is confining. They think it's about rules and living rigidly when all they want is to be free."

"That's true." I nod.

"People don't understand they're enslaved to fleeting emotions and sinful living, which by the way, is the will of the devil. They tacitly reject God in favor of doing whatever they want, no matter how morally wrong, but to what end?" His voice breaks.

"We party hard and indulge ourselves with food, clothes, gadgets, and relationships. Ultimately, we wind up feeling empty and hollow, looking for the very thing we've spurned, in all the wrong places. True freedom is found in Christ alone. Jesus gives peace to the spirit and rests for souls."

"Do you really think the only options are those two extremes, Christ-loving or vain narcissist?"

A wry smile forms on his lips. "No. Most people fall somewhere in between. However, just so you know, all those in-between spaces are outside of communion with God too."

I want to argue, tell him he's wrong. I may not be as gung ho as he is, but I'm not lost either. I want to say those things, yet I can't. Even as I think it, I know, I'm adrift in between.

"I talk to the kids about this all the time. It's confusing for them—for most people, really. With all, we're being fed in the media. That's partly why I started writing." If Brice knows the war raging in my mind, he doesn't mention it; he talks to me like we're on equal footing.

"They tell their lies and misdirect. As God's people, we have the same right, more so, to proclaim the truth. There is only one way, not multiple, and you can't abstain from choosing. If you aren't on that one way, you've, in fact, chosen already. *Broad is the road that leads to destruction, and many enter through it.*

Maybe if I hadn't had months of nightmares featuring two paths and divine voices instructing me to choose the right way, I'd be confused. As it happens, I understand Brice perfectly. I lean my head back against the seat, eyes closed, digesting, marinating on the part about confessing with my mouth. The disquiet in my mind makes me jittery. I fidget and turn in my seat until I'm seated on my side facing Brice. He faces me too. In this position, it almost feels like we're back in the cast house sharing our secrets while everyone else sleeps.

"What if a person hasn't made some grand proclamation about their faith, but they're trying their best to live the right way?" I whisper, not wanting to risk disturbing the energy between us.

"Without Jesus, whatever your effort, it's futile. We can never be justified through our own works. The work of Christ on the cross is perfect and complete. Accept it, LA."

"Hey, I never said me. I said someone."

He chuckles lightly. "Okay. Someone. Do you talk to your mom about this stuff?"

My mom's insightful, but I have trouble talking to her about the real things. I'm afraid she'll see me and be disappointed. I didn't mean for Brice to see as much of me as he has; it happened accidentally, turned out alright, though. He's witnessed me at my worst, and he's still here. Remembering that puts a smile on my face.

"No, I mostly talk to you," I whisper. "Is there something wrong with that?"

"No. Not at all," he whispers back. "You should consider it, though, talking to your mom. I think it'll help."

"I'll think about it... Anyways," I say, wanting to switch the subject to lighter topics. "I meant to ask, what's your favorite color?"

"What's my favorite color?" Brice repeats with laughter, interspersing his words. "Are you seriously asking me what's my favorite color?"

"Yes, I am. A girl likes to know these things about the gentleman she's spending time with."

"Okay then," he laughingly says. "My favorite color's blue."

"Completely typical and boring," I tease. We're so close that his soft laughter moves the stray strands of my ponytail off my shoulder. Wordlessly we stare into each other's eyes, connected by emotions, mutual feelings, and contentedness. It's a rare perfect moment incapable of lasting past this very instant. The thought saddens me; therefore, I try to preserve it a little longer.

"Do you want to come in for a little while?"

"I can't. I have a ton of notes from my editor."

"Right. I didn't mean to keep you." I sit up and gather my things while doing my best to hide my frustration. "Thanks for the ride," I mutter.

I refuse to look at him, although I feel the intensity of his gaze on me. I'm out the door when I finally do. Boys who look like Brice don't pine after girls, but there's no other way to describe the way he's looking at me, which makes zero sense because he just turned me down again.

"I'm looking forward to dating you, you know?"

"Confident much?" I sneer. "What makes you so sure I want to date you?" As soon as the words are out of my mouth, I wish I could take them back. I don't even mean them.

"That's the question, isn't it?" he replies. "Do you want to date me?"

"What's that supposed to mean?"

"You tell me. I only repeated your words back to you."

"I know what I meant, and I don't mean what you mean."

"How do you know you don't when you don't know what I mean?"

Flustered and no longer willing to go back and forth, I shout, "I just know."

"No. I don't think you do," he says with sad eyes.

Completely unsure of what to do or say, I shut the door between us and numbly walk up the short pathway to my house. Because he's Brice, an all-around good guy, he waits until I'm inside to pull off. It's me. I'm the problem. I don't know why I acted the way I did. My feelings for him are undeniable, yet there may be truth to what he said. Maybe my outburst was a Freudian slip, and I don't want to date him. The question is, if I don't want to be with Brice, then who do I want to be with.

"Hey, honey."

"Hey, Mom," I answer, trying to keep the shock out of my voice and the anger off my face. I didn't think she'd be in the kitchen, I thought—hoped—she'd be in her room, and I could sneak past hers down to my mine. I don't want her knowing I had a blow-up with Brice. One good look at my face, and she'll know. She's skilled like that. Several probable excuses for hurrying off cross my mind, then I remember what Brice said about talking to her about some of the things I feel and questions I have. Maybe I could give it a try.

Asking my mother intimate questions, talking to her about extremely personal, not always pretty things about myself is not something I imagined I'd do, yet if it means we can have a relationship that even slightly resembles what Clarissa, Ashley, and their mom have, I'm willing to give it a try.

"Mom?"

She looks up from her plate at me. "Yes?"

My phone whistles three times in a row. Hoping it's Brice, I pull it out of my purse and check it. It's Trent. I have three new texts from him. I should ignore him, but I've been wondering how he's holding up since our last conversation. I saw a different side of him in that green room. Trent isn't as heartless as I thought. Maybe I'm not the only one who got hurt in our relationship. Maybe I hurt him too. I don't want him back or anything. I just want him to be okay.

"You know what, Mom. It was nothing. I was going to ask you something, but Antonia just got back to me with the answer. I'm going to go change my clothes. I'll be back up in a while." I rush past her skeptical face down to my room, where I can read my texts out of her view. I'd prefer not to go through a whole thing with her over a non-issue. We're both agreed. Trent's bad for me.

Trent: *Hey.*

Trent: *The producers loved you. We want you on the team. We're willing to compensate you. Handsomely. What do you say to that?*

Trent: *Hate me all you want, L, but don't pass this opportunity up.*

While I'm reading the last text, another comes through.

Trent: *Maybe you don't hate me @ all, and that's your hesitance.*

I'm barely through reading the text when I hear Pastor Charles's voice clear as day. "Still others, like seed sown among thorns, hear the Word; but the worries of this life, the desires of wealth, and the desires for other things come in and choke the word, making it unfruitful. Be a good ground."

I drop my phone like it's hot. Either I've gone crazy, and I'm hearing things, or I'm hearing God. It wouldn't be the first time the Lord has gone through extreme measures to get my attention. I'm not sure what that was. What I know is this time around, whatever Trent's offering, the answer is no.

Chapter 16

Tell Me Again About the Son Who Returns

"I love your apartment, super chic, super cute," I say, taking a seat in my indigo jeans on the red oak hardwood floor in Cashmere's living room instead of on the white couch or white fur rug.

"Do you really think so?"

"Yes. I love it." It's a beautifully renovated loft. What's there not to love? Actually, there is one thing. "I'm not too crazy about the neighborhood. You do know Trent's condo is only a few blocks away, right?"

"He's never gone out of his way to be near me, so that doesn't really pose a problem for me."

Cashmere stands in her kitchen, too far away for me to read her face, though her voice holds the residual hurt it sometimes does at the mention of Trent.

"Do you want some water?" Cashmere asks from the open refrigerator door, her back to me.

"Yes, please," I respond, hoping the weirdness will pass quickly.

She grabs two bottles out of the fridge and joins me on the floor in the living room. Cash hands me a bottle, then drains her pint before I've got mine open.

"Thirsty?" I joke.

Her smile is tight and un-Cashmere-like. Something's up. I put my unopened bottle down to look at her uncomfortable face.

"What's going on?" I ask.

Cashmere looks away, then back at me. "Don't be mad, okay?"

"Okay. I promise not to be mad at you," I say, keeping in mind that whenever someone starts a conversation with "don't be mad," they're going to say something to make you mad.

"I got a text two days ago...from Trent."

She pauses, waiting for me to react. I don't. I'm not sure I have anything to respond to.

Seeing I'm calm, she continues, "All it said was *Hi.* At first, I wasn't going to respond out of solidarity to you and myself. He didn't treat me right, and I didn't deserve that, but, after a few hours, my curiosity got the best of me, and I responded."

She pauses again, waiting for the reaction I don't give. I'm not thrilled Trent texted her. He knows Cashmere and I are tight, he literally watched us become friends, but I have nothing to be upset about—yet. I believe that may very well change in a matter of minutes.

"He texted back congratulating me on my beauty deal and some other stuff about always knowing I would make it. He isn't really the congratulatory type, so I knew he wanted something and that if I waited, he'd eventually get to it, which he did... You. You were the reason."

"Me?"

"Yes." She nods. "He wanted to know if you'd told me about *Clapback.* Obviously, you hadn't—not cool, by the way," she chides. "I didn't want him to know that, though. Plus, I was getting tired of his games, so I asked him straight out what he wanted."

"What did he say?"

"That he wants to make you happy."

"What did you say back?"

"I told him your happiness wasn't his problem anymore because you moved on to better... This is how he responded." Cashmere picks up her phone from the end table behind her, taps it a few times then thrusts it into my hand. The screen's pulled up to a text conversation, the one she's been describing to me. I scroll through quickly, confirming everything she's told me thus far. I stop on the last message. Trent's reply to her is. *LOL. Nah. She's just upset.*

I reread it, growing angrier by the second. *What does he mean by 'she's just upset?'* I hate that he thinks he knows anything about my situation with Brice. He doesn't. And what was the point of texting Cashmere? Did he really think he'd have an ally in her?

"I'm sorry Trent dragged you into this, Cash," I say, handing Cashmere back her phone. "I've been ignoring his texts. This was probably a ploy to get me angry enough to respond to him."

"What about Brice?" she asks.

"What about him?" I reply, sharper than I mean to.

"Brice is a good guy, and he cares a lot about you."

"Why are you telling me this?"

"Because you're probably my best friend, and I don't want to see you make a mistake."

"I'm—"

"Look, Leah, I get it. Trent's exciting. When you're with him, there's crazy chemistry. It's exhilarating being with a man that powerful and that gorgeous. He can have any woman—every woman—he wants, but he chose you."

I thought what I had with Trent was unique. He fell for me after seeing me once at a party six years ago, but I guess Trent doesn't do sincere. Beverly, Cashmere, me, we're interchangeable to him.

"I understand the attraction, but Trent isn't the man for you. I'm not saying you're interested in him or that you want him back, but he wants you back, so you need to be careful because he won't stop. For him, it's all about the thrill of the chase. In Brice, you have a good man who'll love you for life. Make the right choice."

Sensible and wise aren't the two words I would have chosen to describe Cashmere a few months ago, although that's exactly what she is. I'm touched by how concerned she is about me making the right decisions for my life. I'm not in danger of being sucked back in by Trent, but I appreciate her warning me.

"Thank you for trying to warn me off danger. That is the definition of a true friend. I promise there's absolutely nothing to worry about. I turned down his job offer." Technically, I didn't. I haven't responded to his text. It's implied in my silence.

"And I know as well as you do how great Brice is, but...I don't know. In some ways, it's easier with Trent."

Cashmere's face is a mask of incredulity. It sounds absurd to my ears as well; however, there's truth in it.

"Trent's deceptive. Even when's telling the truth, he's lying. I doubt there was ever a time when he was completely honest with me. With that said, he's also uninhibited. He's not afraid to show me his desire." One thing Trent always did was make me feel wanted. Even now, I feel his longing for me. It's a powerful feeling.

"In our friendship and conversation," I continue. "Brice is candid and attentive. I always know where I stand. But in...other things, he's very measured. Whenever we get to that point where I think, finally, he's going to let me all the way in, he pushes me away. It's infuriating. He says it's me. I'm the reason he's holding back. I don't believe that, though."

214

"You're keeping me at arm's length, Brice. Every time we get close, you pull away from me. Why?"

I was surprised to get Brice's call after our spat. He said he wasn't happy that we fought. I admitted it wasn't a bright spot for me either.

"I charge you, do not arouse or awaken love until it so desires."

"I literally have no idea what that means. I tell you how I feel, and you respond with some quote I barely understand even on the most basic level."

"Don't pursue love before it's time. It'll happen on its own."

I thought we were making progress, then he says, whatever it is he said, which I still don't understand though what I glean from it aggravates me. After all, Brice is the one who while I was still engaged to Trent declared his love for me.

"It's from Song of Songs."

"Where?"

"It's in the Bible after Ecclesiastes." He sighs lightly. "It's a caution to guard my feelings until you're ready to reciprocate. If you're ever ready." He speaks barely above a whisper. "I'm not sure you are or that you've decided who you're going to be and be with. I can't decide those things for you, but I can give you the space to do so."

"What makes you think I haven't decided? I left Trent, didn't I? And I'm with you as often as you will allow. The way I see it. I'm very decided. Maybe the problem is that you aren't as ready to move on as you thought you were, and now you're projecting your issues on to me."

I don't know how much of what I said I actually believe and how much was reprisal. Either way, it was a low blow and beneath me.

"I made my peace with my happily ever after not being with Seriyah a while ago. Now when I dream, it's of you, but I can't handle the heartache of losing the woman I...I survived it once. I couldn't a second time."

The woman he what? I wonder.

"I listen to you when you speak. Always you ask the same question: What are you going to do? You ask it when you talk about your career, your faith, and us. I don't hold it against you that you're still trying to figure things out; I just can't consent to be collateral damage."

"What makes you think you'll be collateral damage?" My voice breaks with the ache in my chest. "Where is all this coming from?"

"I'm not blind, LA. Sometimes I think you are, though. Everyone except you can see how much you matter to me. I want a relationship with you, but I need to know that's what you want too. Right about now, I don't think you know what you want, let alone who you want."

"What do you mean by I don't know what I want?"

"I mean, you're caught in between two worlds, but that can't last very long. Eventually, you have to decide which world you belong to."

We didn't say much after that, unable to defend myself or refute his claims. We hung up without any promise to speak again and absolutely no mention of the party he invited me to.

"You know what I think?" Cashmere asks, pulling me out of my head. I shrug. "I think none of this has much to do with Trent or Brice. It's about you. You're still figuring things out, what you're going to do." There goes that question again. It's become as daunting as my nightmares once were.

"Take your time. It will all work out." I sigh, a loud, audible sigh. "When did you become so levelheaded?"

"I've always been, what word did you use? Levelheaded. I've just matured enough to learn to obey my better judgments." She winks.

"When I grow up, I want to be like you," I say.

She smiles, picking up her phone. I'm proud of how much Cashmere has grown from the time we met to now. I pray I can grow into a woman who obeys her better judgments too.

"What are you doing?" I ask.

Cashmere's tapping away at her phone like her life depends on it.

"Reading through my comments. I asked for suggestions for a church home again. Everyone keeps bringing up In the Garden."

"You're not enjoying it anymore?"

She does something between a nod and a shake of her head. "Yes and no. There are things I like, mainly the music, which I can hardly enjoy. I'm always being asked to go live."

"You're not sitting in VIP?"

"I am. That's what makes it worse. Either my neighbor is recording, or once, in the middle of the service, the pastor stopped and said we people with great influence should go live for the far-reaching of the message."

"Cash, maybe he was sincere."

I don't believe that, but I try to give him the benefit of the doubt.

"That could be true, but I don't believe it is. I think it was for clout. After service, Pastor Jackson had the ushers escort us VIPs to his office to take a group pic for the church's Instagram. I don't know, shouldn't a church page big up Jesus, not celebrity guests?"

I didn't enjoy the one service I attended. Something was missing for me. Despite the bright lights, studio music, and crowds, In the Garden was missing the most crucial part of a church service, fellowship with God.

"You should come to church with me."

"Where?"

"Onward Christian Soldiers."

She puts her phone back down on the end table above her. "Sure." She shrugs. "Why not?"

"Great." I get up from the floor and dust off my jeans. "I have to get out of here, or I'm going to be late," I say while heading to the fancy coat rack. "Auditions for the play Brice is directing start in an hour, and I have to be there."

"I forgot you were helping Brice out with that. How's it going?"

"So far, so good. There was a hiccup with this one girl, Ella—mean, rude, and a bully but protected from consequences by her charisma. She's not so bad though. She's just suffering from a little crush on Brice."

"Well, who hasn't had a crush on him?"

I raise a questioning eyebrow Cashmere's way. She throws her head back in laughter. "I said, 'hasn't.' My crush is strictly past tense."

"Yeah, well, it had better be." Still laughing, she puts her hands up, palms facing me.

"Anyways," I say, moving on. "What are you getting ready to do?"

"I need to edit some content. I have hours' worth of moving in and decorating footage I need to put together. I'll probably order some food and tackle that."

Since she's moved to New York City from Los Angeles, Cashmere doesn't party or hang out like she used to. I think it's good for her to get away from the old scene, though sometimes I worry she's lonely.

"Why don't you come with me? I'm sure Brice won't mind." He'll probably even be happy to see her.

Cashmere's up and at the coatrack in seconds. She takes a dark leather jacket off a peg and throws it on over her Athleisure. She runs back to the living room, grabs her phone, and her keys from the bowl on the coffee table then hurries down the long hallway leading to the bedrooms.

"I'll be right back," she shouts when she's almost out of sight. "I need to grab some shoes. I'll be two seconds, then we can go."

Cashmere's mad dash confirms I did the right thing. Within a minute, she's jogging back down the hall.

"Ready," she says, panting.

"Okay. Let's go."

"I'm so happy to see you," Brice says to Cashmere, pulling her in for a big hug. He smiles at me over her shoulder. "I'm glad Leah brought you. The more, the merrier."

"Thank you for having me."

"Don't thank me yet," he says, smiling. "I'm about to put you to work." Brice leaves us standing off to the side while he calls rehearsal to commence and introduces Cashmere.

"We'll be testing for the character of Avani, the female lead, first. You were each given sides, which included one of her monologues. Everyone hoping for this role will audition with that piece." He gestures to where Cashmere and I are standing. "Cashmere will have extra copies of the sides if you need it... When I introduced you all to Leah, I told you how talented of an actress she is."

Usually, I'd be flattered by the compliment, but I get the feeling I'm not going to be too thrilled about what he says next.

"If we ask her nicely," Brice says, "I think we can get Leah to show us how it's done."

"Please, Leah," someone says in the first row.

"Come on, Leah. Please show us how to audition," someone else says.

"How about it, Leah? Will you do it?" Brice asks.

I nod, although I feel like saying no. I've done little more than glance at the sides I distributed two weeks ago. Now I have minutes to put something together that dazzles.

"Before we get to auditioning, I want to talk to you about the play," Brice says. "Are you all familiar with the story of the prodigal son?"

Most people, myself included, nod. A few others, like Cashmere, remain quiet. Brice stands in front of the sanctuary, silently taking note of our responses.

"Most of you have. For those of you who haven't, don't worry, I'm getting to it. For reference, you can find the story in your Bible—Luke chapter fifteen, verses eleven to thirty-two."

Brice pulls an empty chair from the end of the first row and sits facing us. Cashmere and I sit as well.

"Jesus tells his disciples a parable. How many of you know what a parable is?"

I have a vague understanding of the term. Judging by the blank stares, I'm not the only one.

"A parable is a simple story used by Jesus to illustrate a greater spiritual or moral lesson," Brice explains. Collectively we nod, permitting him to move forward with his explanation.

"There was once a man of means who had two sons. The younger son, deciding he no longer wanted to live at home subject to his father, approached him, demanding to be given his inheritance. He demanded from his father what he felt he was owed, with the intention of taking it, leaving, and never looking back. His father did what he asked, and soon after, the younger son, left his familial home. The scripture says, 'he quickly squandered his money on wild living.' Yes, Joshua, do you have a question?"

Joshua lowers his hand. "I was wondering what kind of wild living did he squander his money on."

"I imagine he spent his inheritance on the same things we irresponsibly blow our money on now and call it fun or living our best lives," Brice says. "Partying, alcohol, companionship."

Joshua nods.

"After he'd spent all he had," Brice continues, "a severe famine spread across the land. Because he was in need, he hired himself out to a farmer who set him to feed his pigs. While he worked and starved, he remembered his father's servants, who lived more comfortably than he currently was. He reasoned his action made it impossible for him to return home as a son; however, he could go and work the fields."

"Why does he think he can't return home as a son?" Ella asks.

"Because," Brice answers, "he didn't leave home on the best terms. He left with arrogance. Now he's been humbled, and he feels embarrassed about what he did and what he's become."

My throat is thick with unshed tears as I listen. I see myself in the younger son.

When I left home to go film *Star Quality*, I was determined never to return again. I told my mom Trent and the show were my portion. Like the prodigal son's father, my mom didn't try to stop me. She warned me about getting mixed up with Trent, then she let me go.

The first night I was away from home, I spent it with Trent. I relished the freedom. I felt like I'd broken out of prison. Gradually the freedom I thought I gained revealed itself to be a mirage. Neither Trent nor *Star Quality* was what I thought they were. I knew I had to quit and go back home—that's what God wanted me to do—but I felt too ashamed of myself to call my mom. After weeks of not speaking, I called Amanda instead. I had alienated my oldest friend because she disapproved of Trent, but she didn't hold that against me. Amanda picked me up and drove me home, no questions asked.

I was terrified my mother wouldn't accept me back home, and I wouldn't have blamed her if she didn't. I didn't even use my house key. I rang the doorbell and waited for her to answer it. I wanted to give her the option of letting me in. I didn't have to wait long, though it felt like an hour. By the time my mom got to the door, my shirt was soaked through with sweat, but she hugged me anyway. I didn't want my mom to touch my sweaty shirt. I told her not to, but she held on tighter as if she hadn't heard me or felt the moisture. She was glad I'd returned.

"While he was still some distance from home, his father saw him approaching and was filled with compassion toward him. The father ran out to meet his young son who had gone away. 'Father,' he said, 'I have sinned against heaven and against you. I am unworthy to be called your son.'

"His disobedience disqualified him from being a son. He didn't return in that capacity. He asked to be allowed to return as a servant. Being a man of grace, his father would not receive him as a servant, but he would accept him as his son. His father was so relieved to have him back that he told his servants to dress him in the finest robes and sandals and put a ring on him. The servants were also told to prepare a feast in celebration of the return of this son for he was lost, but now he is found."

The silence is profound. We sit mutely, undoubtedly thinking of the story we just heard. The tale isn't foreign to me, but was it always this personal? The story couldn't have changed. That means I must have. Between when I last heard the parable of the prodigal son, and now, it went from scripture to my real life.

Chapter 17

Avani

"Brice?" Every head turns in Cashmere's direction. "What does the parable mean?"

Brice steeples his fingertips together, leaning forward in his seat. "I think a lot of us are like the younger brother. We demand freedom from God, go far away from Him, and spend our days living wildly until we're depleted. Drinking, drugging, partying, free-loving. As fun as all that stuff may seem at first, there's a price. Eventually, you can no longer afford to pay it. Ultimately, you find yourself enslaved to an unfulfilling, spiritually starved life."

Cashmere's knee bounces up and down with the effort of keeping from crying.

"It's okay," I whisper while patting her on the back.

She nods, though she seems just as distraught.

"If we're fortunate, we remember we have a wealthy Father and out of necessity return home. It was need that brought the prodigal back; however, grace received him. What gets me is that, while he was still far away, his father saw him." He shakes his head. "God is so good," he says with awe.

"Our heavenly Father sees us, even when we're a great distance from him because he never stops wanting us to come back. By grace, we are not turned away. We are happily welcomed into the body of Christ not as servants—as sons and daughters."

I don't know what kind of impact this has had on the young adults. They're quiet and contemplative. For Cashmere and me, who are about a decade older than them and have lived more, it's life-changing.

"I've always loved this parable because of how beautifully it explains grace," Brice says. "The play, *When I Returned*, deals with what happens after the celebration of, in this case, the prodigal daughter's, return. It's about her learning to be a child of her father again but really for the first time. You'll be auditioning with the monologue from a scene where Avani is having a heart-to-heart with her pastor. In spiritual agony, she confesses the conflict of her heart."

Brice turns his head in my direction, quickly finding me in our small group. I notice a difference in him. I picked up on it earlier. It's clearer now. He doesn't only look the part of a teacher; Brice is a teacher. I appreciate him on a whole new level.

"LA?"

"Yes?"

"Are you ready?"

I nod and slowly walk to the pulpit, one foot in front of the other. They're only teenagers, but their eyes feel like tiny pinpricks against my skin. *What are you nervous about? You do this every week in class. Andy says you're the best acting student he's had in years. You can do this.* I keep my head high and my back straight as I remember Andy's advice, "If you believe it, we will too." Right now, I believe I can do this.

I climb the three steps up to the pulpit and sit in the lone chair. From what I remember, there are usually six chairs on the pulpit, one for Pastor Charles, the other five are for the deacons. Brice must have set up the pulpit for the auditions before we got here. I sit, close my eyes, draw a deep breath, and let it out in short puffs. *You got this.* I open my eyes and say, "scene."

"You know, Pastor." I direct my words to the space I imagine the pastor will be once his part is cast. For now, I use my imagination. "I think I've heard you preach that sermon about a thousand times."

I deliver my line with a slight twang. When I skimmed over the sides, Avani felt like a southern bell. I'm not sure if that's what Brice had in mind when he wrote her, but that's who she feels like to me.

"I sat at a Sunday school desk, slightly smaller than this," I say, laughing, "the very first time I heard of the prodigal son." Pretending the empty space in front of me is a desk, I stretch my hands across the width of it.

"Sister Lilly, may she rest in peace, stood at the front of the small classroom downstairs wearing a yellow dress with pink sunflowers and a big ole sunhat. She looked at us with her big eyes and said, 'Children, today we're going to learn something very important. Y'all are very young, so you may not understand it right now, but you will eventually. When the day comes that you need to return home, your father will be waiting to welcome you back.'"

Head tilted to the side, I say, "Pastor, imagine being eight years old hearing a thing like that." I laugh shakily. "I was confused and afraid because, you know, I didn't have no daddy. I pictured myself walking all the way home from school, then realizing I'd misplaced my keys. If my only hope was my daddy, *hmmph*." I shift in my seat. "I'd be locked out forever. I tried to forget what I heard that day, but the things you want most to forget are the things that you most remember. I'm happy I did. Fifteen years later, those words would lead me out of a club back home." I look off into the distance, remembering.

"Now, now, Pastor, don't be jealous. Many of your sermons haunted me during my darkest moments, but Sister Lilly's words, they reminded me my daddy would be waiting to let me in." My voice breaks.

"Much to Mama's delight, I came back home. For the first few months, every day was a good day. Then something happened. I took a real good look at myself, and you know what I saw? The same girl who made all those mistakes. That brings me to why I'm here. I need to know what happens after the prodigal returns," I declare.

I mime pulling out a Bible and turning to Luke chapter fifteen. Looking at the pastor, I point to the page. "How does he live with the shame and guilt of the things he's done? How does he now handle the desires that led him astray in the first place? And how—" My voice deflates as I get to the root of Avani's distress. What is it she needs to know more than she needs to breathe? I lean across the invisible desk. "How...How does he become a man his father can be proud of?"

"You were amazing, Leah."

If a week ago, anyone would've told me Ella would shower me with praise, I'd never have believed it. I should be thrilled to have gained her respect. I need that if I'm ever going to have an impact on her life. At present, I don't have it in me to be thrilled. I'm too raw from the monologue. It's all I can do to nod my thanks.

I shuffle past Ella, away from the lobby, where I escape to cry after I had more applause than I could handle. Leave it to Brice to unknowingly, perfectly capture me. Avani, like myself, knows what it feels like to be determined to be different, better, but not know how.

"Leah." I turn around. "Are you okay?"

Ella's made up her mind that I'm not. She's no good at keeping her thoughts secret. Her face gives her away.

"I'm fine," I reply. "The scene got the best of me. It happens to all actors; no big deal. I'm sure that's not what you wanted to talk to me about though. What's up?"

"You're right," Ella says. She doesn't completely buy my story. She won't pursue it any further either. "I wanted to ask..." She hesitates, "if maybe you could give me a few pointers."

I don't feel like talking. It takes more energy than I currently have. Nonetheless, I can't pass up this moment. There'd be no getting it back. It took a lot for Ella to ask for my help. Either I speak now or forever hold my peace. I push my personal stuff aside and mentor.

"The best advice I can give you is don't act. Feel."

"What kind of airy-fairy mumbo jumbo is that?"

"It's not airy-fairy or mumbo jumbo. It's sound advice—quit rolling your eyes and listen. When someone pretends to be nice, pretends to cry, or pretends to care, don't you feel how insincere it is?"

"Yeah, I guess so." Ella shrugs.

"Spare me your guesses. I distinctly remember overhearing you whisper to your friends that I was only pretending to be sweet."

To my surprise, she looks down at the carpeted floor, unable to meet my eyes. I'm moved by how embarrassed she is by her behavior.

"It's fine," I assure her. "I've had far worse things said about me. Matter of fact, you've heard worse things said about me."

Ella bursts into laughter, probably remembering some of those things. I can't find it in me to be upset. Ella's no longer a snotty kid working my last nerve. She's my mentee, my responsibility. I want to help her.

"Okay. Yes, it's hilarious," I say in a tone that expresses the opposite. Ella composes herself, although a faint smile remains. "If you act," I say, "you'll be pretending, and we'll all be able to tell. However, if you feel what Avani feels, we'll feel it too."

"But what if I can't feel what she's feeling?"

"Lucky you," I mumble to myself.

"What'd you say?"

"I asked if you tried?"

"I don't know where to begin," she says, lifting her hands and letting them fall to her sides.

"Close your eyes," I whisper.

"Are we back to the airy-fairy stuff?" Ella's expression says I'm crazy, and she's not about to listen to a crazy person.

"Just do it." I huff. She obliges. "Imagine the worst thing you've ever done. Not the worst thing you've done and tell people about, but the thing you're so ashamed of, you tell no one, and if you do, you keep the details private."

I follow my own instructions and find myself going down a rabbit hole of memories I'd rather forget, many of which involve Trent, yet a lot of my regrets involve me alone and the things I've wrong. I close my mind to my own follies to focus on Ella's.

"Do you have it?" She nods uncomfortably. Whatever it is it hurts to think about. "Now, imagine your mom found out." Her face becomes panic stricken. "But she's forgiven you." She relaxes a bit. "But you don't know how to forgive yourself, how to move on from the past."

"This is the worst."

"Yeah, well, be happy you're only temporarily borrowing those feelings."

She opens one eye. "How are you sure I'm borrowing those feelings, that they're not mine?"

I'm sure. Anyone who's felt as Avani does would need no coaching on how to feel that way.

"Because I know." I stop short of adding what it feels like. "How old are you?" I ask.

This exercise has reminded me how young she is. Without the cloak of her attitude, Ella's just a child.

"Seventeen. I'll be eighteen in two months" she says, grinning widely.

"I remember being seventeen, eagerly awaiting my eighteenth birthday because it meant I'd be an adult. The big day came and went, and exactly nothing changed, except I was a year older. I still lived with my mom, I was still her responsibility, and I still couldn't do any and everything I wanted."

She searches me, questioning my point.

"Don't grow up too fast. Enjoy being young. You'll miss it one day. And good luck with the audition," I say, walking away from her, back to the sanctuary.

"You were my favorite."

"I was your favorite what?"

"Contestant. You were my favorite contestant...until you stole my man."

I'm not sure who starts laughing first. Either way, we're both hysterical. When I can catch my breath, I say, "For starters, he isn't my man, so I couldn't have possibly stolen him from anyone. Secondly, you're a solid ten years too young for him."

"Some men like younger women," she answers, the ease of the previous moment ebbing away.

"You're not a woman. You're a young lady. Men like women, predators like young girls."

She puts her hands on her hips. "You're telling me when you were my age you weren't interested in older guys?"

"Of course I was. Thankfully they were all decent enough not to be interested in me." Mostly true. In my younger years, I crossed paths with stand-up guys who laughed at my attempts at flirting and treated me with sisterly affection. However, there were one or three who weren't so stand-up. I was too young and dumb to understand, though. Thank goodness for Antonia talking sense into me. She'd say, "If a man can't attract and keep a woman his own age, something's wrong with him." I share that advice with Ella.

Her hesitation, thoughtfulness, and reserved demeanor lead me to believe we aren't talking hypotheticals. I think she might have another crush on an older guy, one a lot less noble than Brice. Teenage girls hate being told what to do, especially regarding guys they're interested in. I know this from experience. Still, it would be negligent not to say something.

"I won't pry by asking, but if you ever want to talk to me about anything, you can. No judgments."

And because I can't bear the idea of Ella opening up her naïve heart to the wrong guy, I say, "This time in a young lady's life is...complex. You're too old to be a child, not old enough to be an adult, though you're beginning to have adult wants. While you're growing into the woman you will be, there are many people out there willing to take advantage of your greenness."

She hugs me. Ella actually hugs me. I guess I did have something to say worth listening to all along.

"Come on," I say. "Let's head back to the sanctuary. We should have been back ages ago."

Ella's still a child. She doesn't realize that, though. I don't know what or who she's mixed up with, but I'm afraid of what will happen to Ella if Brice's plan doesn't work. What if community service and mentoring aren't enough?

Cashmere, Brice, and I sit pretzel legged in a circle on the floor in the sanctuary long after auditions have ended and Brice has sent everyone home. We debate who we should cast as Avani. Three hours ago, when we all sat down to discuss it, each of us thought the answer was obvious. We were wrong.

"I don't see why this is even a discussion. We all know who should be Avani."

"No," Brice says, replying to Cashmere, "we know who did best. That doesn't necessarily translate into who should play her."

He's losing patience with the discussion. We've gone back and forth on the subject for hours. Round and round, the argument goes without any conclusion. Unlike Brice and Cashmere, who are obstinate in their choices, which is the problem, I listen to the case for each possible Avani with an open mind, despite my leanings.

Skylar was unsurprisingly amazing. At least, I was unsurprised by her talent; everyone else was. She's petite, young, and shy, but she delivered. Just like when Brice picked her to pray, the mousiness that usually characterizes her was replaced by boldness no one would have ever guessed she possesses. She had the strongest performance; still, there are others to consider.

Ashley and Jade were good as well. Each had strong auditions, Jade more than Ashley. Jade is also one of the older girls among the youth group. She looks old enough for the words to be true coming out of her mouth. Needless to say, she's a serious contender.

Last but not least is Ella. She wowed me. Skylar had a better command of the script. Jade looks most convincing, but Ella evoked the most emotion from the story and us. Our talk must have worked because there was no sense of pretending from her at all. We've talked in circles for the last two hours, bringing up the same points with no conclusion.

Ashley lifted right out the conversation for those in the running almost immediately in light of the strengths of Skylar, Jade, and Ella. They each have something integral that she's lacking. Cashmere's vote is for Jade.

"She had the best performance if we consider the monologue and her look. Really, guys, it's a no-brainer."

Technically speaking, she doesn't really have a vote—even my vote's courtesy. The decision's Brice's. Right now, he happens to be leaning toward Skylar.

"She has something, and I think this will be good for her, help her come out of her shell."

He's made that same argument over and over only to have me rebut it because she's simply too young to deliver with conviction. The story is compelling, dealing with poignant under-discussed feelings, regardless of age. Jade looks like she's lived, but she doesn't deliver with passion, and I don't know if that's something we can teach. But Ella, she bridges the gap.

Brice hasn't said it, but I think his hesitation is that he doesn't want to contribute to her already sizeable ego. Every time I bring her up, he says, "We want to do things differently than they're done in Hollywood. Let's decide based on merit."

It's an innocuous comment, at first, though after the third time, I decide it has a specific target. I didn't imagine the scenario when I was Ella's biggest champion, but that's exactly what's happened. So now the three of us sit in a semi-circle on the carpeted floor of the church, everyone gone but us. Brice rubbing small circles at his temples, Cashmere silently fuming, and me unmoving on my decision that Ella is our Avani.

"I have an idea," I say. "Let's pray on it."

Cashmere's slightly less willing than Brice, who quickly closes his eyes and bows his head, but she's new to this. The notion of praying to God about something so trivial is foreign to her. Truthfully, it's new for me too. I've always saved my prayers for the big stuff. Although the last few months have been teaching me all our stuff, big and small, none of it goes unnoticed by God.

"Go ahead, Leah, pray," Brice says.

When I suggested we pray, I meant that Brice should lead us in prayer, not me. It's too late to clarify my meaning. I close my eyes, bow my head, and pray.

"Dear Lord, we come before you at this moment to—" I pause to think about what exactly is the reason we're praying. What outcome are we hoping for? Decision. We need to decide. Through our own reasoning, we haven't been able to come to one. With God's intervention, I'm certain we can.

"We're seeking your wisdom, Lord. Please forgive us for not including you in the process sooner, for there is nothing above your notice or too minuscule for your care. We want to glorify you with this play and edify those who witness it; however, we cannot do that apart from your Holy Spirit. We need your help, Lord, every step of the way, including right now in choosing the lead. We are foregoing deciding by man's standards, which can only account for what's outwardly seen. We want to choose whom you have chosen. Please, Lord, reveal that person to us all that we may be unified in doing your will. We pray to you humbly, in complete submission, in the name of Jesus Christ. Amen."

In the moment between saying amen and opening my eyes, I feel an even greater conviction that Ella is Avani for reasons that lay outside of talent. I trust this strong feeling. There's no telling if Cashmere and Brice will also since she's whom I've been pushing for from the beginning. I won't withhold what I'm sure is an answer given in response to prayer, but I'll let the others speak their minds first.

"Thank You, Lord." Brice doesn't exactly whisper.

It wasn't said loud enough to be a group comment either. A peaceful expression replaces the frustration he wore just before prayer. "I have my answer, ladies. Do you?"

I nod, inwardly praying his is the same as mine.

"Yeah," Cashmere adds. "I think I do too." Her voice sounds as rattled as she appears.

"Are you alright," I ask.

She nods, which I don't find particularly reassuring. "I'm fine. It's just...I think the prayer worked."

Neither Brice nor I ask what she means, probably because we've all just had the same experience, a peaceful certainty that this was God's say-so, not our own.

"So we're all in agreement that Ella is Avani, right?" she asks.

"And Skylar is the understudy?"

Though I did not have that revelation myself as soon as Brice says it, I know it's true. Skylar is the understudy. Cashmere must have received the same edict because she vehemently agrees.

"Thank you for being here today, Cash," Brice says.

"It was honestly my pleasure."

"And Leah..." Our eyes meet for what feels like the first time since I ended the scene. "Thank you for reminding us of the power in including God in our decisions." After a beat, he says, "I'll make the announcement at our next rehearsal. Here's a complete copy of the play."

Out of his worn leather messenger bag, he pulls out a fairly thick script and hands it to me. *When I Returned,* written by Brice Young.

"I'm sorry, Cash, I only have one copy for Leah."

She waves his apology away. "It's fine. I'm not part of this production, and I'm not much of a reader anyway. I'll let Leah read it and tell me all about it."

"Do you want to be part of the production?" Brice asks.

"No. I'm super busy with my channel and new partnership. I don't have the time. I would like to come see it, though, and maybe revisit the church during service next time."

"We'd be happy to have you at the show and service anytime you're ready to come," Brice says. "In the meantime, let's get out of here. I'm exhausted."

I lag behind Cashmere and Brice. I watch them joke as they walk up the sanctuary aisle to the doors leading to the lobby. A year ago, I didn't know either of them existed. Today, they're my best friends. I didn't win *Star Quality,* but I gained friendship. I look at Brice's handsome profile. Maybe more. I pick up my pace and catch up with them. I bump Brice lightly with my shoulder. He looks at me and smiles.

Chapter 18

New Opportunities

Andy Strapp's acting studio is the back bedroom of Andy's apartment in downtown Manhattan. His place is kind of drab and messy. Fortunately, though, looks can be deceiving. I absolutely love my acting classes with him. Andy can be intense. He's exceptionally talented, though, and he knows how to get a good performance from me and my nine classmates. I've been studying with Andy for six months, and he's never had a bad word to say to me. I suspect that's about to change. Andy's asked me to stay after class, and I think I know why. I think he found out about *Star Quality*. To serious actors, there is no greater affront than reality television.

"Thanks for staying back after class," Andy says, collecting the scripts we worked with today off the now empty chairs. I have a sinking feeling I know why he's asked me to stay behind.

I shrug. "You asked me to. I doubt 'no' was an option."

He laughs at my brashness, reminding me that I like him. Andy's always appreciated my sometimes surliness. That makes me slightly more comfortable—as comfortable as I can possibly be, while I wait for Andy to get to the reason he asked me to stay behind. I'm positive Andy finally learned about my participation on *Star Quality* and now wants to disassociate his actor's studio from me. Like Cara did when she fired me from Jolie.

"I caught your rendition of Delores Claiborne on *Star Quality* last night." I nod. It's as I suspected. "It was exceptional."

"Excuse me? What did you say?" No way did Andy just compliment me on my performance. He's supposed to call the show a disgrace to actors everywhere and send me out of his studio, not praise my performance.

"I said you were exceptional," he cries. "Don't you think you were exceptional?"

Seconds pass with Andy staring expectantly at me until I realize it's not a rhetorical question. He's waiting for an answer. I guess I did a good job. Everyone said I did. I haven't actually watched any of my performances. Aside from the few minutes I watched of the first episode, I haven't kept up with the show. Neither has Cashmere or Brice.

"I don't know about exceptional," I answer. "I did a good job."

"I'll take your word for it," he says, looking deflated. "After all, who knows your potential better than you? If you insist that it was not your best work, that it was merely a good performance, I eagerly look forward to what you deem exceptional. This brings me to why I asked you to stay behind."

Andy directs me to two empty chairs. We both sit.

"A good friend of mine has written a brilliant coming-of-age tale. It's about a young woman named Marie. She's from a Caribbean island but visiting her family in New York City for the summer, as she has every summer since she was seven. The summer she turns eighteen starts off like any other— hot, boring, long days spent between her aunt's cramped Brooklyn apartment and church. It's completely typical until she meets Jamal, the boy who would be her first love and inevitably turn her world upside down. He's all wrong for her, but she loves him hard anyway."

The hairs on my arms stand up. This is it. This is the project for me. Even if Andy weren't as passionate as he is, I would still feel the same. I'm meant to play Marie.

"I've been telling Leslie about you since you first started attending my classes. She didn't believe I had someone half as talented as I told her you are.

Then she saw you on *Star Quality*—she caught your Jordan Belfort performance. She's been keeping up with your performances ever since. She's producing this film independently, and the financing is small, but if you're interested, Leslie wants nothing more than for you to audition for Marie."

"I am..." I'm on the verge of saying "very interested" when I recall the last few times I rushed into an opportunity. I regretted it. "I am," I begin again, "willing to audition with Leslie."

"The audition is a week from today. I'll email you the details and sides. I can help you prepare for it if you want."

"I appreciate the offer, but I think I have a handle on it."

The smile on Andy's face slips. I'm sorry to hurt his feelings, but I don't want another man in my life wanting to further my career for their credit. One is enough.

"Okay. Well, look out for my email."

I hold up my phone. "I'll watch it like a pot."

Andy's email comes about an hour later, and not alone. I receive an email from the producers of *Star Quality* informing me of a party in two weeks commemorating the season finale and formally introducing the winner. Truly, I can think of very few things I would rather do less than celebrate Beverly's sham of a win. The producers made sure to remind me at the close of the email that I'm "contractually obliged to attend." I pull out my phone and send a text to Cashmere.

Me: *Did you get this email about our mandatory appearance at Beverly's celebration?*

Yeah. *You going?* Cashmere texts back.

Me: *I don't see that I have any other choice. That's what happens when you sign your life away for the promise of fame. You going?*

Cashmere: *I signed that very same contract, remember? Why don't you get dressed at my place? I'll have my glam squad work on us both.*

Me: *You know I can't resist a glam squad.*

Cashmere: *Who can? What are you thinking about wearing?*

Me: *I haven't given thought to what I'll wear. It'll be tough since I can't spend a dollar on a new dress with my financial situation being what it is.*

Cashmere: *I have an idea.*

Me: *Oh, brother, I'm scared. What is it?*

Cashmere: *Borrow something from me. Designers lend me dresses all the time, especially since this partnership with Face Cosmetics happened. All I have to do is credit and tag them on social media. You can look through my loaner dresses, choose something fabulous, wow in it, and return it to me.*

Me: *And I thought fairy godmothers didn't exist.*

Cashmere: *Uh, fairy godmothers work for free. I do not. I fully expect you to repay me in help picking out my own outfit. You know I'm no good at the whole sexy yet reserved thing.*

Me: *Fortunately, you have me. I have rehearsal with Brice every day except Sunday for the rest of the week. Does that work for you?*

Cashmere: *Sure. Help your boyfriend first, then you help me.*

Me: *Not my boyfriend, and sure.*

Cashmere: *Not your boyfriend—yet.*

Me: *Things are still a little weird between us. We're talking, but since the fight, our conversations have been guarded.*

The approach of opening day promises more opportunity to change that, though. Between rehearsal three days a week and our volunteer hours, we see a lot more of each other. Hopefully, constantly being thrown together will help get us past the weirdness and back to us.

"Why didn't you tell me putting on a play is this much work?" Brice laughs softly as he makes a U-turn and starts in the direction of my house. "Don't laugh at me," I protest. "When we're not blocking scenes, we're figuring out costumes and set design, not to mention everyone's questions, especially Ella's."

"She's really embraced the mentor-mentee relationship, hasn't she?"

"She has. She's become my annoying yet loveable little sister." I've gone from being her least favorite person to the person she seeks out for advice—Skylar and me, that is. "I'm proud of all the ways she's grown in these past weeks. She's been sweet and kind to everyone."

"Hmmm," Brice says, momentarily taking his eyes off the road to look at me. "I wonder whose great idea it was to put you two together."

"I'll admit it. You were right."

He cups his ear and leans closer to me. "What did you say? I didn't hear you over the traffic."

I playfully push him away. "Yeah, yeah, yeah. But you know everything isn't all good. Something is definitely up with her."

"What do you mean?" Brice asks, becoming very serious.

Being involved with the youth ministry and the play has changed her, but something's tugging at those changes. "She's always on her phone texting. She no longer wants a ride home after rehearsals, no matter how late it is, and she's moody. One minute she's flying high; the next she's typing away on her phone at an impossible speed, too distracted to deliver her lines."

Brice nods. "I have noticed those things, but she's seventeen. Aren't seventeen-year-olds moody?"

I pat him on the shoulder. "Good thing you had the good sense to bring me on because you are so clueless when it comes to seventeen-year-old girls."

"I should be clueless about seventeen-year-old girls," he protests.

I roll my eyes. "Brice, she's a textbook case of a girl in love with the wrong guy."

"What?" he asks, his voice colored with emotion. "Are you sure that's what's going on?"

I nod.

Long gone are the days when my greatest concern about Ella is some flirtatious behavior toward Brice. There's a new guy on her mind, and whoever *he* is, I don't like him.

"What are we supposed to do? How do we handle this?"

"For now, keep a watchful eye on her. I'll have to confront her soon. I only hope she heeds my warning. I've lived my own version of this story before. I know how it turns out."

Brice takes one hand off the steering wheel and grabs for mine. "I'm not sure if I've said this to you or not, but I'm happy you're my partner in this. I couldn't have done it without you."

Brice and I are busy with the play all the time, but when it's just us two, underneath the conversations about the kids, lighting, and sound, there's the thing I feared we'd lost. The connection between us remains despite how little we acknowledge it.

"You know what I'm happy about?" I say.

"What?"

"That we're not fighting."

Neither of us has brought back up our fight until now. I think we've both been content to move forward.

"I'm happy about that too. By the way, only twenty-two more days to the party. I can't wait to see you in another beautiful dress."

I turn my gaze out the window, hiding my smile. "You won't have to wait for twenty-two more days for that."

"Huh? Why not?"

"The *Star Quality* party." He nods. "I picked out my dress with you in mind."

Now Brice is the one biting back his smile.

In between rehearsals, job interviews, and volunteering, I ready myself for my audition. I've prayed about it. I think this is the opportunity my mother promised would come. I asked her to pray about it too. Three whole days went by with no answer.

On the fourth morning, while in the kitchen eating breakfast, she says to me, "The plans of the heart belong to man, but the answer of the tongue is from the Lord.'"

The cup of coffee she hides her smile behind doesn't quite do the job. She received an answer to her prayers, a favorable one, which can mean anything. She's never been keen on me pursuing such an "inconsistent" line of work.

"I take it you received an answer," I say.

"Yes, I did."

Trying hard not to lose my patience, I ask, "What is it?"

"Commit your work to the Lord, and your plans will be established."

"So... is that a yes?"

"That depends on you, doesn't it?" she says, taking a sip of coffee.

My mom can be very insightful when she wants to be. I need now to be one of those times.

"Mom," I plead, "can you please give me a straight answer for once?" My voice rises. "I'm really trying my best to do things the right way. Please, help me to."

The end of my sentence gets lost, swallowed by my attempt to hold back my tears. My emotions are close to the surface these days. I cry at the drop of a hat. Almost everything sets me off. I hate that I've become so emotional, but this time, my tears do the trick.

In the exasperated voice I'm so used to hearing her speak in, she says, "It really does depend on you." She motions for me to take the seat next to her at the kitchen island.

"The time has come for you to decide if you're in or out." I answer with a look of question. "Either you're going to submit to God in every area, giving Him all the pieces, or you're not. It's impossible to live with two purposes contrary to each other. You can't glorify God and yourself. It has to be one or the other. If your purpose is to live for God, He will establish all you do, if it's not then..." She shrugs. "This conversation doesn't really matter because you'll do as you will."

My mom takes my hand in her own calloused hands, rough from twelve-hour shifts of bending, lifting, and scrubbing hotel rooms in Manhattan. She's committed her ways to the Lord. Would she consider her life successful? I don't. I'm sorry to think it, but I don't want to end up like her—divorced, living hand to mouth, at a dead-end job, and in relative obscurity It's not enough for me. I want more, and I don't know that I could ever be content with less.

"I know what you're thinking," she says, staring at our locked hands. "Success may not resemble the picture the world has shown you. If your measuring stick isn't God's, you're always going to come up short. You'll never be satisfied."

Before I can think about it too much, I say, "What about your life? Are you satisfied?" At first, I think I've offended her, then she smiles—a rare, happy smile.

"You have to remember I wasn't born in this country or this generation. I came here from Haiti without a plan or a dollar, only my great desire to glorify Christ in song. That desire got me my plane ticket here, gave me community, and eventually, a family. Can I say life has been easy or that I always feel happy? No, I can't." She pauses for a long time, thinking.

"Life has been difficult. I suspect it will never stop being that for anyone, but it has also been rewarding. I have a peace that's implacable. No matter how hard the storms of life toss my boat, I remain convicted in the saving power of Christ in all situations, and that, my dear, is what I call a successful life, one filled with the glory of God."

I welcome the feel of her rough warrior hands as they clutch more tightly my smooth, barely tested ones. Compared to my mom, I've had it easy. At sixteen, she became the head of her household, responsible for herself and her three younger siblings. Nothing I've gone through even compares to the life she's lived, and yet she's steady. I want that.

"It's not a sin to want to be prosperous. I think it'd be a shame not to want that, especially at such a young age. Just don't want prosperity more than you want Christ. Many make that choice to the price of their downfall. *'But godliness with contentment is great gain. For we brought nothing into the world, and we can take nothing out of it. But if we have food and clothing, we will be content with that. Those who want to get rich fall into temptation and a trap and into many foolish and harmful desires that plunge people into ruin and destruction. For the love of money is a root of all kinds of evil. Some people, eager for money, have wandered from the faith and pierced themselves with many griefs.'*"

"Where's that from?"

"First Timothy chapter six, verses six through ten."

"How do you interpret that?" I ask. Although I understand it all too well, particularly the part about "piercing themselves with many griefs."

"It means there's no reason not to believe that God will bless you abundantly but *'seek first the kingdom of God and His righteousness and all else shall be added unto you.'* So, honey, what will you seek?"

"I don't know," I answer my mom honestly.

Her face falls. That's not what she expected to hear, It's not what I meant to say either, but the truth always has a way of coming out.

Tonight's festivities are by far the swankiest *Star Quality* event I've been to yet: midtown location ballroom, sit-down dinner, Swarovski crystals, tall floral arrangements, cast photos, swag bags, and the who's who of the REALTV network. I try to relax and mingle. The problem is my heart's not in it. I don't want to be at another *Star Quality* event, I had to be because of a stupid contract. I'm anxious about seeing Trent, dreading watching Beverly gloat, Brice is nowhere to be found, and I haven't heard back about the part yet. I should have heard something by now. I left the audition confident I'd nailed it. The more time passes, the less sure I grow. In the days leading up to the audition, I lived with the sides. I laid it all out on the line. If Andy could have seen my audition, I believe he would agree *that* was exceptional.

That was also a week ago. I've heard not a word back. I've just about given up hope. What little hope I can manage, I hold on to as tightly as I can. It's not an easy feat in a room of people boasting of their success when you have none to boast of yourself.

I sit at table number one with Cashmere, Aiden, Zack, and Corey. The two empty chairs belong to Brice and Beverly, neither of which have arrived yet. I zone out while everyone else at my table talks excitedly to each other.

I can probably leave after the president of REAL TV makes all his speeches.

A large tanned hand swipes vertically in front of my face; I bat Aiden's hand away.

"Leahz, where are you tonight?" Aiden asks.

"What? I'm right here." I guess I'm not doing a very good job of hiding how much I don't want to be here.

"Don't sweat it," he says.

"Huh?" I ask.

"We all know who should have won."

Aiden thinks I'm sulking about Beverly winning *Star Quality*. I'm not happy about that, but what I'm feeling is deeper than that. I feel lost.

Chapter 19

So We Meet Again

Thank goodness for Cashmere's glam team. She only uses them when she has a special event. I'm happy today ranked because being pampered by them has been the best part of my day. Growing up, my mom would tell Antonia and me we didn't have to look like our situation. I've held on to that. Just because I'm feeling stretched doesn't mean I have to look it.

Candice, Cashmere's hairdresser, styled my tresses in large finger waves with little curlicues fixed on my temples, à la the 1920s. The makeup artist used a light hand for my face—except on my eyes. She made them dramatic and smoky, especially set against the rose gold shimmer of my skin, also her handiwork. After I was dressed, she added a mole to my right cheek, to complete the look, she said.

My hair's beautiful, makeup's perfect, but the showstopper is my dress—a floor-length, billow sleeve, illusionary see-through gown. The neckline is a tastefully executed deep V. The bodice is snug, fitted through my waist, looser on the hips. The material, a heavy nude-colored lace, is thicker on the torso. It thins farther down my legs.

The shape is lovely and alluring, but the crystals take it over the top. They're plentiful. Sparse in some places like the sleeves and abundant in others like my waist, the effect is shocking against my skin on the parts of the dress where the lace is virtually invisible. I glimmer, sparkle, and shine. Tonight, I've been transformed into the star I've always dreamed of being.

"Tell me again why I didn't keep that dress for myself," Cashmere says after another partygoer, for what seems like the millionth time, compliments me.

"Because it was too conservative, according to you."

"Right. I did say that." She presses her lips together. "Next time, ignore me."

"Note to self," I say. "Ignore Cash."

She's joking, of course. Cashmere's choice in outfit, a provocatively low-plunging metallic jumpsuit with gorgeous draping in the back, is just as attention grabbing as mine.

"You look great, and you know it."

"I never said I didn't," she answers, tossing her hair. "I'm not blind."

Months ago, Cashmere's playful bluster would have driven me crazy. Now, it only makes me laugh.

"What are you ladies so happy about?"

"Nothing," Cashmere replies to Corey. "What are you so happy about?" she counters.

I haven't spoken much to Corey all night. Last I saw him, he was chatting up a redhead a few tables from ours. He pulls out the chair next to Cash and drops into it. His usual partners in crime, Aiden and Zack, are currently in deep conversation with some network honcho. They're probably getting offered roles in new projects. I try not to feel too bitter about that and remember mine will come.

"What is there to not be happy about?" Corey asks. "Good food, good friends, beautiful women," he says, eyeing us not so subtly.

Corey's had a hopeless crush on Cashmere since day one. She pretends not to know, probably because while he's good-natured, affable, and cute, he's also very younger brotherish. Fortunately, his attachment to her is too shallow to invoke bitterness or hurt feelings.

"Remind me to teach you the delicate art of flirting," I joke, not without affection.

"I thought I was flirting."

"That's the problem," I say.

"Are you saying I've been doing it wrong this entire time?" I laugh heartily enough to forget I'm having a bad time.

Thanks to my castmates, I'm having an okay time. It would be better if Brice were here, though. I scan the faces at the tables around Cashmere and me and those walking by again, hoping he'd slipped in unnoticed.

"Who you looking for?"

"Hmmm?" I respond distractedly.

"I said, 'Who are you looking for?" Cashmere repeats, speaking a little louder to be heard over the music.

"No one. I'm not looking for anyone."

She rolls her eyes. "Yeah, sure. If you're not looking for anyone, why do you keep scanning the crowd every few minutes?"

I didn't realize I was doing that. Though I'm sure she's guessed by now, I tell her anyway. "I'm looking for Brice. He said he was coming, but he's late. If he isn't here by now, he's probably changed his mind."

"Why don't you call him?"

I hold up my unreasonably small purse. My ID barely fits. No amount of turning, flipping, or cramming could get my cell phone in there too. "I didn't bring my phone."

"How could you leave the house without a phone?"

"Well, it's not unheard of. I've done it before. As a matter of fact, I spent the first sixteen years of my life without one. Do you know whole generations before us hadn't even imagined such a thing as a mobile phone? They contented themselves with home phones, payphones, and some people resorted to sending letters."

"True," she says drily, "but I bet you wish you had one now, don't you?"

I shrug.

"Here." Cashmere hands me her jewel-encrusted iPhone. "Use mine."

"It's okay," I decline. I'd like to keep some dignity. I can always call Brice when I get my phone back if he doesn't show. I hope he does.

"Okay. If you change your mind, the offer stands... Also," she says, her eyes flicking past me, "Beverly's on her way over. Ignore her and keep your cool."

My resolve not to acknowledge Beverly is broken the instant I see what she's wearing. She's in a dress with a slit so high up I can't fathom how she walked all this way without an accident of indecent exposure.

"You two look..." She surveys Cashmere and me from head to toe, which doesn't take long since we're still seated. "Nice," she finishes lamely.

My instinct is to say something snarky back, but *he* beats me to the punchline.

Saddling up to Beverly from out of nowhere, Trent says, "Yes, they do."

Beverly jumps into his arms with reckless abandon while Cashmere and I look on.

"You look fantastic," Trent remarks to Beverly. She loops her arms around his neck, snuggling close to his ear. "I'm happy you like what you see."

"That I do," he says.

"You look good yourself," she says, nibbling his ear.

I have to agree with her on that. Trent's as handsome in black tie as he is in any of his other fashion choices. No surprise there. But their display is ugly. They're all over each other, yet nothing about their situation says genuine commitment or love.

"I see someone I want to go talk to," Beverly says. "I'll be right back." She looks at me, "Don't stay over here too long," she says to Trent, walking in the direction of the swag bag table.

"I'm right behind you," he calls to her.

Trent puts on a show of being so engrossed in watching Beverly walk away that he doesn't notice me, which is a lie. He sees me, though it's Cashmere he addresses.

"You've never looked more beautiful," he says to her.

If Trent and I survived, my friendship with Cashmere could not have. She loved him. She was desperate to be loved by him. Trent didn't feel the same way in return. Behind her mask of indifference, I recognize trepidation. After all this time and all the hurt he's caused, her name spoken from Trent's lips still pulls at her heart. She doesn't acknowledge his remark, though. Like me, Cashmere seems unable to make out his intentions in paying her such special attention. Trent's not ignorant of the wound he's caused her or the desperation she felt to be loved by him. Singling her out feels mocking, like he's laughing at her.

"I told her the exact same thing earlier." The smile briefly slips off my face when his dark eyes finally turn my way. "She has the glow and confidence of a woman who has left behind toxic people and relationships."

He grins, revealing, once again, this entire interaction was just to get a rise out of me.

"Sounds to me that you've finally realized what you're missing," Cashmere says, unaware of what's truly happening, Trent's weird version of cat and mouse.

"I think you might be right," he says. Without explanation, I pull Cashmere up from our table, leaving Trent standing alone, though I doubt he'll be that way for long. If it's not Beverly, he'll find another woman to stand at his side. I can't explain to Cashmere that Trent was only complimenting her to make me jealous. She would be devastated. I can't explain to her the truth of what that was. It would devastate her. I also won't let her be used for sport. I let Cash think I need to get away from Trent and lead her across the room to the bar.

We carry our drinks back to our table. It's full except for Beverly, who's still attached to Trent, and Brice. He still isn't here yet. He must've gotten sidetracked doing something for the play. Beverly takes her seat with us when dinner is announced.

After dinner, before dessert, Scott Perry, president of Real TV, rises from his table and calls the room to attention. I met him earlier in the evening. He complimented my work, my dress too.

"Ladies and gentleman, I hope you've enjoyed your meal. I'll let you get back to it soon." He laughs. "I wanted to take this opportunity to thank the fantastic crew and cast.

"Aiden, Corey, Zack, Brice, Cashmere, Leah, and Beverly, the show wouldn't have been a success without you. Or you, Mr. Producer Extraordinaire." Perry raises a glass high above his head. "To Trenton Shaw and his continued success." The room erupts into loud applause.

Trent rises from his seat at the table for network executives, addressing the room. "Thank you all. Each of you in some way, shape, or form has made my success possible." He scans every face as if he genuinely means it, which he doesn't. The only person Trent credits for his accomplishments is himself. His eyes meet mine. I want to look away. I haven't managed to when he says, "I'm nothing without you."

Why can't Trent simply fade into ex- fiancé obscurity? The more I say I'm done with him, the more he objects. The moment I think I've forgotten him for good, he bullies himself back into my thoughts. I'm tired of the merry-go-round that is our relationship. I just want it to be over.

I'd go home, but I can't leave without Cashmere—we rode together— and I left my things at her apartment. She excused herself a little while ago, and I haven't seen her since. My clothes I'm okay with collecting later, my phone I need.

Trent takes his seat while Scott remains standing. "Thank you all again for being here," he says. "Enjoy the rest of the night, and Deejay," Scott looks to the deejay table, "play something we can dance to."

"May I have this dance?"

I didn't notice Aiden approaching. I thought he was still on the dance floor. At the rate he, Zack, and Corey are going, between the three of them, they'll have danced with every woman here by the end of the night.

"What's the matter," I reply, "run out of women to turn you down?"

He puts his hand over his wounded heart, pouting. "I want to dance with the most beautiful girl here, and you too." Laughing, Aiden hops backward to avoid a kick to the shin. "Come on, Leahz, you owe me a dance. It's time to pay up. Let's go."

Before I know it, Aiden's got me out of my seat headed to the dance floor. I protest the whole way. "These shoes aren't really made for dancing. They're made to be admired."

Aiden spins around, his gaze on my shoes. He pushes the damp hair off his forehead and grins. "Okay, shoes," he says, eyes never leaving my feet. "I like your sparkly quality." To me, he says, "How's that for admiration?"

"It's a start." I laugh.

I figured someone so determined to dance would actually be good at it, not Aiden. He's terrible. Luckily he laughs easily, especially when it's at himself. When the song's over, I'm corralled into dancing with Zack, who's only slightly better. Slightly.

"No. Just stop it," I shout at Zack over the music. "It's like this. You see. A nice two-step." Zack tries and fails miserably to stay on the beat.

"One. Two. One. Two." He does slightly better with me coaching him through the song.

"No man, it's like this," Corey says, doing a crazy bop.

"What in the world is that supposed to be?" I ask.

"It's the latest dance craze. I learned it on TikTok."

"Dude, you're totally doing it wrong. It's like this," Aiden says, doing an even worse interpretation than Corey.

"What are they doing?" Cashmere asks, watching Zack, Corey, and Aiden with a bemused expression.

"Dancing. I think. Where did you get off to?"

"I was mingling," Cashmere says.

"Come on," Aiden says, grabbing Cashmere and me both. He drags us to Zack and Corey. Together we butcher the latest line dance. I laugh and dance until I forget I want to leave.

"I'm gonna grab a seat," I say to Cashmere.

"Are you okay?" she asks over the music.

I nod. "Girl, you know how it is when you're on hour four of your two-hour shoes."

"Ouch. I know that pain too, too well."

"Come find me when you're ready to go." Cashmere nods and goes back to dancing.

The dance floor's crowded with couples having a good time. I'm jostled left and right by dancers.

"Sorry. My bad," I say to the person I bumped into.

"Don't be. I'm not," the person responds.

My mouth falls open. Why is he always exactly where I am? I don't have the energy to deal with Trent right now. I turn around and try to walk back the way I came but find my way blocked.

"Get out of my way," I yell over the music. After our last meeting, I thought we could be civil, that we'd finally reached an understanding. I was wrong. Trent doesn't respect my decision to not be in a relationship with him anymore, and I'm tired of explaining it to him.

"Ouch. Are you trying to make me cry?"

"You? Cry? Yeah, right."

"What, you think I don't cry or hurt? I'm not a sociopath. I feel."

His voice is too smooth and his face too controlled for me to believe him. Less angry, I say, "Why are you making this more difficult than it needs to be? We've done this already. We know how it ends in betrayal. Please, just leave me alone."

"I can't. I need you, L, the way I need air."

I make the mistake of looking at him—really looking at him—and *wham,* I'm pierced in the heart with longing. I clutch my stomach so I won't double over with it. The space between us closes emotionally first, then physically. Somehow my arms end up around him and his around me as we sway to the music.

"I had a dream about you last night," he says.

I nestle closer to him, settling into the familiarity of him. "What did you dream?"

"We were at my loft the night before filming began. I watched you sleeping peacefully, positive I would love you every day I live."

As forcefully as I was overcome with longing for him is as forcefully as I'm smacked with the truth. I never had peace with Trent. I spent my days convincing myself I was doing the right thing and my nights waking up out of one nightmare to fall into another. I jerk away from Trent, resolved to bulldoze through him if need be.

"Excuse me," I say, "and before you refuse, know this: If you don't move, I'll make an Oscar-worthy scene."

"LA." My head turns quickly enough to cause me whiplash. Only one person calls me LA, the one person I wanted most to see tonight. Brice, beautiful and right on time, parts the crowd with his stature and determined stride. He reaches me in no time and pulls me into a tight hug. I'm so happy to see him I can hardly stop the words from tumbling out of my mouth.

"What are you doing here? I thought you weren't coming."

"I came to see you." He intertwines our fingers and leads me around Trent like he isn't even here.

"The casting directors need your answer, L," Trent says as we walk past him.

Neither Brice nor I respond. We keep walking until Trent is swallowed by the sea of people.

I thought Brice was leading me off the dance floor. Instead, we end up in a less crowded corner where we dance slow. We've never been this close to each other without the motivation of fear. In the cast house, when I couldn't face another nightmare, I'd find peace with him. It wasn't romantic, not at all. It was comfortable and safe. Since we've reconnected and our relationship transitioned to a gray area, Brice has been careful not to get too close, but tonight is different. He holds me as tightly as he can, the way you hold on to something you're going to have to let go.

"What's wrong?"

He shakes his head. "Nothing."

It would be easy to choose to believe him, let whatever it is pass, except deep down inside, I know it won't. I pull away, enough to look into his troubled eyes, devoid of their usual luster.

"You've always kept it real with me. Don't change it up now. Tell me what's wrong."

"Okay," he says with a half-grin I don't believe.

I know what his happy smile looks like. This isn't it. I regret it. I regret asking him what's wrong. I don't want to know. Whatever it is, I don't want to know. I press my head against his chest and start moving to the music again, forcing him to do the same.

"Tell me later," I plead.

"Leah."

"Tell me later," I shout, tightening my hold around his neck. If I hold on, everything will be okay. Brice holds me back, but he doesn't stop speaking.

"Maybe what I told your mom was wrong. Maybe if we hadn't both ended up on *Star Quality,* we wouldn't have met. You would have lived your life, and I would have lived mine. I don't know anymore. I know that if I hadn't come tonight, I would have regretted not seeing how beautiful you are."

My mind tries to reconcile what Brice is saying with how it makes me feel. My arms fall from around his neck. They're too heavy to hold up any longer. "Why does it feel like you're saying goodbye?"

He doesn't say anything, and I'm too afraid of the answer to repeat the question or insist he respond.

When I think it's safe—that neither one of us wants to continue our current course—Brice says, "I'm going to ask you to do something."

With a careful finger, he traces the S-patterned wave of my hair. I look up into his eyes, wondering how someone so cautious with my heart could cause it this much pain.

"The last time I was this afraid, life as I knew it, ended," he says softly.

"Then don't ask," I reason. "We can just forget about whatever you were going to say."

"I don't think I can do that, LA."

"Yes, you can," I half shout. He hugs me, a wasted attempt at consolation. How can I be consoled when I know the death blow's coming?

"Look at me, LA." I refuse. "Leah." Gently he forces my eyes to meet his. "I once asked you to pick between him and me. When you didn't get married, I thought you had, but you're as undecided today as you were then."

"I'm not undecided," I interject. "I've decided."

"By default," he says. "I can't be your backup, LA, and you can't have us both. I won't tell you who to choose. I won't even tell you how much I want it to be me *or* how much I—" He hesitates, then stops altogether. "I can't do what we're doing, with you one foot in and the other foot out the door. You have to choose."

"There's nothing to decide. I'm here with you, dancing with you, having this insane argument with you, not Trent."

"So what was he talking about, LA? What casting directors?" I open and shut my mouth, regretting my decision to not tell Brice the truth when I had the chance. "Here's an easier question for you: Do you still want to be with him?"

We're not dancing anymore or holding on to each other. Every second that passes without an answer, Brice slips farther away from me. I take his face in my hands, forcing him to see how much I don't want to lose him.

"I've been waiting for you all night. I got dressed with you in mind, not Trent." I speak calmly despite the urgency I feel. We're getting odd looks from the partygoers nearby.

"But you were with him when I got here," Brice says, pulling free of my grip. "I don't know if it's love, infatuation, or a sense of obligation. Whatever it is, you're not done with him yet. Maybe you'll never be."

Panicked anger rises in me. I lose all cool. "How can you tell me how I feel?" I ask too loudly. The couple dancing next to us stops and stares. I recognize the guy as someone I met earlier, although his name escapes me. He looks at me curiously, probably trying to decide if I'm drunk and having a moment. I'm about to play the angry drunk girl with him until I feel myself being pulled away.

I let Brice lead me away because I'm burning mad, and I don't want any witnesses to what happens next.

Chapter 20

Forgiveness

We take the stairs because most people won't, especially not in their finery. Brice leads me a few flights down. When we stop on the small, narrow landing, I yank my hand out of his.

"We're alone now. Are you ready to tell me how you can dictate to me how I feel?"

"Fine. I won't tell you. You tell me," he says.

"I–I–" I can't say what I know I should. I can't tell Brice I'm over Trent.

The light goes out of him. Somehow, he seems less than what he was a second ago, less sure, less tall, less vibrant. I've crushed him. Despite his insistence, part of him hoped he was wrong and is devastated he isn't.

"What about you? Are you over Seriyah?" Bringing her up is cruel, but it's the only way to make him understand the pull an ex can still have over you.

"It's not the same thing. Seriyah's gone. And when she was alive, she never gave me cause to doubt her."

"You doubt me?"

He turns away from me, backing all the way into the recess of the landing. Brice would rather his elegant tuxedo jacket brush up against the wall of a dusty old stairwell than stand close to me.

"I doubt," he answers, "I'm who you want." His voice is small and tired. "I'm sorry if it felt like I was comparing you to Seriyah. I wasn't. What I was trying to say is how I feel about you is unique to you."

"And what I feel for you is unique to you. It has nothing to do with Trent, so why can't we move forward?"

"Because," Brice says, "what I felt for Seriyah is not in competition with what I feel for you. Your heart, on the other hand, is conflicted." I look away but don't deny it. "It's okay, LA, I'm not mad."

He looks at me across the tight space, and something shifts. Brice isn't angry or sad. He's done. He walks over to me and places a feather-soft kiss on my forehead, then I'm listening to his footsteps retreat. It's over before it ever began.

I surprise myself by making it back to the party. I hardly know how I do. I vaguely remember ending up in the lobby trying to leave. A security guard asks if I didn't want to get my coat first. He smiles and points me toward the elevator bank. I'm too numb to do anything more than follow instructions. I follow a kid with a dead flower on his tee shirt into the elevator and end up back at *Star Quality* event ballroom

I'm bumped side to side by people having a good time. They say things to me, compliment my dress, ask me to dance, announce their surprise that I didn't win. I hear it all detachedly. Perhaps I respond though I don't think I do. I have one goal: Find Cashmere so I can leave. I regret not asking her to go when I had the chance. I would've been home by now, and everything would still be okay.

I can't find her, and everything's beginning to blur. The music's too loud. I can't breathe. Belatedly I realize I'm panicking. It's been months since I had a panic attack. I can't remember what to do, making me more anxious.

Someone's here—Brice. He came back for me. He's by my side, holding me up, asking if I'm alright, and leading me to the restroom.

I stumble into the restroom, on to a couch in the sitting area. On the rose circular plush couch sits two women. One's on her phone and the other with her head in her hands. I plop down, not being careful of how. I sit, desperate to be seated. I lean my head against the back of the couch, and close my eyes. Soon, I feel a little better.

Now that I'm of a clearer mind, I feel everything I was too numb to before. I let Brice go. Why did I let Brice go? I hate myself for the part of me that can't wholly write Trent off, that tiny, minuscule part of me that couldn't choose Brice. I replay the conversation repeatedly and see it happen differently in my mind's eye time and time again.

I should have told him how much he inspires me, that his fervent faith has challenged mine to grow. I should have told him how safe he makes me feel. I should have told him that even though it frustrates me most of the time, I love that he's slowly courting me, taking the time to love properly absent of lust. I should have told him I've never valued a friendship as much as I value his. I should have told him not to go because it would break my heart. I will tell him because he came back for me.

I exit the restroom feeling shaky on my feet though excited to see Brice, but he's not here. Trent is, though. For the first time ever, his face offends me.

"Ugh," I say, unable to contain my disdain.

Somewhere deep down inside, I know it's me I'm disgusted with, not him. That knowledge doesn't extinguish the rage kindling in me against him for being here and Brice because he's not. It only further upsets me when Trent—with a gentleness I forgot he's capable of—asks if I'm feeling better.

"What's it to you?" I push past him and his extended hand, slowly and unsteadily walking back to the ballroom where Brice is probably waiting for me. I'd rather crawl than let Trent help me.

"I can't believe you would ask me that. I'm the one that saw you wobbling around, looking seconds away from colliding with the floor. I waited for dude to swoop in, and when I realized he wasn't coming to your aide, which is ironic because he always seemed to be glued to your side when we were together. I got you to the bathroom, then I waited out here forever for you to come out, just to make sure you're okay."

"What? You helped me? Why?" I thought it was Brice. I thought he came back for me.

He lets out an exasperated breath. "Because you mean everything to me, L. You should know that by now."

"Well, allow me to mean less, then maybe I might have a chance at a healthy relationship." I go off like a grenade, not caring who hears or sees us.

Trent's eyes narrow the way they do when he's piecing something together.

"Where is he? Where's Brice?"

"Gone."

It takes saying it aloud for it to sink in. Brice isn't in the ballroom waiting for me. He's gone. "G–O–N–E," I shout. "Gone, and it's all your fault."

"How's it my fault?"

"How…How is it your fault? Are you kidding me? Every time you come around, you ruin my life. You refuse to leave me alone. Why couldn't you stay on your side of the room? Why did you have to talk to me? Why won't you just let me be?"

"Because I'm still in love with you," he screams. "I love you enough to fight for you. What about him? He leaves you alone and unwell. That's the guy you chose over me?" he says, sneering. "Are you serious?"

My chest heaves with anger because he's right. Brice left me.

"L, I'm sorry. I really am. Can't you see that?"

I don't know what I see when I look at him. He's beautiful, but it masks deep darkness. I'm afraid of him. I'm also drawn to him. I have always been, try as I might to fight it.

"We can start over, do things differently," he pleads.

Trent takes my hand and brings it to his chest, over his heart, exactly like he did last time we met. I don't pull away though I usually would. What's the point? I quit the show, left him, and got nothing out of it. I'm back at square one, so why not be with Trent?

"We can still have everything we wanted, except this time around, I won't hurt you. I promise."

My head's spinning. I can't think straight. How can I with Trent so close?

I try to put some distance between us by stepping away, but he clenches my hand. I don't know if I should be holding on or letting go.

"What's it going to be?" he asks.

"Time," I say. "I need time."

I wake up in an unfamiliar bed in a strange room, dazed and confused. I close my eyes, forcing myself to focus and recount what I remember. Everything comes back: Brice, Trent, being too distraught to go home. Cashmere suggesting I stay the night in her guest room and readily accepting.

Sunlight streams in through the windows across the white coverlet. My hands curl around a small patch of light warming my cold fingers, though it does nothing for the cold numbness in my heart. I stay that way until Cashmere appears at the door with a steaming cup of coffee. Without an invitation to come in, she crosses to the bed in her fuchsia robe and sits at the foot, feet curled up underneath her. She hands me the larger of the two mugs she carries. I'm not thirsty. I'm not anything actually, though I take it, if only for something to focus on.

"So," she says, "feel like talking about it yet?"

I shrug. I don't really feel like talking. I just want to sit, so we do, until I break the silence with a question.

"Do you think people can change? Not their taste in music or something else equally trivial. I mean change deep down—change their inclinations, their nature?"

She doesn't answer immediately. She sips at her coffee, taking her time, coming to a decision. Finally, she says, "I do. Though not without a deep desire for change and actively working on it. But," she pauses, "if you're thinking about whether or not a specific person—maybe Trent—can change, my answer is no. I don't believe he can change his nature, not because he's incapable, because he's unwilling."

I wasn't thinking about Trent—well, I was, but the question was about me, not him. All these months, I've tried to be someone different, better than the girl who made all those stupid decisions because of a guy and ambition. I wonder if that better person exists. If she does, that's who belongs with Brice. This girl—selfish, single-minded, impetuous—she's better suited for Trent.

"I don't know exactly what's going on with you right now," Cashmere continues, "although I think I'm correct in guessing that you're caught in between two people. You have no idea who to choose, right?"

I nod though the two people I'm caught in between aren't Trent and Brice. I'm caught between who I am and who I want to be.

"Earlier, when I said people could change, I was thinking about myself." She clears her throat. "I spent the first part of my life as a neglected child, the next couple of years living out the consequences of never knowing love, and the last two years as a celebrated social media star. Throughout all the changes in my circumstances, I personally have not changed. I've been an abused, neglected, insecure girl all my life—childhood to adulthood. I've just been packaged differently. The day... " She falters then begins again. "The day . . ." She falters then begins again. "The day I tried to...to . . ."

"Cash, It's okay. I know what you're talking about." The day she tried to take her own life, that's what she means. Cashmere nods, looking relieved she doesn't have to say the words aloud again.

"That day, I realized I couldn't go on living like I was. I needed to change, and I finally understood how to do that. Jesus saved my life, not for me to go on like I was. I was meant to live a different life than the one that almost killed me."

A single tear falls from her eye onto the bedspread. She doesn't look sad though. She seems determined.

"It's hard, Leah. It's so hard trying to change and let go of what was for what can be. With the right support system—people who encourage your growth—I pray, have faith, believe that I'll be so different one day, I won't recognize the old me. That's my advice to you. Choose the person who helps make you better and encourages your growth. Life is too short to spend it with someone who helps you self-destruct."

"I'm having trouble with this scene. Daniel and I have tried it a dozen ways, but it always comes out flat."

"I'm sure it's fine. You're doing a great job with it," I say. Ella brushes off my reassurances that it can't be as bad as she thinks maintaining it is.

"Brother Young admitted it was falling short," Ella says. "This is the most important scene of the play. If we don't get this right, the audience won't understand John's love for Avani or the complexities of their relationship."

Ella's melodramatic explanation does what Cashmere was unable to, make me smile. I'm proud of how far she and I have come. Ella wasn't a fan of mine when we first met, now I'm someone whose advice she values. Only her desperate text messages coming in every thirty seconds could have cajoled me into being in the same room as Brice this soon.

His surprise at seeing me was all over his face. He waved but has kept his distance since. Thus far, we've been able to stay at opposite ends of the church. I work with the leads; Brice with the lighting crew. It's weird how I do and don't want to be around him at the same time. I'm furious with Brice though seeing him is the only thing that's eased the weight in my chest. I don't ever want to hear his name again, but every time I do, hope springs up in me that he'll say he's sorry and take back everything he said last night. I stop myself from scanning the room for him and focus on Ella and Daniel.

"Let me walk you through what's happening in this scene, explain it to you. That should help."

"Brother Young did that already. It didn't help. We were hoping," Ella says, gesturing to Daniel, who has let her do all the talking thus far, "that you could show us. like you did during auditions. You and Brother Young."

Working with Brice is absolutely out of the question. I can't look him in the eye. How would I do a whole scene with him?

"Please, Leah." I haven't said no yet, and she's already begging. "I really need your help and…" She looks over at Brice. "He's already said he'd do it."

"Did he really?" I ask.

"Yeah, he did. Did you think he would say no?" Ella says.

Ella and Daniel both look at me like I'm a complete idiot, which I am for having this conversation with a pair of seventeen-year-olds. I'm a bigger idiot for doubting that Brice would do anything for these kids, even work with me.

"Why you keep coming 'round here?" I slur as a drunk Avani wobbling around the pulpit, doubling as our set. It's dressed in a starry night backdrop with two porch chairs. The scene takes place late in the evening on Avani's veranda.

"What do you want from me?" I ask Brice, playing the role of John, the boy Avani left behind when she skipped town.

"Nothing," he says softly. "I don't want a thing from you, except for you to be okay."

I tighten my grip on the neck of my prop beer bottle, bring it to my lips, and take a swig.

"Oh yeah? Be okay with you, I suppose? Right?" I stumble closer to him while maintaining my grip on the bottle. "Well, let me tell you something. I've been places and done things your little green ears can't handle hearing. The sweet, innocent girl you knew before I left this here town is gone," I say, sneering, "so stop coming 'round here."

I throw the plastic bottle at him. He ducks. The bottle smacks against the carpeted pulpit/porch floor and rolls down the stairs into the grass/congregation.

Rage I've never seen in Brice flashes in his eyes. "Why are you doing this to yourself?" he thunders.

"What am I doing? Huh?" I slap the palms of my hands against my chest. "What? You don't like this version of me?" I mockingly ask. "Well—" I shrug—"I don't much care for it myself, although you might have liked me better two drinks ago." I stumble away from him. He follows hot on my heels.

"If you don't like yourself, change." He's less angry, more pitying.

"You think it's that easy?"

"Yes, I do. You changed into a haunted shell of who you once were, so you can change back."

Brice kicks the legs out from one of the porch chairs and topples it over. I want to scream but Avani, she laughs sinisterly at the love John has for her that sends him into a rage at the sight of what she's become. I walk over to the cooler beside the fallen chair, making me inches away from Brice. I pull out another plastic prop beer bottle. "Want one?" I taunt.

What happened to you?" John looks at Avani with such disgust, it's hard to fathom he ever loved her. I try to walk away, but he catches me by the wrist, forcing me to stay. "Tell me," he yells, "what happened to you out there?"

"Life," I yell back. I pull out of his grasp but stay where I stand. "There's more out there in the world. I've seen it, lived it, but it's a lie. At the end of the yellow brick road is regret, so I came back home to the same ole house with the peeling paint, the same ole church, and the same ole boy I would have married if I hadn't left. You're all here, exactly the way I left you, perfectly content. I'm trying to be the old me, too, but I can't. I can't. I've tried to go back out there." I fling out my hand, indicating life beyond the spot we're standing in. "Who I was out there, that isn't me either," I say, sinking to the ground, "so here I am, stuck in the middle, unable to go back, unknowing how to move forward."

Hot, thick tears come down my face, fast and steady. My vision blurs. I can't see, but I hear Brice walking toward me—John running to Avani. He sinks to the ground next to me. Shakily, his arm goes around my shoulder. In his embrace, my tears turn into sobs. When they slow, he pulls back to look into my tear-stained face. We look into each other's eyes for the first time since last night. I'm unsure if the pain I see belongs to Brice or John.

"Give it to Jesus, then let it go. That's the way forward." Through ragged breaths, I ask how.

"Surrender to Jesus. Whatever it is you're searching for, it can't satisfy like Jesus can. Tell Him how much you need Him, that you can't make it without Him. Make Him the Lord of your life and rest easy in His peace."

"Do you think God listens to people like me?" I ask with all the innocence of a child.

"I'm positive He does. I'm living proof of it. Jesus bore death on the cross for the sick, not the healthy, for the people like us who know they need Him. Don't be afraid."

"Of what?" I ask.

"Forgiveness."

Chapter 21

One Hundred Minus One

I regret not having had Brice as a scene partner during the competition. He's good. There were times he was too good, too believable. Was that John's eyes glistening with unshed tears or Brice's? Does he see me the way John sees Avani? Did I inspire her?

Brice and I spend the rest of rehearsal working on the scene with Ella and Daniel without interacting with each other. One of us makes a suggestion that the other agrees with, all while avoiding direct conversation. We're both obviously feeling weird about last night then doing such an emotional scene together. We go on dodging each other until the end of rehearsal.

Standing in a circle, hands joined, heads bowed, Brice says, "Leah, would you lead us in prayer?"

My stomach plummets to my feet; my mind blanks, I don't know what to say. *God, please help me talk to you* then, from a place within me I didn't know was paying attention, prayer bursts forth.

"Holy, Holy, Holy. Three times Holy. Father in heaven, to You, we come in adoration and praise. I thank You for allowing me, the least deserving, to speak Your hallowed name. I thank You, God, that You so loved the world that You sent Your one and only Son, that whoever believes in Him shall not perish but have eternal life. Thank You, Lord, for forgiveness and redemption. Thank You, Lord, for second chances. Help us today and every day to live redeemed and forgiven. I pray to You, Lord, not by merit or because of virtue, but humbly in the precious name of Jesus Christ, our Savior. Amen."

My Uber home is thankfully quiet. I'm in no mood for conversation. What I need is space to think, to work out the nagging thought in the back of my mind fighting its way forward. When I'm very still, I can almost discern a faint whisper urgently rousing me toward something. I'd be ready to act if only I knew what to act on. I spend the night praying harder than I ever have before. I ask God to grow the whisper into a shout so I can hear Him.

I wake up late and disturbed. I must've dozed off a dozen or so times last night to wake up shortly afterward until falling into a weird dream. I was in Trent's brownstone. He was stooped in front of a closet on the second floor I didn't know existed. He pulled out clothes—mine, I think—and throws them into black trash bags. I could see him though he couldn't see me. On the verge of saying something to him, a beautiful dark-skinned woman dressed in a striking white dress stopped me. She spoke in a language I couldn't speak but understood.

"Follow me," she said.

I had a choice either way. I could stay with Trent or go with her. it was entirely up to me. I listened to my instincts and left Trent behind. She led me into a bedroom—a walk-in closet, really. Row upon row of dresses, blouses, and skirts of vibrant colors, varying patterns, and rich fabrics hung neatly in the bright, spacious room. It was impressive on its own, moreso considering the state of the clothes I just saw Trent stuffing into bags.

"Change your clothes. Put on whatever you like," she said. I opted for a white sundress almost identical to hers. I put back on the pale lime green and sequined cardigan I was wearing when I walked in over it.

Wordlessly, she led me out of the house onto the street. We walked around a familiar Brooklyn neighborhood, not Trent's though equally affluent. The woman said something to me I'm having trouble remembering now. I don't recall my response either. We went on for a while in a conversation that's vanished from memory except for the last part.

"If you've moved forward, why are you holding on to a piece of what was?" she asked.

"I have moved on," I protested. "No part of me is holding on to the past."

She turned her discerning, permeating eyes on me. "Then why throw off the old clothes in favor of new, only to again cover yourself with an old worn garment?"

I looked down at myself, at my sweater. It was sparkly and brand new when I put it on—at least I thought it was. Just then, it's ratty with holes and torn almost completely away at the hem. I woke up before I could take it off or respond.

I'd love to put it out of my mind, but I've had enough experience with dreams to know sometimes a dream is just that. Other times, it means something. This dream is meaningful. Outside of wanting to clean out my closet, I'm struggling to make sense of it. Maybe I'll dream about it again tonight and wake up with more clarity. For now, there's somewhere I have to be.

"Suppose one of you has a hundred sheep and loses one of them. Does he not leave the ninety-nine in the open country and go after the lost sheep until he finds it? And when he finds it, he joyfully puts it on his shoulders and goes home. Then he calls his friends and neighbors together and says, 'rejoice with me; I have found my lost sheep.'"

Pastor Charles looks up from his Bible. For a long time, he looks out at the congregation. I've stood on that pulpit for rehearsal. I personally know

271

it's possible to clearly discern every face from where he stands. That isn't exactly comforting. Right about now, I'd gladly take the anonymity of a megachurch.

"Sheep," he begins, "have very poor depth perception. They cannot see in front of their noses. For that reason, they are led by shepherds. The shepherd takes care of the sheep, leading the flock to graze in green pastures and driving them to a safe place to rest. It is also the shepherd's job to protect the sheep. If one loses its way, the shepherd searches for it until finding the sheep. When he does, the shepherd carries it back to safety on his shoulders."

"Amen," is heard all around the congregation.

"Like sheep, we don't always see well and may wander off the path, but we also have a shepherd—the Good Shepherd, Christ Jesus, He is merciful to seek and recover us."

With tears in her eyes, the woman beside me lifts her hands in praise of Jesus. Is she a sheep gone astray or recovered? I wonder, then I think, *What am I?*

"Little children," Pastor Charles calls, "I submit to you that you are not too far gone to be rescued by Christ. The nature of sin is to separate man from God and His love. The more we sin, the more tempted we are to hide from the Lord. The farther away you go from God, the more difficult it becomes for you to turn back, but glory be to God. The Good Shepherd will leave the ninety-nine sheep gathered to Him in security to seek out the one lost." Pastor Charles pauses and looks at each of us.

"The lost sheep," he says, "is a metaphor for our fallen state and a parable of Christ's grace and love. Jesus is our hero, our Savior, who came and saved all of humanity that had gone astray. Christ sought us all the way to the cross and carried us to safety with the sacrifice of His body. Now all who come to the Father through faith in the Son have forgiveness of sins. They gain liberty from their old self and past mistakes, newness of life, wholeness, healing, hope, a future, and a blessed assurance." My shoulders shake as tears flow from my eyes.

"You who have sinned, who have fallen short, whatever it is that you have done, whomever you have been, Christ has atoned for you."

"Thank You, Jesus," someone whispers from the row in front of me.

"What Jesus did on the cross was for once and for all. For all people in all times. Christ stood in our place, accepting the judgment that was rightfully ours. Christ paid the debt we couldn't, carried the burden too heavy, and set us free to be His. You may have left the flock and gone away, but Jesus has not given up on retrieving you. Turn with me to Proverbs twenty-four, verse sixteen."

When the sound of pages turning stops, he reads, *"For though the righteous fall seven times, they rise again.'* Falling isn't righteous; getting back up is. Only the righteous discerns that they need not remain fallen. Stop waffling, believing there is no hope for you. Jesus Christ has defeated your sins on the cross. Run to the Savior and receive healing for your soul." Pastor Charles walks out from behind the pulpit to stand in front of us.

"*'I tell you that in the same way there will be more rejoicing in heaven over one sinner who repents than over ninety-nine righteous persons who do not need to repent.'*" He continues reading from Luke chapter fifteen, verse seven.

"My message to you today is this: Throw off the weighty sin that easily encumbers. Repent and receive the grace of God by faith in Jesus Christ. God sent His only begotten Son to seek the one in one hundred, the one who has gone astray. Relinquish whatever it is that holds you back. Choose life, and allow the Lord to put you over His shoulders and carry you to the safety of His pasture."

I bite my lip, trying hard to stem the sobs rising up in me.

"I invite anyone who has not yet accepted Christ as their Savior to come up for prayer." He turns to the left and right, looking for those who would approach the altar. No one does.

"Perhaps you're a wayward sheep who's left the flock. You want to come back but don't know how. Don't remain lost. Grace is available for you too.

Come back to your Father, confess your sins, ask His forgiveness, and be welcomed home as His returned child."

Pastor Charles stands at the pulpit detailing what it means to have new life in Jesus at the same time as the congregation, led by Sister Carol, sings "Amazing Grace." The thing I felt the first time I visited, the power of the Holy Spirit, I feel it again, as well as clarity of mind. I understand my dream now. It's not enough that I quit the show and ended my engagement to Trent. Yes, God wanted me to do those things because they took me farther away from Him. What God wants most is a commitment from me, a relationship—not a fickle connection dependent on how things are going in my life.

Since I've been home, I've put on a new dress while still wearing the old battered sweater. New wine cannot be poured into an old wineskin. My new desire to live a life more attuned to God cannot prevail alongside my old self with its old habits, desires, and people. I've prayed for new life. God wants to give it to me, but I can't half step. I have to make a decision to either follow Christ or myself. I can't serve two masters at the same time.

My life flashes before my eyes. In the time it takes to walk to the altar, I experience every moment of my life again, and it comes up wanting. I watch the mistakes and feel the pains borne of them, wanting nothing more than to be whole again, released from the past, restored, and forgiven.

Eyes shut tight, I kneel before Pastor Charles. I've never done this before—confessed aloud Jesus Christ as my Lord. I sat in church every week without having personal conviction. What little I did to honor God was out of habit, not relationship. That's about to change though. Whatever comes next for me begins with this moment.

"Young lady," Pastor Charles says in a voice intended only for me, "do you know what you're doing?"

"Yes," I say, opening my eyes. "I'm surrendering my life completely and wholly to Jesus."

"It is indeed a surrender," he replies. "The giving up of your old self along with its baggage. Yield yourself to Jesus—mistakes, hurts, insecurities, scars, addictions, wrong ideas—and become a new creation in Him. Redeemed not by corruptible things like money, rather purchased with the blood of Jesus. You are made brand new, and in Him, you have forgiveness of sins and hope. This doesn't mean your life will be perfect," he says with a meaningful look. "You will face obstacles and have difficulties, but as a child of the Lord, you are the recipient of a blessed assurance. Do you understand?"

"Yes."

"Then let us pray."

I close my eyes and bow my head.

"Lord, we bring these young souls to You in rejoicing. For Your Word tells us there is much rejoicing in heaven when a sinner is repented. From this day onward, Lord, please allow them to carry the name of Jesus in their walking, talking, and existing. Please, Lord, help them to believe in the power of the blood of Jesus that sets them totally free from the power of sin and death and classifies them as your own."

My tears flow unchecked as I think about the freedom I'm receiving in Jesus.

"Lead them, Lord, in their walk with You, though it won't always be easy."

"Yes, Lord," someone says.

"Help them not to depart from the good way. They knelt before You, Lord, as sinners but please, Lord, permit them to rise as servants in Your kingdom, never to be parted from You again. Create a new heart in them belonging to the new man, the one crucified with Christ and surrendered to Him. We thank You, Lord, for drawing them near to You and Your salvation. We ask You to please hold their hands and lead them through life, from now to forevermore. We pray humbly in the name of Jesus Christ, our Savior, the Crucified and Resurrected One. Amen."

I feel like a newborn seeing my parents and the world for the first time. I may not be able to physically see God, but I feel Him. A work has, without question, been done in me. I feel brand new.

Sister Carol is the first congregation member to welcome me into the body of Christ with a tight hug. She looks at me with those knowing eyes and says, "I knew you would come to this decision. The Holy Spirit showed me how much your spirit yearned for closeness with the Lord. I thank God for His grace." I try to wipe away my tears, but she catches my hands. "No," she says. "Let them fall. Those are tears of joy. Let them glorify the Lord."

She's right. I'm not sad. I'm happy—happier than I can remember being. I rest my head on her shoulder, although she's at least three inches shorter than me, and let the tears do their work. When they stop coming, Sister Carol smiles at me.

"God's been waiting for you," she says. "Now go greet your sister in Christ."

I turn around and am stunned. "Cashmere," I ask. I can't believe my eyes. Without question, we greet each other in Christ with an abundance of joy at the decision we've both been coming to for a while.

"Leah," she says, smiling radiantly. "Do you feel it?"

I nod. "Do you mean the lightness of spirit?" She nods, still beaming. "I think...I think that feeling is freedom."

Member after member congratulates us on our homecoming, including Brice. I'm sincerely taken aback when I see him. For a moment, I forgot he was a congregant.

"This doesn't surprise me one bit," he says, beaming.

Whatever weirdness there was between us is gone. He's happy to see me finally choose—and wisely. We don't talk much. It's not the right place or time, but I suspect we will eventually.

Chapter 22

The Play's the Thing

"You look different."

Scooping a forkful of rice and beans onto my fork, I say, "Really? How so?"

I didn't tell my mom what happened at church today when I got home, hoping this very thing would happen, that she would discern the difference in me.

"You look...lighter. Peaceful."

"You know what, Mom, I wouldn't have used that word, but it is completely apropos."

"My goodness." She lets her fork clatter to her plate. "Please tell me you didn't go out and do something crazy. It's not another reality show, is it?"

I laugh at the horror on her face. "No. I didn't do anything crazy. That I didn't do it before is crazy."

"What did you do?" she asks with a raised brow.

"I gave my life to Christ."

"Hallelujah. Thank You, Lord. Thank You, Jesus, for answering my prayers." Her hands are raised to God in praise. "Thank You for reconciling my daughter—Your daughter—to Yourself."

I praise God along with my mom for His faithfulness. If it weren't for His patience and constantly seeking me, things would have worked out differently. From my room, I hear my phone ringing. I ignore it and continue thanking God for never giving up on me, although I've given up on Him more times than I can count.

With tears in her eyes, my mom hugs me. "I'm proud of you, prouder than anything else you will do could ever make me. Today we are not only mother and daughter, we're sisters."

I would not have thought of myself as being on an equal footing with my mother; however, that's exactly what she means. Jesus Christ is the great equalizer. Man or woman, rich or poor, educated or not, parent or child, we are all sinners saved by grace. I lift my hands in praise to God that the revelation of His salvation is available to all.

"Hey."

Brice looks up and quickly locates me standing in the doorway to the sanctuary. I hate breaking his concentration, but his intense focus on the notes in his hands is beginning to creep me out.

"Hey yourself," he says, grinning.

We've been talking again, the way we used to—with ease. Outside of my mom and Antonia, he's the first person I told about being cast in the role of Marie. Right when I stopped feeling like I needed it, Leslie called to offer me the part a week ago. It's not so much that I stopped wanting it. It's just that I started wanting God's will more, whatever that might look like. I have to admit I'm over the moon that His will includes the movie. Rehearsal starts in three days, filming in ten, but tonight is all about Brice and the youth who worked hard to put this play together.

"Nervous?" I ask.

"Not exactly—I mean a little. I'm nervous but not about anyone's performance. I'm nervous about the message not coming across. I pray the production glorifies God while resonating with those who need it most."

I walk down the aisle to the front of the church. Brice is sitting on the steps of the pulpit, now dressed to resemble a sanctuary for our opening scene. I sit next to him and lean back with my forearms on the steps behind me.

"Why don't you put your notes away for a bit and relax?" I suggest.

"I'd love to, but there's too much to be done."

"Five minutes won't bring the production to a screeching halt. Plus, the kids aren't here yet. Their call time isn't for another half hour. Just take a minute."

Brice pretends to be inconvenienced but sets his papers down next to him and leans back with me. I put my head on his shoulder.

"*Shhh,*" I say.

"I didn't say anything." He laughs.

"Good. Now be quiet and enjoy the peace." After a moment, I feel the weight of his head leaning against mine. "What time are you picking me up for the party?"

"I didn't think you still wanted to go to that."

"I never stopped wanting to go, but you were right about everything you said that night at the *Star Quality* party." I bow my head, unable to maintain eye contact with him. "I needed to decide." Meeting his eyes again, I say, "And now I have."

"Yeah? What have you decided?"

I put my head back on his shoulder. "I've decided," I say, taking my time, "that we should color coordinate our outfits."

His fingers intertwine mine. "We can color coordinate," he says, "as long as I get to wear a black suit."

Blissfully happy, I say, "We'll talk about it."

"Ninety minutes to curtain, people. Hair, makeup, and wardrobe need to be completed in the next half hour," I announce mostly to myself since no one is paying attention.

They're all too busy getting dressed, running lines, or in Ella's case, furiously texting. Seriously, I wouldn't be surprised at all if she were to get a finger injury, like a sprain or something.

I tap her on her shoulder. "Come on, Ella, you're up."

She says something I don't catch then follows me back to my workstation. Wherever her head is, it isn't on her debut performance. I have my suspicions about the nature of her distraction. Regardless of how much she's grown to trust me, she's still a seventeen-, almost eighteen-year-old girl. Nothing will drive her into the arms of the wrong boy faster than objections from her family—in our case, her mentor—so I keep my concerns to myself.

It's a madhouse in here. Downstairs in the smaller meeting room usually used for small group sessions, we've set up hair, makeup, and wardrobe. I touch up hair and makeup. Cashmere, who volunteered to help, does the same. Sister Carol, a seamstress, operates the wardrobe station. Nerves are running high as patience wears thin.

"Ella," I say, with a note of warning in my voice. With my numerous other duties, I can only designate seven minutes tops to each girl. "Would you put the phone down and look at me? You know we're pressed for time."

"Sorry." She puts her phone down on the vanity and turns it over. That lasts about ten seconds, exactly how long it takes for her to receive the next text. I take the phone away from her. She doesn't resist me though she does look put off.

"You'll get this back when I'm done doing your makeup, okay?"

"Okay."

"So, what's new with you?"

She shrugs. "Nothing really. Just nervous about tonight."

"Don't be. You'll do great. You've really come a long way from when we first started rehearsing."

"Thank you," she says with feeling. "I couldn't have done it without you. I know I gave you a hard time at first, but I'm happy we met."

"I'm happy we met too."

"You know what else I'm happy about?"

"What?"

"That you and Brother Young worked out whatever it was you were going through." Ella smiles mischievously at me, looking more like the girl I first met than the one I've gotten to know.

"Don't bother trying to deny it," she says. "I noticed how you two went from looking at each other with stars in your eyes to complete avoidance."

"We did not," I object, barely able to keep a straight face.

"Whatever you say." She grins. "Just don't do anything else to mess it up with Brother Young. He's a great guy."

"Okay." I accept her wisdom and take the opportunity to offer some of my own. "I'll keep that in mind if you consider—and I mean, really consider—my advice to you."

Her confident smile fades in anticipation of what I'm about to say. Ella knows where I'm going, and as I suspected, she doesn't want anyone's advice about him, whoever he is. I give it to her anyway.

"You're young, beautiful, and gifted. A lot of boys will show interest in you. That doesn't mean you have to entertain them." She looks away from me and down at her hands. "Protect your spirit from leeches—people who if you allow them to attach themselves to you, will suck your spirit dry. You may not be thinking about your spiritual life right now... I get it. You want to be carefree and enjoy your youth. That doesn't mean your spirit should be neglected."

I lift her head to meet my eyes. "Ella, take it from someone who had all the wrong priorities in life for a long time. 'Seek first the kingdom of God and His righteousness.' Just because you can doesn't mean you should. Whatever you do now does and will have consequences. What feels good in the moment can bear you a lifetime of pain, so be selective about your friends, stingy with your romantic affections, protective of your body, diligent in your schoolwork, determined about your career, and above all else convicted in your spirit."

I accept her simple nod as proof she's heard my warning. I feel I've gotten through to her when her phone chimes and she doesn't answer it. I'm not sure it'll stick, but I gave her something to consider. I dab her lips with a nudish pink color. "You're all done."

"Thanks, Leah," she says, getting out of the makeup chair.

"Ashley, you're up next."

"Hey, Leah," Daniel says, "Brice sent me to get you. He asked if you could come upstairs."

"Thanks, Daniel. I'll head up there in a second. In the meantime, go ahead and get your costume on." Daniel nods and walks away. "Ashley, I have to head upstairs for a few minutes. I'm going to get Cashmere to work on you, okay?"

"That's fine," she says.

"Cash," I say, approaching her workstation, "do you mind holding down both stations for a while? Brice needs to see me."

"Sure. I'll finish up so you can go rendezvous with your completely gorgeous boyfriend."

I roll my eyes, but I'm laughing too. My relationship with Brice has absolutely graduated from will eventually happen to definitely happening. Brice is a romantic guy; however, I highly doubt his reason for summoning me upstairs is because he misses me. There's simply too much to do.

"Whatever, Cash. I'll be back in a few minutes."

"*Ummm-hmmm,*" she says. "Take your time."

I shake my head at her all the way out the door.

"You know she's only slumming it with you because she's mad at me, right?"

"I can't speak to your situation with Leah, but I can tell you that she's 'slumming it' with me because she wants to be here." I slow my pace realizing I just walked into the most unlikely scene, Trent and Brice verbally sparring in the lobby of Onward Christian Soldier Ministries.

"Yeah, whatever, man. Just know she's leaving with me, bruh."

"If that's what she decides, I won't try to stop her."

"You really think you're better for her than me, don't you?" Trent gets up in Brice's face, but Brice doesn't back down. "You can't do a thing for her. Me, I can give her the world. She'd never want for a thing."

"Leah doesn't need things. If that's what she needed, she would've stayed with you."

"So you think you're tough," Trent asks, getting loud.

"Stop it," I shout.

Trent and Brice both turn in the direction of my voice. They stare, waiting for me to do something, each with their own idea of what it is I should do. Finally, Brice walks toward me and meets me in the middle of the hallway, his face concerned.

"He showed up a couple of minutes ago demanding to see you," he says. "I agreed to get you." He hooks his thumbs through his belt loops. "I guess I'll leave you to it then."

I grab Brice's hand and hold it firmly in my own. Our eyes meet, and without words, much passes between us. He's uncertain about what I'll do but determined to let me do it. I release his hand but hold his gaze. He nods, then turns and walks to the sanctuary, then through its doors. Once he's out of sight, I walk the few remaining steps to Trent.

"What are you doing here?" Maybe I could be kinder in my approach, but to Trent, any hesitation or what he perceives to be weakness on my part is an opening to needle himself through.

"What am I doing here?" he asks. "I came because of you."

"Yes, but how did you know to find me here?"

"I follow you on Instagram," he says, waving his phone at me.

"I didn't post about this on Instagram."

"You were tagged in a post about a play happening here tonight. The flyer said you were co-producing it with Dude," Trent says, referring to Brice. I nod, remembering some of the kids did create a digital flyer for the play and post about it on social media to get people to come out. I didn't notice my name on there as a producer, though.

"Okay. Well, you found me. What can I do for you?"

Silence. He just stares at me. I cross my arms over my chest and stare back at him. I take in his leather bomber jacket, dark denim, and flashy luxe sneakers. Everything about him is eye-catching, but now when he looks at me, I don't swoon, and my heart doesn't patter. What I see is a tattered old sweater I won't put back on.

"Why are you here?" I ask again.

He walks from his side of the hallway to mine. Trent leans up against the wall next to me, purposely trying to disorient me with his nearness. "I'm here," he says in the low, throaty voice he uses when he's trying to be sexy, "to pick you up."

"Pick me up?"

"Yes. You asked for time. I gave you that. Now time's up. I'm not going to be chasing you around New York City, having arguments with clowns like Brice."

"I'm glad we're finally agreed on something. You absolutely will not keep tracking me down. Furthermore, the only reason you're attacking Brice is that you feel threatened by him, and I'm not going anywhere with you."

"What do I have to feel threatened about? I'm wealthy, growing wealthier by the day. What's he got, a chitlin circuit play? I mean, really, L?"

"He has things you can't even begin to understand, let alone value. That's your problem. Your priorities and values are all wrong, which is why we would have never worked."

"So what do you call the months we were together, the days..." He leans into me suggestively, "and the nights?"

I push him away from me. "You're disgusting."

"If I'm so disgusting, why do you still want me?"

"I don't," I say, not backing down, "and you know it. That's why you're upset."

"Six years, L. Six, it took for you to walk back into my life." He takes a step in my direction but keeps a safe distance away from me. "Now, you're just going to leave again? Don't you know how happy I can make you? With me, you'd never have to struggle. You'd have whatever you like whenever."

I listen to him and nearly weep for how without a clue he is. He doesn't realize I'm not the girl he met almost seven years ago and spent the next six years pinning after. I'm not even the girl he knew for a short time while we dated. That girl, she loved him and the things that came with him. She's gone now, and by the grace of God, she's never coming back.

"We're not right for each other," I say, "I'm sorry it took six years for you to discover that. There was a time when I rested my hopes and dreams on you because I was as lost as you are. You were able to give me everything I wanted, but none of what I needed. And that's not your fault. It's mine."

"You know what, L? I'm getting really tired of this mess you're talking. I'm not lost, I know exactly who I am, and I like it. The only thing missing in my life is you. Yeah, I didn't handle my jealousy well. I shouldn't have cheated on you with Beverly or hijacked your chance at winning the competition, but we were good together. The only reason you're spouting all this nonsense now is that you're upset with me."

"This is not about me getting back at you because of Beverly and everything else you did. The truth is I'm not even upset anymore. Those things feel like they happened to another person."

He turns facing the wall, then back. Before he says a word, I know he's lost his patience. He doesn't know what to make of an uncompromising version of me.

"L, you're talking crazy. You're the same beautiful, talented, and hot-tempered girl I fell in love with. Those things aren't still true?" he asks.

"They are. Now let me tell you something you preferred to not notice. I was flailing, discouraged, and out of touch when we met, but I found what I've been looking for. I pray one day you find it too. It's life changing."

"What is it? What did you find?" he asks, raising an eyebrow.

"Grace."

Stumped, he opens his mouth then closes it. There's only one more thing to say. "I'm not going to say bye to you again. I did that already. I'm letting you go. Please do the same for me."

He looks at me for a long time. I can tell he finally sees it. His L is gone. He walks to the double doors and stops. "I did love you, you know."

"Not the way I needed."

Trent shakes his head and walks out without looking back. As I watch him go, a scripture I happened upon a few days ago comes to mind. *I do not consider myself yet to have taken hold of it. But one thing I do: Forgetting what is behind and straining towards what is ahead. I press on toward the goal to win the prize for which God has called me heavenward in Christ Jesus.*

I chose not to go backward, to keep moving forward. I am determined that I will strain ahead and win the prize.

"Are you alright?"

I didn't hear Brice come up behind me. I smile up at his anxious face and nod. He holds out his hand to me. I take it.

"Ready?" Brice asks.

"Ready."

Epilogue

"Wait." Brice tugs on my arm, pulling me back toward the black Suburban Jael, his agent, arranged to chauffeur us to the book launch party.

"Are you okay," I ask.

"Yeah," he says with an easy smile. "I wanted to tell you something now in case I forget to tell you later."

"Yeah," I ask, feeling slightly apprehensive. Brice takes both my hands into his, interlocks our fingers, and stares deeply into my eyes. "Thank you for being my date," Brice says. "Tonight's already one of the best nights of my life."

"It's one of the best nights of my life, too," I say.

Everyone in my life has made this night special in some way or another. One day I'm telling Kelly, the head of wardrobe for the movie, I had a book release party to go to and nothing to wear. The next, she's fitting me for one of her custom designs, a moss green sleeveless one-shoulder gown. I don't think I'll ever wear another dress that isn't a trumpet again.

Vanessa, who's been doing my hair every day for the last ten days, insisted that it should not change, which was fine by me. I love what she's been doing with my hair. Tonight is no exception. She gave me jade extensions reaching the small of my back with a deep part and huge barrel curls she shaped into lush beach waves.

My sister, Antonia, and my mom helped me get dressed. Then Amanda and Cashmere came over. Amanda and Antonia began questioning Brice's intentions toward me the moment he arrived to pick me up. But by the time we were ready to go, he'd won them over.

They were actually warning me not to hurt him. I pretended to feel insulted. In actuality, I was over the moon to have my family and friends know about this great guy, possibly *the* guy, and be in full support of us. I've never had that before. I've made such horrible choices in men that I've had to downplay or outright hide my involvement in past relationships. It's refreshing doing things the right way. I was all smiles as we drove off.

Brice lets go of my hand to wrap his arms around my waist. I drape my arms around his neck, realizing the warm feeling expanding in my chest is happiness. I'm happy.

"You look like a dream," Brice says. "I'm half afraid I'll wake up and find I only dreamt you were here with me taking my breath away."

I duck my head, hoping to hide my blush. Brice always knows the right thing to say. Truthfully, he's the dream.

"You don't look so bad yourself," I reply.

Jael has good taste. She personally picked out and delivered a single-breasted plaid suit to Brice. I was suspicious of her at first, but Jael's actually pretty okay. She's happily engaged and seems genuinely invested in Brice's success. Plus, she respects what he stands for and doesn't try to get him to compromise. Brice couldn't ask for a better agent than her. Neither could I if I agree to it.

Jael's expanding into representing actors as well. She's been trying to get me as a client. As a trial, I let her handle the negotiation of my contract for the movie. She was amazing. Tomorrow I'll tell her I want her to represent me on a more permanent basis. Tonight, Brice and I enjoy the party and each other's company.

My hands fall from around Brice's neck to the crook of his elbow. "You know what I was just thinking," I ask as we begin walking toward the venue.

"What," Brice says, glancing my way.

"Sometimes life is hard. You rage against the wind without making a dent except in yourself, then you surrender it all to God. Life is still hard, but it's also infinitely better. I praise the Lord for not giving up on me, and thank you for not giving up on me either."

We stop in front of the restaurant where the party is being held. Brice steps in front of me, blocking my view inside. "I prayed," he says. "I asked God to bring us to this exact moment if I was the man he intended for you, but if I wasn't, that you'd find peace with the right man."

"Well," I say, sniffing, "I'm thankful God chose you."

The doorman notices us and flings open the doors wide. Brice smiles at me and steers us inside. I glimpse the beautiful décor, smiling faces and think this must be a small taste of what it's like when heaven celebrates the return of one sheep.

Bible Study Prompts/ Group Discussion Prompts

1. A central theme in the story is redemption. What are some ways in which you see redemption played out?

2. Pastor Charles delivers a sermon about the parable of the sower (Matthew 13 vs. 1-23). Leah identified with the seed that fell among the thorns. What ground do you identify with? The seed that fell on the rock? The seed that fell on the path? The seed that fell among the thorns, or the seed that fell on the good ground?

3. Leah's mother tells her, "Success may not resemble the picture the world has shown you." What is your picture of success, and how does it align with the Biblical view of success?

4. Brice retells the parable of The Prodigal Son (Luke 15vs. 11-24). Has there ever been a time in your life when you 'left' God momentarily or for an extended time?

5. Trent is Leah's greatest temptation despite being detrimental to her. Have you ever been in a relationship that drew you away from God? Are there relationships in your life at this moment, romantic or friendship, that are a hindrance to your faith?

6. Brice breaks down how Jesus had to have gone out of His way to seek the Samaritan woman at the well (John 4 vs. 7-29). Recall one time when Jesus has gone to great lengths or acted extraordinarily to reach you?

7. Brice and Leah talk about the adulterous woman in (John 8 vs. 3-11) and the Samaritan woman (John 4 vs. 7-29). What does this say to you about how Jesus deals with women struggling with sexual sin?

8. We see Leah tempted by Trent repeatedly, with his physical appeal and his worldly possessions. What are your greatest sources of temptation?

9. Brice has a tense conversation with Zack about the gospel. Have you ever shared the gospel with a friend that was a non-believer? How did that conversation go? What are some other ways to witness to someone about Christ?

10. Leah grew up in church and had a faithful mother, but she wasn't. After realizing she had been in an inconsistent relationship with God, Leah accepts Christ as her Savior. Have you surrendered your life to Christ?

Made in United States
Orlando, FL
17 December 2022

26976547R00163